T0043148

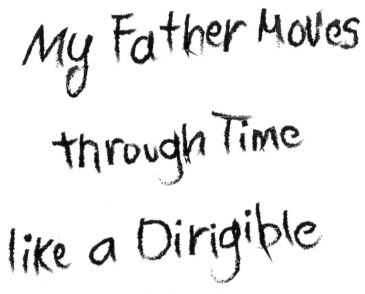

My Father Moves through Time like a Dirigible

and other stories

Gregg Cusick

Livingston Press
The University of West Alabama

Copyright © 2014 Gregg Cusick
All rights reserved, including electronic text
isbn 13: 978-1-60489-138-6, hardcover
isbn 13: 978-1-60489-139-3, trade paper
isbn: 1-60489-138-6, hardcover
isbn: 1-60489-139-4, trade paper
Library of Congress Control Number: 2014939695
Printed on acid-free paper.
Printed in the United States of America by
EBSCO Media
Hardcover binding by: Heckman Bindery
Typesetting and page layout: Joe Taylor, Amanda Nolin
Proofreading: Joe Taylor, Emma McClung, Verdie Coleman III, Teresa Boykin

Cover design and layout: Emily Edwards, Amanda Nolin

Cover photo: NH 82257, USS Shenandoah, courtesy Naval Institute

Acknowledgemtns of previous publication:

"Gutted," *Saturday Evening Post*, May/June 2011; and *Tartts 5*

"Clay Pigeons," *Florida Review*, Summer 2011

"Schrödinger's Cat for Inmates and Barristas," *Inkwell*, Spring 2011

"Ghosts of Doubt," *Bellevue Literary Review*, Spring 2010

"Have You Seen Me?" *North Carolina Literary Review*, Summer 2009

"My Father Moves Through Time Like a Dirigible," *Wordstock Ten Anthology*, *Fall 2008*, and
Short Story America Anthology Vol II, Sept. 2013

"Balance," Hemingway Festival program and
www.ernesthemingwayfestival.org, Sept. 2005

"Looking for Things in the Courtyards of Oaxaca," *Chelsea 77*, Feb. 2005

"Dozen Wheelbarrows," E.M. Koeppel Award, on-line publication Writecorner
Press, www.writecorner.com, Summer 2004

"Diagramming Wyatt," *Alligator Juniper*, Summer 2003

"Mendacity," O.Henry Festival Stories, Greensboro College, Spring 2003

"Wake," *The News & Observer*, Raleigh NC, Jan. 1, 2001

This is a work of fiction. Any resemblance
to persons living or dead is coincidental.
Livingston Press is part of The University of West Alabama,
and thereby has non-profit status.
Donations are tax-deductible.

first edition
6 5 4 3 2 1

TABLE OF CONTENTS

My Father Moves

through Time

like a Dirigible

My Father Moves Through Time Like a Dirigible

Lakehurst, NJ. September 2, 1925. 2:52 p.m. Despite objections of Commander Zachary Lansdowne, an Ohio native, fearing line squalls and late-summer storms, the navy orders the 682-foot blimp Shenandoah *to set off for its tour of Midwest state fairs. As Lansdowne and his crew of forty in the rigid airship sail out over the pine woods of New Jersey, his wife watching from the ground turns her head away. So do wives and families of the other crewmen who have come to the field. It is considered bad luck to watch your husband's ship fade out of sight.*

I always sit down gingerly in the principal's office, into a chair surely more often reserved for the rumps of 13-year-olds. We smile, the principal and I, perhaps appreciating the same irony at the same moment. See, I'm 83 years old, while the principal of the Sam Houston Middle School is about my son's age, about 43. We've met before, and he knows what I want to discuss, again. My proposal for a school play. It's historical, and really about how time and memory work, I tell him again. *As if anyone knows that,* he's thinking, I know.

But I can see it all, I tell him. At least the scene, the set and props so clearly, the illustration of the smooth movement of time. I don't, at first at least, mention my responsibility for the crash of the dirigible *Shenandoah* in 1925, nor my responsibility for my father leaving just a few months later, although this is not because they have nothing to do with the story. It's more that if you go before a producer, say, to pitch an idea for a movie, if you start off with ramblings about guilt and responsibility and not fiery crashes and drama, you've pretty much shot yourself out of the air before you get a chance to fly, don't you think?

"So it's to be the Commander's, Lansdowne's, it's *his* story?" Principal Constantine asks. "Or is it *your* view of it now? Or is it the boy's, the four-year-old's—is it *his* story?"

"No," I say. "History," I say.

The principal is a smart man, and we've known each other for years. We live in the same Austin neighborhood and sometimes wave to one another as we put our recycling by the curb. He knows my son, I believe, though we've never discussed this. My son and I have been, I guess you'd call it estranged, since the divorce back now almost twenty years, but we still talk at the holidays and I call on his birthday. Maybe *estranged* is the wrong word, since we communicate, but it's like some form of distance or at least things unsaid, maybe *emotional estrangement*, you could call it. For my part, I wish we were closer but I'm not sure how to get there. I wonder if I may be like my own father in this way.

Speaking of whom, my father, did I tell you of my earliest lasting image of him? It was that afternoon, September 2, 1925. We're an Austin family, but my father was teaching then in Gettysburg, Pennsylvania, and we rented a little house outside of town, on what seemed to me then to be a huge tract of land but was actually less than an acre. I didn't know all this at four, of course, but I didn't recognize my father until then either.

I can hear his whistle this moment, cutting through the air on a bright, early fall day of much sun and scattered clouds, visibility probably fifteen miles or more. I've always been preoccupied with weather—I flew bombers in both WWII and Korea, was a commercial pilot after that. I've been forever fascinated by flight. But I was inside the house that afternoon when I heard my father calling my name and the name of my brother. My mother came running, too. I skidded to a stop at the huge unmoving feet that held up the statue that was my father, and I ran my eyes slowly up the legs, time-creased khakis, worn at the knees and white-paint spattered, up to his plaid wool shirt, to shoulders and across the outstretched arm that pointed toward the distant sky like one of those memorable statue-stances of Stalin or, more recently now, Saddam Hussein. Pointing off into the glowing future. The sun behind my father haloed his head so that I could not see the features of his face, only shapes in bronze light. My eyes followed the line of his arm to see what my father, like a circus barker, was presenting to us.

It was of course the blimp, one of the great "rigids," an airship named *Shenandoah*, an Indian word meaning "daughter of the stars." My father always knew these facts, the details that make a story. And the dirigible, she was beautiful and massive but somehow seemed also light, moving smoothly, so distant across our view as if attached to my father's hand by some invisible, mile-long cable. I might've even imagined then my father being carried away by the blimp, like a clown by a handful of balloons. This was late afternoon, still hours before the *Shenandoah* would encounter the storms that would bring her down.

In the play, I tell the principal (Mr. Constantine his name is; mine's Joe, by the way), in the play it can be just as vivid.

Or if I were seated in an adult-sized chair before the massive glass-topped desk of the film producer, pitching the idea—I'd mention of course the natural forces, the storm and winds, and the looting after the crash. The looting could be a major sub-plot, sad and fascinating to a generation gobbling reality TV shows. Later, the surviving officers of the *Shenandoah* tried to keep watch, but souvenir seekers and worse materialized from the nowhere of rural Ohio and carted off the remains of the dirigible, leaving not even the skeleton as a fish picked by sharks, since there was really no flesh to the craft and the structure itself was all that was exploitable.

But I hesitate, and then I realize I'm asking the producer, the principal, for another chance, a new start to my spiel. I take a deep breath, and I hear my voice again, like an NPR reporter smart, confident, serious:

It begins and ends, and begins and ends again in my mind—I tell the principal. Curtain up, and it's the Jersey launch scene, wives and families crowding the stage while suspended upper right is a plywood cut-out blimp. Which is pulled, from the audience's right to left, smoothly across a clothesline, in front of a backdrop of clouds and blue-sky interspersed. Some plywood "clouds" are suspended in front of the backdrop, to give the scene depth and allow the "blimp" to pass through, at times "disappearing" behind "clouds." If your head conjures the tune, the words 'it's only a pa-per moon, floating over a card-board sea,' then you're getting it.

I tell all this to the principal, for the third time, I think, it's got to be three times at least. He could be my son, I guess, him forties and me eighties, his grown kids my grandkids if I had them. I tell Constantine for the third time that the school kids could really learn something from my play and, no, not just about the great "rigids," the airships, but about time and memory, about relativity, about personal responsibility. I can see what Constantine is thinking. At my age, maybe this is one of the few perks—I know he thinks I've got a whale of a story or, well, a decent tale, and a story that works on several levels. And I know he thinks I don't see it all.

"Your story works on several levels," he says then.

Three-quarters of a mile above Philadelphia, PA. September 2, 1925. 4:18 p.m. The Shenandoah *passes over the city through scattered clouds, heading west toward the Alleghenies. She passes over central Pennsylvania in the late afternoon, cruising at 4,000 feet, the critical "pressure height" at which the ship's helium gas bags are 100% full. Lansdowne tries to rest but a brewing storm in the northwest has him back in the control room shortly after 3 a.m.*

He's probably forty-three, Principal Constantine, as I said, though I'm a lousy judge of such things. As I was even before I got to the stage where everyone was decades younger than I, though I'm not looking for sympathy. He's got a peppery beard and big gray-blue eyes. He looks more like an actor who would play a middle school principal in the movie version. Divorced just a couple years, Mr. Constantine sports a once-white, wrinkled button-down shirt, pleated slacks the same age and creases. He smiles, again, at my pitch for the Sam Houston Middle School's spring play. I know the two kids with the beeping cell phones in his outer office await his discipline. I can see in his face, his eyes that he thinks he knows me, and maybe I am the old man he sees. Still, I don't think he understands the *Shenandoah* story, what it means to the boy or what it meant when it crashed in 1925.

"Again," he says to me. "Fascinating." And there's both patronizing and admiration in the word voiced. "Think," he says to me as if I wasn't there. "Hundreds, maybe thousands saw it flying over that day, but how many are still alive? It's kind of a 'last Confederate widow' sort of thing, isn't it?"

I can't tell if he sees me as this widow, or if I'm the young writer, to his saavy producer. I can see the cardboard (*plywood*, I say) blimp on the clothesline. And the first scene—Jersey, right? With the wives and families watching the dads fly away. Next the blimp is pulled slowly across, about center stage, where the father, *your* father, points upward and the boy and his family watch it pass. "Interesting," Constantine says, "I like the symbolic images of the 'blimp-father' leaving the families. Your own father was about to leave his family then, right?" He pauses, picturing it, and I can't deny the images, yet of course I feel he's distorting my intentions for the play, reading too much in.

I think Constantine will ask then if I somehow caused the crash, caused my father to leave, but he does not. Instead he asks me about my health, what the doctors I've surely seen must've said about my declining health. And I tell him—I don't know from where inside me these outbursts come—that he can fuck himself. He laughs at this, tells me to come back and talk again soon, that he always loves my company. My mind is recounting the events in the life of the boy, but Mr. Constantine is on his feet then, extending his hand. Again, he's the producer behind the desk.

"About the play," I say.

"I'll pitch it to the drama teacher," the principal says, though I think this assurance is a falsehood. But as I'm leaving, my back to him, he calls out:

"About *flight*," he says, "have you thought about your passion for flight? And your father's running away from your mother and his kids, or yours from your wife and son?"

Divorce, irreconcilables, I could scream. She cheated, the rumors were rampant, all over town, I could inform him. Instead I ask him if he's a certified psychoanalyst. And again, I remind him that he can screw himself, knowing still that he's a smart man and that he thinks he's seeing some levels I haven't considered.

A mile above Caldwell, Ohio. September 3, 1925. 5:05 a.m. Battling headwinds, the Shenandoah *slows. Rising two meters per second, her ascent can't be checked. She is forced into a squall, the clash of opposing winds—one moist and warm, the other dry and cold. At 5,000 feet, the blimp is pointed up 15 degrees and still rises. Lansdowne orders helium valved off to check the ascent. Then, at 6300 feet, the cold force of the squall pushes the ship into a steep descent, 25 feet per second. Lans-*

downe orders tons of water ballast dumped to halt the plunge.

And what I didn't get to describe to Principal Constantine (because while we met for an hour it seemed like seven minutes—is that the ratio of actual to perceived time, the formula I'm looking for?):

In this vision, *if you would*, I tell Constantine, substitute *time* for *sky*, sub it just as you sometimes will mashed potatoes for salad; it's that easy. And simply allow the plywood blimp to move ever smoothly but *between* a cloud or two, so that it's not always visible to the viewer on the ground or, I mean, to the audience.

September, 1925. I know, I know, it's an unbelievable amount of time to go back. But we must remain flexible, my yoga teacher tells me repeatedly. 1925, can you imagine what *hasn't happened yet*, not new VW Beetles or even the original ones, not Desert Storm or Vietnam or Korea even or WWII. Not yet even a Depression, though we're sitting flat in the middle of Prohibition, not that it stopped us. But I'm four, okay, four years old, and I don't have any idea who my father is. Until I hear that whistle. Thumb and index finger moist and pressed together, you know the sound.

I'm eighty-three, but I hardly feel it, isn't that crazy? And I know I sometimes fail to connect my thoughts, but that's only because I hope my listener knows the connectors that are, thus, unnecessary. You follow?

Yet in this college town sometimes girls of eighteen or forty-three look at me and I'm still at least mentally giving it a chance and they're casting aside glances, rolling eyes, or snorting like I'm a doddering fool. They probably talk about me, pass rumors about my war stories and my eccentricities. But, point is, I feel pretty fit, intellectually in step, yet from their view, their perspective, I'm a crazed old man, a wild card. Like right now, I'm sitting, scribbling in my notebook, in a restaurant I lately favor. I've ordered the salmon entrée and what I'd have thought was a pretty smart glass of pinot noir. But my pretty young server seems hesitant, stays back a foot more than she has to her other tables, I can tell, don't tell me I can't. The air begins to smell of grilled pork, the special. And fall leaves, and late season grass clippings, when the door opens again and again then as the place gets louder and very busy.

Now at this late age I believe my father to have been, like all of us I guess, many people. He was gifted and angry, a reluctant father, a frustrated philosopher, a romantic maybe of the second kind—the first being those who pass away or are dramatically taken before the vision gets crushed; the second those who live the whole time believing or at least wanting to, that something or other could happen in this way or another, both rightly and beautifully, like an editor clips a movie. Me, I see them both. I wonder does my own boy know me in these vague ways, or something more specific? And I think my father's violence and self-hatred were nothing of romance. And listen: when he moistened fingers to blow, and near-connected right thumb and index finger to whistle, that brought you running, lemme tell you.

Get out here this is something to see get out here come on!

And so we ran to the yard and looked up to where he was pointing, my brother and mother and me not knowing what we were looking for, be it geese (we'd seen, but still beautiful), a funnel cloud (also seen, and we lost a garage this way), or something our father may never have seen with objective eyes (we'd been called to plenty of these false alarms, four-alarmers of his mind, and we so wanted to see them we nodded always as if we did but he knew, he knew). But we looked at his finger pointing, like hunting dogs, then beyond it into the sky and saw it. All of us saw it, we decided for ourselves and confirmed to each other later.

One couldn't forget such a sight, against such a painter's background blue sky, this buoyant blimp, some five decades before the Goodyear version showed up at sporting events, can you imagine what a sight the thing was? And I was four, did I tell you? What does one recall about being four? Nothing, I'd have wagered, yet I had this startling all-sense image: feel of warm wind, sound of father's whistle, touch of my brother's hand on my shoulder pulling me, smell of lye soap my mother was making, taste of the grit of blowing dust that was always in my mouth I think now at least, and the sight of the dirigible (I know now that's what it was), floating overhead, beyond my father's outstretched index finger (strangely his right, though he was left-handed). An observer of the scene could have drawn a straight line from my upturned head through my father's that was turned toward me, along his right arm that he wasn't looking at, through into the air and to the blimp that from that distance, in the vision of an observer standing perhaps ten feet from me, might appear to be not distant and huge but close and just a scale model or even a well-painted plywood cut-out maybe three feet long.

Mrs. Lansdowne—she was at the time just 27—spoke unrevealed words to her husband, in Lakehurst, NJ, and then she looked away as the ship sailed from sight. I had no reason, I think now, to believe that somehow I had caused the crash. Or that either of the above—words not spoken or the accident—had anything to do with my father's disappearance some months later. As much my fault as the damned Depression that was already part of our lives then but that they'd have you believe didn't really hit until '29, several years later. But I was just four then, when the blimp went over. And of course I digress. We were talking about my father.

Near ground, near Dayton, Ohio. September 3, 1925. 6:27 a.m. Opposing wind forces wrench the Shenandoah. *Amidships, steel girders tear and two crewmen are pitched out into space. The blimp falls, levels off, then again rises precipitously. Struts supporting the control car snap, the ship spins rapidly in a circle, Lansdowne and seven others in the gondola plunge to their deaths. Weighed down by three engines, the separated stern section falls like an arrow, glances against a hillside. Remarkably, the engines are scraped off by the earth, and the loose stern section floats up again. Men tumble from the wreckage, leap to the ground trying to avoid the crashing, disintegrating ship. Crewmen release helium and actually crash-land a section and survive. Debris is strewn over an area of twelve square miles.*

So remember that I said that it begins and ends and begins and ends, and begins again. I realize for a moment now that I may be repeating myself. But each version's different, yes? And I only humbly wish to make the point that we're all, every one of us, full of fact and fiction. The waitress before me now may not even believe I was shot down over Germany in '43 and, hell, maybe I wasn't. And just as much, I mean it depends as I may have said on one's point of view, where one places one's tripod and starts (and stops) the camera rolling. And see how perspective-talk leads us around and back right back to *TIME*? And of course its buddy, the great manipulator of time, memory. Memory that can leap forward and backward minutes, months, decades in single bounds that only take seconds.

On the next visit, or perhaps the previous one, I say to Constantine (like a kid, one whose tiny frame would fit this chair I'm in, would): "Did I tell you it was really all about time, that is, time and memory?"

His look is both pensive and somehow still patronizing. Does he want me out of here? Is he comprehending my pitch, my theme? That is, either he's thinking of time, or of how to ask me to leave without offending me? His comments can be taken at various levels of seriousness.

"Right," he says to me, in a tone impossible to read, "about *time*," he finishes. I'm thinking he definitely italicized that *time* there. "Interesting," he says.

A plywood blimp, I say. Smoothing across a sharp cloudy late summer blue sky. The sky subs for time, the dirigible then being any of us, my father for instance, moving through it. Yet my father doesn't seem to move at all—he's there with his arm outstretched, whenever I look up. But he's actually moving daringly fast—rotating with the earth at 1037 mph, and revolving with the earth around the sun at a speed that is relative to the center of our galaxy, just as our galaxy is moving relative to the nearby galaxies.

But I too, just a boy of four, I'm moving at the same speed. So we're like the two motorcyclists speeding down the road side by side: we can toss a tennis ball back and forth, and to either of us the other seems to be motionless, relatively speaking. Which is simply to try to explain perhaps why my father seems to be motionless, and time seems the thing moving smoothly behind him. So we're back to point of view, as the dependent factor in measuring motion and, can we say, measuring time as well?

On the ground near Dayton, Ohio. September 3, 1925. 6:45 AM. All of the Shenandoah *is now down. Fourteen men are dead. The fragments of the ship and its 29 survivors are scattered over the flat Ohio landscape. First come the rescuers, followed closely by the curious, and the looters. By noon thousands of scavengers, armed with knives, hatchets, pliers, wrenches, make off with logbooks, steel girders, yards of fabric, and the ship's instruments. The still-dazed officers and enlisted men try unsuccessfully to keep guard. The gondola, miles from the other sections of the ship, is picked clean by nightfall. Even Lansdowne's Annapolis class ring is missing from his lifeless hand.*

I leave principal Constantine's office, sit down in a regulation-sized adult chair in this restaurant in town, where I watch my hand scribble these words that you might read in what might be described as real time, the description of our meeting. I know, again because I've known it before, that he won't be recommending to the drama department that they put on the *Shenandoah* play I proposed. And I'm not really agitated. Knowing, as I do, that I have my image. I have my father, moving in and out of the clouds, smoothly through the years, the sun behind him haloing his head.

Balance

Ever since she shot her husband, Bonnie has felt better about their relationship. First, of course, because he'd survived—a fortunate outcome she'd been in no way sure she wanted, until after she'd fired the shots. And in fact after the seven months of recovery it was the bullet to the back of his thigh that still bothered him. Not the two in the chest, frontal, or the two that pegged his midsection as he turned his sometimes sorry, sometimes irresistible ass to her and stumbled down the front steps into the yard. The point, in Bonnie's mind, is that some kind of equilibrium has been restored.

It's a rainy Tuesday in October, and they're on the way to the university where Bonnie used to be a student and Harold used to be a maintenance worker. It's 9:27 a.m. by the Corolla's dashboard stick-on clock, and they need to be on High Street in less than ten minutes to see the spaces fill up. They don't need to find a place to park, but really just a good vantage point to idle while the students and faculty pull in. They'll watch the vehicles and the owners, note who carries a handbag and who points a key chain at their car as they leave, activating an alarm system. Certain vehicles they won't even mess with, while others are worth a bit of risk.

"Sum-bitch," Harold tells the driver he's tailgating in front of them, braking, wincing at some imagined pain in his right thigh, the one Bonnie shot. White, tall-coiffed hair is visible above the headrest of the Buick station wagon, its license tag bearing the icon of a figure in a wheelchair. "I think I know that guy, and he sure as hell ain't handicapped. Works maintenance at the law school," Harold continues. "Bowls in the league—good, too. Got this little girly throw, swinging down the lane. But he can pick up a spare, I'll tell you." Some grudging admiration in the voice.

Harold likes to say he knows everybody in town. Knows everybody's story, everybody's business. Grew up here, and he does shake a lot of hands on the street. He offers little details about everyone, stuff Bonnie figures he mostly makes up. 'Went to high school with that dude,' he'll say. 'Was in the Chess Club and ran track. Pretty good miler, for a nerd.' This town is Harold's world, and the people all fit neat categories. Bonnie sometimes envies the clean simplicity of his view.

He tails the Buick onto High Street that intersects with the university six blocks up. Until 9:45 each morning the inbound side of the street is a bike lane, after which it's open for parking. Harold pulls the Toyota wagon to the curb squarely in front of a fire hydrant, waiting with the students who will pull into legal parking spaces.

Sometimes there's a little Traffic Services golf cart that cruises the street at about 9:40 to make sure no one jumps the gun. The meter maid's a woman named Norma whom Harold dated in high school, and he always has to remind Bonnie about her (cheerleader, yearbook staff) and shake his head at how much weight she's put on. Today, in the drizzle, there's no golf cart in sight.

They watch the Buick wagon parallel neatly into a handicapped space in front of one of the brick administration buildings. A well-dressed matronly figure with a white beehive hairdo unfolds herself and, leaning against the car, pulls an aluminum walker from the back seat. She locks up and begins a three-minute, fifty-foot crawl up the brick walkway.

"Damn, I know her," Harold tells Bonnie. "Used to teach my sister violin. Nasty attitude. Man, she was eighty *back then*," he whistles. "We can forget about that car, though. Shit, she was always stingy, and poor. Bet we'd find your buddy Jim Beam under the seat though," Harold whistles again, about the only thing he still does that gets on Bonnie's nerves. Used to be he was always walking in on her in the bathroom, interrupting her when she was talking to her mother on the phone or reading in bed. But these days it's like he's going through a period of respect, is what Bonnie thinks.

"That bourbon breath, man," Harold's in reverie. "She'd stand by the window looking out while Ruthie played. She'd steam up the glass, and the plants on the sill would be wilted for two days after each lesson. Now *she's* one you could've shot," he laughs, then winces, rubbing his thigh. "Damn."

"Just keep watching, will you," Bonnie tells him distractedly, lighting a cigarette. Noting the dashboard clock reads 9:42. "I coulda put a slug in your other leg, too," she says blandly but smiling. "Then *you'd* need the walker." Silently, they're both picturing Harold, hobbled, creeping up the walk.

Harold and Bonnie study the line of vehicles pulling one behind the other along the curb like some kind of military exercise. The clock digits blink and change as they watch the cars in front. At exactly 9:45, perhaps twenty driver's side doors open nearly in unison, and from both sides of their Toyota students and faculty step out, many with backpacks, most in jeans, slickers, hiking shoes. They do look like a kind of army, Bonnie thinks. A unit Bonnie had been a part of. That is, until the accident.

Harold would never admit, though Bonnie suspected, that the shooting was about the best thing that ever happened to him. Funny how things work out. He was a "martial arts expert," that's what his business cards said, but he couldn't find a job teaching that, and he didn't have the cash to start his own place, which would be a sure fire hit if he could just get started. So he was working maintenance at the university, rotating shifts three days and two nights, squeaking by. Days off, when Bonnie was at school studying psychology of all the useless things, he stayed home and made plans.

The Academy of the Martial Arts, it would be called, maybe "International" before it, if he could get Billy Lee from the Chinese take-out place to throw in a few bucks and teach with him. Then it could be the IAMA, and Harold liked the sound of that. Harold had a flair for marketing, and he envisioned the initials on tee shirts and ball caps, even stitched to karate belts.

So one Tuesday Bonnie gets her classes cancelled and comes home early to find Harold and Billy Lee hunched over the kitchen table, studying a blueprint they picked from the trash of an architect—a recently transplanted Minnesotan, a cartoon-talking Swede named Halvorson— who lives a few streets over where Harold walks the dog. They're passing a joint back and forth and drinking Pabst tall-boys, reworking the blueprint so it looks a little like the plan of the building they're fixing to buy for the IAMA. And in walks Bonnie who usually goes straight from school to her waitressing job and gives Harold some peace on his days off.

Harold loves Bonnie to death, but he knows she's got no head for business, and she never had understood about the Academy. He would've thought she'd found him in bed with the checkout girl from the Kwik-mart—the one with the sweet eyes who was class secretary his senior year, whose family was in poultry—for the way Bonnie overreacted.

Billy Dee slips out before the shouting and Harold's got to give Bonnie a little head-butt to calm her down, just a light pop forehead-to-nose to remind her she's busting in on him for once. He knows just how to do it, being an expert, and is surprised to hear the little popping sound that is her nose crunching over toward her left cheek. He storms out then, thinking he'll drive over to Billy Lee's and she can find her own damn way to work.

Midway down High Street, Harold and Bonnie continue to wait, the wipers on intermittent, studying the line of cars, each silently cursing the daddies who buy their kids new rides with auto-locks and security systems. But they spot a couple "likelies," a late-'70s Honda and a Chrysler K-car convertible, which causes Harold to snicker. They nod silently to one another, and Bonnie grabs her bookbag (packed with a couple old psych texts and a notebook) and the thin steel T-square, a drafting tool that works great on car windows.

She's dressed like the rest in jeans, slicker, new hiking boots purchased with the credit card of one of the young co-eds whose car they hit last week. She hops out, smiling at Harold who's only the wheelman, seeing as how he's still disabled. "Hey, see if you can't score us one of those handicapped tags off a rearview mirror," he tells his wife, rubbing his thigh as he pulls away. The skies, perhaps clearing, idle somewhere between rain and shine.

So what happened when Harold stormed out was he left his car keys on the table beside the blueprint. Halfway across the yard he says Shit! and turns back. It's the grand exits he can never pull off. And he's given Bonnie a chance, of course, to chain the door. He doesn't know he also gave her time enough to grab the pistol—the .22 they bought and registered together and spent many a fine afternoon at the target range with—so that when he busts the door chain and steps in, Bonnie blasts him.

Twice in the chest and he's feeling this dull burning, smiling at her in a crazy way proud. "Damn, bitch," he says almost admiring, and steps back as she plugs him again, this time in the stomach. Harold turns and sort of stumble-runs the front steps out into the yard. Bonnie pops him twice more, once in the back and once in his right leg. The last one drops him in the yard, where he lays there fully conscious but dazed, as the neighbors gather round him. And then Bonnie, who's lost the gun and rushes to kneel beside him, the grieving wife.

Harold rides up High Street and makes a left onto University. Waves at Norma Childress, the meter maid, her expanding buttocks balanced on her golf cart writing a ticket. He glances at the meter, which still appears to have time on it. But as he passes, and she waves back, the red flag flips up in the meter's little window: "Violation." Norma begins writing on the ticket again.

Around the block and back onto High, Harold sees Bonnie in the driver's seat of a white Corolla, the sedan version of their own car. He thinks she could get into that one with a skate key, for all the times they've locked the keys in theirs and broken in. In high school when they'd started dating, Bonnie had asked Harold to the Sadie Hawkins roller skating party in the gym. She'd been so cute, wobbling on the skates like a fawn, and he'd been completely smitten. Still was, he thought. He remembered holding her hand—they'd first kept each other from falling—and then how they really started flying around that polished wood floor.

Harold also thought of how things had changed since she'd shot him. What he'd thought, laying on his front yard with the neighbors around and then the ambulance and the police. Thinking how she loved him enough to shoot him *five times*. Damn.

Harold idles beside her now and watches as Bonnie pulls a ten-dollar bill from the glove compartment. She also pockets what looks like a yellow Shell gas card and a Visa. From a checkbook, she tears off the last two checks from the pad in the little blue wallet. She emerges then and shuts the car door without relocking it. She hops in beside Harold all flushed and excited, and she's the little girl at the roller skating party. "That car's almost just like ours," she chirps.

Some in the neighborhood, where domestic violence and even shootings were pretty commonplace, were still surprised Bonnie wasn't charged with anything. Women mostly applauded her guts, standing up for all battered women. That is, until Harold got out of the hospital and she took him back in. Harold's male friends mostly said Damn! though not with all the admiration Harold had. Shot him in the back, too, they said, or commented, amazed, that she took his sad ass back in. Said he'd be sleeping with one eye open for a long time. But they'd really missed the point, Harold thought, about how bad things were leading up to the shooting, and how much better they got after.

And after he got home, Bonnie had nursed him like an angel. She'd quit school to be with him, and while the unemployment didn't pay for everything, they'd found a way to supplement their income. Harold was dying to get out, and to drive, anyway. They'd been out cruising one afternoon when one of Bonnie's teachers had pulled in front of them. The bitch, who'd given Bonnie a C in Abnormal Psychology last semester. They'd watched her park and enter a campus building, and then Bonnie had walked straight to a magnetic "hide-a-key" right in the center under the rear bumper. In the glove box she'd found a gas card, an old driver's license, and a checkbook, and under the mat was a $20-bill. They'd written a check and cashed it at a branch across town, no questions asked, and they were off.

"I want to return these," Bonnie says, meaning the cards from the Corolla. "She had her lip-gloss in the glove compartment right where I keep mine" She opens the box to show Harold, and there it is. He's not surprised, of course, but he loves her considerate side. Loves that she wants to return the cards, which they do, after a fill-up at Shell and a CD player on the Visa, one they'll pawn since they got a nice Kenwood only two weeks ago. Bonnie puts the cards back right where she found them and only uses one of the checks, that for only $50 at a drive thru. She's munching Doritos from the Shell convenience store as they pull into their driveway.

The final gift she saves for Harold, until they're in bed, snuggling beneath crisp new sheets from Belk. She pulls from inside her book on the nightstand a little blue and white laminated tag, a handicapped card to hang from the rearview mirror.

"It's only a temporary," she tells him. "When your leg heals up— and when you're back in the martial arts business—" she smiles, gently petting his thigh, her middle finger finding the soft indent. "Then you'll have to take this down."

"Sure," Harold says. "Like that little architect Halvorson says," he puts on the Swedish, "'You betcha.'"

Dozen Wheelbarrows

Alone in the house—his mother on second shift at the hospital—Hank scrapes his plate of congealing macaroni into the dog's dish. He swaps jeans for shorts, double-knots his running shoes. And he takes off into the October night, down the woods road toward the lake, his breath visible in puffs like those enclosing the words of comic strip characters.

Hank doesn't wear his hearing aid, which is often the case, since he wants the near silence of the woods, the muted sounds around him. He is sure that *less heard* means a heightening of his other senses. The fall air is crisp and oak-smelling, sharp, and the temperature in the forties he doesn't notice. He sees more than a dozen deer over a course of seven miles, big and brazen before the season.

Nearing home, still a quarter mile off through the woods, Hank can see his tiny two-story cabin's front window flashing blue television light and, as he nears, an unfamiliar late '70s pickup in the short gravel drive. The dog's bark he doesn't hear. Hank enters the darkened house and, after two weeks unaccounted for, there is his father on the faded plaid couch. He looks older somehow and thinner—Hank thinks the word *husk*—thinking only puppies could change so noticeably in such a short time. His father is sipping Jim Beam from the last unbroken tumbler, watching the History Channel and puffing on a filterless Pall Mall.

The History Channel is what his father always watches, justifying an attitude he exudes, one he's explained to Hank and his brother countless times, a stance he's earned he says, surviving fifty-odd years in this small, unfair place, a Seneca Indian-named town most people can't even spell. A simple dictum, that today's world is too easy and rewards the lazy, unpatriotic, and false. Tonight's history lesson remembers The Titanic.

In the cold night, running under a cloud-snuffed moon, Hank had felt that one more sense had been removed and he'd loved the darkness. The pain, too. The burning in his lungs from cigarettes and in his hamstrings from the hills, steep enough but glacier-softened, ground down by ice masses moving just a few feet a year, an indescribable but palpable momentum. He enters the house, full of pumping endorphins, a runner's high. Now thinking about what he is returning to, his loaded mind rifling through conflicting emotions that all fit, only able to describe what he feels *physically*. His father smiles a wry, knowing (God knows what) smile, extends the pack of Pall Malls. Hank takes one and lights it, hands back lighter and package, coughs on the first puff. He sits tentatively in a stuffed chair left by the previous renter.

Green water, with that bluish-cold quality, rushes around the boat and into the wake behind it. Not as cold as it looks certainly since the day's early September and the summer sun has warmed it for months. The outside air, maybe fifty-five degrees, is much cooler, Hank knows. Of the three on board—high schoolers, know-it-alls, know-nothings— Banker is unofficial leader, and he's appropriately at the stern of the fourteen-foot bass boat, handling the tiller of the little Honda outboard. Dobey's at the bow. Hank is in the middle, straddling the mound covered by the army-green canvas tarp that hides what's supposed to look like fishing gear. An awful lot of tackle, if you ask Hank.

Green water, not the clear aquamarine you'd expect, or what it looks like from the air, or how the tourist brochures present it in slightly retouched photos and purple-prose text. The lake was formed by glacial movement, a deep crevasse cut by an ice mass moving in ultra-slow motion, cut over more years than Hank can fathom, much less how long back. Not really deep here, maybe twenty-five feet, a wading pool to a real swimmer, he's sure—they stay close to the shore. At the rear of the small bass boat, low in the water and motoring slowly across this Finger Lake, the Honda engine sounds capable as ever, the steady light click like a sewing machine Hank remembers his mother using, the soft sound a comfort to his even-then near-deaf ears. Behind him Banker has his headphones on (of course), listening to a William Buckley novel-on-tape, crazy for a high school junior, like the young Republican on "Growing Pains" reruns. What's up with that, Hank has asked more than once.

Banker's talking, as always, but he of course can't hear a thing Hank

Dozen Wheelbarrows

or Dobey say, not that they're talkative, especially by comparison. It's "Banker," by the way, for his penchant for hugging the shore. He can't swim, having missed the summer lessons like as a student he had ducked Spanish verb conjugation, totally ignorant of the preterite tense. He's Banker, then, not for some known gift with finances. Hank gazes down into the green water, knowing but not seeing the mossy, snaky flora that covers the lake bottom.

It's nearly five on a Thursday, just two weeks into the fall term, the cool air signaling the abrupt end of summer so common upstate. Yet in the breeze is the smell of both summer and winter: if it were fruit, both crisp apples and rotting bananas would blow past. Hank smells these and looks around as if they'd be carried by the air.

As the three pulled out from the lake house dock, Dobey was uncharacteristically exuberant. *Good haul, men,* he says, *best of the season.* Dobey's got a leg an inch and a half shorter than the other from a skiing accident, nearly died and maybe'd be better off. Like the rest, he's handsome in an athletic, boyish way, and like the rest he's flawed, limps only slightly to walk but can't run for shit. But all that's a story for someone else.

Banker guns the engine, and it responds sluggishly, like a runner into an uphill, Hank thinks, a member of their high school's cross country team, though he misses a practice every few weeks for their "runs" on the lake. *They got more than they could ever put in a dozen wheelbarrows,* Dobey had said more than once about the people who live on the lake. And it's true, Hank thinks, though he finds the image odd, disturbing. Hank thinks of *Moby Dick,* their current English reader, how the whalers and others moved their few belongings in the carts, borrowed because they didn't even own them. Hank pictures these now, filled with the electronic toys and *nouveau*-riches of the lake-house entrepreneurs, the soft-handed twenty- and thirty-something computer geniuses. Juxtaposition, Hank's English teacher might say.

Hank watches the lakeside homes pass them, thinking of the comedian, was it Billy Crystal, saying Trump's the only one who can look at the NYC skyline and say *got it, got it, need it, got it, need it, need it, got it.* Thinking as he visually marks the docks and their accompanying houses, *we've hit them but not them, hit 'em, not yet*, etc. He pulls at his left ear's hearing aid, dislodges and pockets it, happier in the steady whir of the engine and no voices at all.

When the tiny overloaded boat tips to port it's no surprise to any of the three. Banker's fond of clowning with the rudder, exercising control, a show of his new-found confidence. Last summer he was the near-blind, Coke-bottle-lensed butt of jokes. Then came the growth spurt and the contact lenses, that transformed him overnight into a popular figure, got him a girlfriend in a matter of weeks. And changed his attitude, too. Banker had become sometimes cocky, sometimes even showing a mean streak that for Hank brought to mind the ones who'd picked on Banker since the early days.

It's not a big tip Banker causes, but an unsteadying jolt just the same. And for Hank, he senses something injected into his system, electric-like, perhaps fear and adrenaline, almost like what he feels before a race. And time slows for him then, movements clipped and jerky like photos on a storyboard he's seen in a film magazine. Like Zapruder's maybe. Or a lazily constructed cartoon, where too-few images are used to represent motion. Hank sees in that second a snapshot, himself racing through the woods on the cross-country course, cool fall and trees a red-yellow blur whipping past, a moment at the height of his training when he is flying. He's feeling that runner's high, his strides seem long as Buicks, and what is more often for him than most, the world is silent but for his steady breathing, so even he might be in sleep. If the photo is a race shot, he could be far behind the pack as easily as leading, since no other runners are in sight; but he's far ahead, with a still-lengthening advantage.

And so slowly then again, as Banker reacts to counterbalance the listing of the boat, the pendulum swings back with slightly more and still slower force. The small bass boat tips back then, a tiny amount of lake water swishing over the gunwale. The three passengers are all well-coordinated, athletic, yet their movements are again jerky, cartoonish, but at the same time slow and overreactive. Hank sees a second flash of remembrance, feels a second larger jolt of adrenaline, more panicked than at the first rocking of the boat not two seconds before.

In this photo Hank sees family, just for an instant, his brother and mother around the breakfast table. His father—this before he moved out to a construction job in the city, to send money sporadically and inconsequentially home—appears, too, workboots heavy on the stairs, then sitting at the table, declining cereal but taking black coffee. Hank's father wears the jeans and flannel shirt of the day before, smells of cigarette smoke and bourbon. But if one of Hank's lakeside classmates had peered in the kitchen window, there would be nothing in the scene that would lead one to think anything different here from their own kitchens.

Hank often doesn't wear his hearing aid at home, prefers the silence, and in it the chance that it just might be that things here in the rented house are as they are in the giant homes on the lake, down the long paved driveways past the iron gates that are padlocked when the residents get away to ski Steamboat or dive the Keys. Dobey works part-time at Sanford Animal Hospital, which offers boarding, so it's simple enough to find a time when this or that lake house family will be out of town, the right time for their boat runs.

In the image, though, Hank sees a flicker of something—perhaps he's right, he thinks, that their home life is no different. But the sameness is not in its contentedness, the peaceful family picture; the similarity may be in the illusion of harmony. The rich and advantaged people in the lake houses drink too much and slap their kids and lose jobs, too, but wear pressed slacks and polished shoes to church, parking the BMW on the end where it's least likely to get bumped by a pickup.

When the boat tips again, Dobey feels it most, being farthest from the fulcrum of the rudder. Bank's laughing, in fear and false confidence, part from the Maker's Mark he swigged off the wet-bar of the last house, part from the joint he lit as they shoved heavily off from the thirty-foot dock, all loaded down. And in this tiny instant that's as strangely drawn out as the other two, Hank sees a flash of their sophomore English class last spring. Dobey and his girlfriend, Julie, both in the class, and they had to write short stories. Hank gets called on to read his aloud, first, and he stares at the pages feeling the eyes on him. Especially hers, Julie's, whom he's barely spoken to, but Hank believes he somehow understands, can hear beneath her tough-girl talk, can see beneath her over-applied makeup. And Hank begins, in a voice he can hardly hear and is sure sounds like that of a deaf person who's learning to talk.

But he guts it out, reads his story about a guy who makes himself what people want him to be, called "Potemkin," using the idea of the Russian soldier who may have built fake villages to impress Catherine the Great. He reads, and Dobey and some others laugh at inappropriate places, but he remembers Julie doesn't

Dobey's not laughing at present, nor is Banker, who'd been playful with the tiller, just for a scare. There's none of that now.

Wish we had your skis, Banker yells to Dobey above the engine noise, over the novel-on-tape in his ears, lamely with false confidence. And Dobey nods his *good one, don't mistake me for someone who gives a shit* head, while Banker keeps futilely at the Honda engine, over-correcting as they veer out away from the shore. The third tip is a doozer, and they're suddenly all wet.

Doozer in the sense of turning things upside down. The three, their cargo, and the bass boat itself, with its unevenly distributed load, its engine blaring, though Hank hears but a low rumble. The propeller spraying, then the motor coughing, then stopping, suffocated. To Hank, the water's not cold exactly, just heavy. Downward pushing, he thinks, not the way gravity must be but more like the way his mother asks things—her vulnerability, his sympathy, how can he refuse—or his father demands with the implicit *or else.*

Water conducts electricity, Hank's thinking, remembering his hearing aid safely in the buttoned top pocket of his flannel shirt. Thinks again of the equipment on board, not that anything's plugged in. When Dobey comes at him, Hank is without normal human resistance, just lets him grab on and feels himself begin to sink slowly, calmly as if he's drifting off to sleep. And they go down together, thoughtless of Banker, except for a last glance over. In his silent vision, Hank sees Banker grab for a big Sony TV, he can see the logo lower right of the screen, grabs it of course like an anchor as it tips last out of the boat. Hank can't know whether it's to save himself, as if the television would float, or if he grabs on to save a piece of their haul, so sure he is that this drowning thing's a lark, a sit-com scene where the most he has to worry about is explaining later why they all got so wet. And at this Hank starts to laugh, soundlessly under Dobey's wrapped arms, laughs and takes a great mouthful of the lake. Not a hundred feet from shore, that's what the *Lakes' Journal* would say two days later. The scene could be so catastrophic, but it's more just quiet.

Hank with the worthless ears, Dobey with his short leg, Banker did we mention, besides just eyesight, had the reading problems (and was supposed to be listening to Melville tapes for school). And the paper called them "models." Which Hank would have found funny, too.

If I was a reporter, Hank thinks, I'd write the story of the haves and the have-nots, of the things that gotta be done to level the playing field. I'd let them know that it's not fair, not fair that the water fills the mouths of some and not others. Hank thinks, he wishes, he longs suddenly for his mother and father, and not Dobey hugging his neck. His parents—who at times lately asked Hank *howya doin*; and if he'd answered at all it was *fine*, no problems, no shit. Because what could they have done, he thought.

Into a very relatively shallow amount of water the three went, not so deep but deep enough in the green lake that they had to be dragged up.

And quite unexpectedly said the *Journal*, the dredging revealed two Sony TVs, a JVC CD player, a couple receivers of unknown make. Enough equipment to flip the Queen Mary, somebody at the BP on Lake Avenue said, one of the first to the scene, an hour later when the water's surface was back to smooth, glass. Good kids, others said, putting the blame on the schools. Or the parents, fine. All doing fine, thanks.

And the scene Hank never recalls is one his father would have thought he would. When Hank came in not two weeks ago from a run along the lake and his father had been watching the history channel on television. A feature on the Titanic. Hank had come in, had lit one of his father's cigarettes and sat for the end of the story. Spellbound. A granddaughter, an infant survivor, voices her grandmother's perceptions: screams of the sinking, the dying, horrible. And then after the ship disappears beneath the icy surface, worse, so much worse: the silence. Haunting. Something you'll never, whatever joys life holds for you, forget.

And his father beside him, now passed out, snoring comically-loud like the fourth Stooge, Shemp. But his father will remember every bit of it, Hank knows, could recite it back some day, word for word. Stuff no one would recall but him, just like the stuff he uses against people. Again, the emotions Hank can't name, only the physical he could describe.

Hank sits smoking in the television light and thinks, wanting to cry out or to head into the woods running again, that a few more miles and more sweat and it will all have changed somehow, in some way, he's sure. Even if just that he'll be a different person then, older by minutes, or that the arrangement of atoms beneath his unblemished skin will be somehow altered because of the cry or the perspiration or the exertion or the night air. And Hank thinks there's something serious here, between the silence and the snoring, and maybe he has no choice but to laugh.

Looking for Things
In the Courtyards of
Oaxaca

In the tiny darkroom of the offices of *Diario Oaxaca* sometime after 2 a.m. Saturday, March 14th, three American architecture students work feverishly. They're coming down from ecstasy highs but more smoothly than they'd expect, since the *cervezas* and the mescals they sip ease the transition. They develop the photographs, some seventy from which they'll choose just twelve. Once the oversized, 11 x 14 prints emerge, they must carefully crop them to fit 5 x 7 frames. And slice them precisely so that each photo includes the old man but does not include the city police, both of whom can be found in the background of many of the negatives.

At this same early hour some blocks away, a lovely plump innkeeper irons linens because she cannot find sleep. Upstairs at her hotel, a young gringo writer does sleep, dreaming elaborately. A half mile from the hotel, next to placards bearing angry slogans about injustice, tour drivers and cabbies doze in their idle vehicles parked in a strike line in front of the 2nd Class Bus Terminal.

And also nearby, a still-impeccably dressed Mixtec—one sharing both native Amerind and Hispanic heritage—sips his own mescal hoping it will bring sleep. He is the one whose drug network supplied the methamphetamines to the students. He's known in the historic city, around the square, the *zocalo*, as Dios-padre, the godfather, or more often Don-zoca, the Don of the Zocalo. Sleep will not come for him tonight, because he has as much on his mind as in his heart. But there is an element of celebration in his solitary sipping of the Oro de Oaxaca, the mescal. He thinks of the students he's depending on, wishes them *suerte en sus es-*

fuerzos. But we get ahead of ourselves, thirty-six hours at least.

* * *

Thursday, March 12. 9:15 a.m. The professor of architecture meets with his eleven students in the courtyard of the Hotel Azucenas, delivering a short lecture before he takes them on a walking tour of some of the spectacular courtyards of Oaxaca. "Just a few things to look for," he begins, a glance to his watch as the last of the students hurry from their rooms that surround the small open space already bathed in angled morning sunlight. "Note the exterior façade, often diametrically opposed to the space within," he continues.

His students yawn through his talk in waves, that is, one begins at his extreme left and this triggers yawns left to right, around and then back exactly like in a crowd at a stadium. For them, 9:15 is 6 a.m. their home time, and yesterday they'd left the east coast of the U.S. early in the morning. A flight to Mexico City, then a seven-hour bus ride south to Oaxaca. An entire day of travel is behind them. The professor's lecture continues for perhaps twenty minutes. "Note the threshold," he says. "See if the surface material changes from street to *zaguan*, or vestibule, to inner space. Check the light, the temperature. Sunlight and shadow, warm and cool, and note the time of day." A student thinks he means the ungodly hour of morning they stand now in, and groans.

"We're at 16 degrees north latitude—the sun's angles are much more direct than you're used to," the Professor continues. "Taking in the courtyard itself, note opposing concepts at work: formal versus organic—which is it? Symmetry versus asymmetry. Colonnade versus arcade. Colors and materials contrasting or blending. Note column proportions, drainage solutions, plantings, sounds, smells…" and on he goes. At length, finally, he leads the students from the cool of the shady hotel courtyard into the warm concrete-and-cobbled streets. Meanwhile, on opposite sides of the rooftop terrace, the widower and the husband of one of the students sit at iron tables half beneath umbrellas, partly in the morning sun, both with open notebooks, pens poised.

The widower sits in an iron chair on the second story terrace of the Hotel Azucenas in the historic district of the city. An American, he sits with coffee, surrounded by lime trees bearing fruit and outreaching bougainvilleas and all types of flowering plants and cacti that flourish in the arid climate of this place. An ancient city of a quarter million sits between mountains like a giant dimple, like the uneven hollow between thumb and forefinger in the top of a fist. The widower sits in the morning warm and soon to be hot sun, its rays quite direct at 16 degrees north latitude, a notebook and a plastic water bottle beside his coffee cup. The clear liquid half-filling the plastic bottle is mescal.

On the otherwise blank notebook page, the widower has written a quotation from the guide who yesterday took him around the city and to the historic site at Monte Alban. The tour drivers and cabbies of Oaxaca city are currently striking—the local police have been stopping them and demanding payment of a hundred or two hundred pesos, bribes of ten or twenty dollars to let them pass. The widower's guide had agreed as a favor to his sister, the *patrona*, the hotel innkeeper, to take the widower to the famous pre-hispanic site. It is not uncommon, the widower remembers from previous visits, for native Oaxacans to blame Cortez and the Catholic conquistadors for the area's problems past and present. Convenient scapegoats, he thinks, but in every version of history are both lies and truths. The widower smiles at the words on his page: "Spanish bastards!"

At the farthest iron table from the widower, a younger man sits, he, too sipping coffee, and he with a pair of notebooks open before him. Also American, he reads from handouts regarding architecture and history of Mexico, notes from his wife's professor. Both men listen to the sounds from below—the man in the back of the flatbed of giant water bottles singing "Aah-guu-waah!" and the uneven whirring of Volkswagen beetles that are everywhere here, seemingly half the vehicles—and both feel a slight violation that the other is present on the rooftop in what should be each's own private space. The younger man reads:

The courtyards of Oaxaca, and courtyards in general, oppose the urban plan of recent residential developments. The popular design of American architecture features the centered building surrounded on four sides by grass yard, while the ancient and world-wide model has a building on a lot a quarter the size with an interior private, open space, a kind of outdoor living room. A space, significantly, that is inside and outside, public and private, at once.

The widower sips at his coffee, then from his water bottle, hearing now the call of a seller of compressed gas, his unique song offering nothing he can look up or translate—not *gaseas* or *asfixiante* or *gasolina*—but better, a refrain that signals to all his singular presence on the street. The younger man on the rooftop hears this, too, as well as the whirrings of the Volkswagen engines, the Beetle he owned as a college student twenty years back coming strongly to mind. And similar reminiscences for the widower, who as a young English major-turned lawyer in 1967, had owned a red bug. The same year he'd read that novel so many writers bring up as influential, the story of the last day in the life of Geoffrey Firmin, a story that takes place right here in the Mexican state where the two men sit. Each scratches something in his notebook.

The widower knows he is an outsider here, an American away from home, an English speaker in a Spanish speaking land as well. He thinks of other outsiders, Cortez and his Catholic thugs, torturers and murderers and stealers of the native culture, their riches, their beliefs. Almost five centuries back, the atrocities, yet in the minds of many—the guide, the widower himself at this moment—those crimes in the name of Christianity seem fresh. Yet they're split, these people, most sharing blood of both the native peoples and the Catholic conquerors. Both extremes within the same people, such a difficult position. Like having one's mind drawn and quartered, the widower thinks, knowing the invaders committed even worse acts. Spanish bastards!

The widower sips from his water bottle, feeling the need to get up and move, to walk to the zocalo perhaps, somewhere he will interact with others. Anywhere outside the concentric spinnings of faulty reason in his own head. A shame crosses his sun-reddened face, what he thinks is shame for his drinking; his wife would have disapproved. Strange, he had thought that after her death, after all the years of her presence somehow now the opposite would be true, that he'd only be conscious of her absence. But there are times daily—just then, for example, as he raised the mescal to his lips—that he feels her with him. Times he feels her presence so clearly. He does not think explicitly that he is looking for something to fill the void left by his wife, and that like Firmin and others he's using drink. But with some hazier version of this thought, with difficulty he rises, steps carefully down the stairs and through the hotel courtyard and out onto the street. Walking slowly then but as smoothly as he can muster east along Avenue de Metamoros, destined for the square.

And as suddenly as his dead wife had been with him on the rooftop, on the street then she is absent.

Hot breath rises from the cracked concrete of the sidewalk. The widower stumbles briefly but rights himself, pauses. He's staring through open double doors into a large yard filled with all types of machinery, car and truck parts, boilers and furnaces and tractors, an open-to-the-sky but interior spaced filled with rusting and greased and multi-colored steel parts, a mechanic's giant shop. Pointing through the doors, the professor of architecture might have asked, "Is *this* a courtyard, yes or no. Why or why not?"

Back on the hotel terrace, the younger man sips at his coffee and resists accompanying it with a cerveza. He scribbles more notes on his spiral pages, lights a cigarette and listens. Scribbles some more.

Until his wife emerges from the stairwell to the rooftop, back from the walking tour of courtyards, in khakis and cotton blouse hand embroidered and white and fresh from a vendor at the zocalo. Sun-flushed, lovely, she asks, a kiss onto his concentration-pinched forehead, "How'd your morning go? Do you want to tell me about your writing?"

The younger man, the writer, smiles sheepishly, looks across the rooftops to the distant mountains. "You see, I've got this incredible setting," he turns back to her. "And some good characters. The widower, for example—" He motions over to the far side of the terrace toward a now-vacant table, " a rich character for sure." She frowns.

"But the problem," he laughs under his breath, thinking she knows what's coming, "I'm looking for the action. But I just can't seem to get the widower off the terrace with his mescal."

"Trying to fill the empty space—his body's courtyard," she smiles in offering him the connection, "with tequila."

* * *

In the courtyard shop of the *mechanico*, perhaps the most beautiful courtyard in all Oaxaca to some, at sometime after 2 a.m. on Saturday, nothing is happening. Well, perhaps that's exaggeration—mice roam beneath the *decrepito* car engines and around the broken down boilers and furnaces and stoves and conveyers. Cats—rare in Oaxaca while dogs are plentiful—cats look for and fix on prey. Moonlight plays against shadow like the cats against the mice; more is visible than one might think.

At this hour, as the students work in the *Diario Oaxaca* newspaper's darkroom, the don sips mescal. Also sleepless, the patrona rises to iron bedsheets, and the professor lies in his moonlit room in the Hotel Azucenas, worrying for his students and himself, wishing for luck in the events that will culminate in a few hours at the photography exhibit opening. The widower and the cabbies, their parts played, their work in the plan finished, doze. The widower thinks of his patrona, while the cabbies, looking only for justice, wait in their strike line at the bus station and reflect on the previous day's events—the drug deals they've driven the American students to—and the way their lives should be different after the exhibition. All the while, just blocks away, this most beautiful and functional of courtyards, this mechanic's shop is near silent. But, again, we've slipped ahead of ourselves.

* * *

Yet where were we? Thursday afternoon, walking down Avenue de Metamoros with his wife, the young writer is still trying to make the ongoing story become active. "I promised in the introduction," he tells her, "that there'd be intrigue and amusement, both." He trips on the uneven pavement, peering into yet another courtyard, the best yet he thinks, this one filled with engines and machinery of all kinds—a mechanic's shop. "And I told you so far I can't seem to get the character of the widower off the rooftop with his mescal in the Desani water bottle."

"Nice detail, *Desani*," she says.

He pauses on the street, exasperated. "But the old man doesn't seem to care, I swear! It's as if he wants to die, because his wife did, he wants to pull this pitiful 'Leaving Las Oaxacas' sort of thing, doesn't seem interested in saving himself. But he's either saved or he's dead, right?" he asks her, and she laughs at him.

And a few blocks later while they wait for their cervezas at an outdoor café overlooking the square, while his wife studies her notes on the courtyards they'd visited that morning, the younger man opens his notebook. Pausing for inspiration, looking toward the center bandstand and out from it, at the clothing and curio vendors and balloon sellers and shoe shiners kneeling at the bases of their wood and iron thrones. An impeccably dressed, silk-suited mestizo, having blood of both the native Amerinds and the Spanish mixed, reads his newspaper while the shiner buffs his Italian loafers with a soft cotton rag. The young man at the café table looks down at his notebook's empty page, then begins scribbling.

The Don of the Zocalo, the Dios-padre, flips a coin to the man his same age, 41, who shined his shoes—ten pesos plus a two-peso *tipo*. The Don's father and the father of the shoe shiner, both of Zapotec origins, both also Catholics as the vast majority of people here are, had worked together way back, before the Don became powerful enough that his father no longer needed to work. Now Don-zoca and the shoe-shiner's relationship is some complicated version of master-slave, not unlike the Spanish and the Zapotecs five hundred years before. They need one another, coexist because of the existence of the other, yet they resent each other—the Don that his childhood friend reminds him of his beginnings, the shoe shiner because he envies the Don's power and wealth but not his methods or his business. Each feels both superior and inferior to the other, and the resulting tension shows in the clenched jaw muscles of the shiner, in the averted eyes of the man reading the newspaper, the one with the highly glossed Italian loafers.

Stepping down, the Dios-padre chooses the prime corner café table at the restaurant facing the square, a selection based not on which table is unoccupied because this makes no difference in his choice. He could just as easily find a car he wants to buy, and his stature and wallet would land him behind the wheel, probably before the traffic light changed. Standing a few feet into the square, the Don of the Zocalo motions a gold and gemmed index finger toward the back of the restaurant, with a sidewise glance toward the prime table where a sandy-white haired man of perhaps seventy is finishing his meal. At the Don's signal, a waiter and a manager step briskly from the back, with respectful nods toward the don but a lack of eye contact similar to the aversion of the shoe shiner.

The older gentleman, an American tourist, looks up from his enchilada to find the waiter and the manager sliding half of his table outward, the new prime corner table. The old American finds himself now in row two, his salt and pepper and mole and verde sauce split off, too, to adorn the table of the don, the Dios-padre, who seats himself then, while the waiter slides the chair in from behind. The don then pulls from his suit jacket pocket a pair of cell phones, which he aligns carefully on the table in front of him. Don-zoca's face shows irritation, as if the creation of his table took entirely too long.

A second waiter hustles up with two bottles of white wine. The Dios-padre points to one, barely looking up from the cell phone on which, having checked messages, he now plays a video game. Cell phones are rare on the street, so expensive none but the wealthiest can afford—yet he holds two. Besides trafficking methamphetamines and marijuana, the godfather is preparing to launch a cell phone network business that will have thirty-five percent of Oaxacans using his product within the year. Across the zocalo, three payphones sit in a row, two or three locals waiting in line to use each. This, the godfather notes with satisfaction.

The waiter disappears and reemerges with an ice bucket on a steel stand for the wine. No one else in any of the cafés has such a privilege. He presents the dripping bottle to the Don, who touches the back of his hand to the glass and shakes his head, gives a little laugh, disdainful. Of course the wine isn't cold enough. Rebuked, his face a dark reddish brown pout, the waiter spins the bottle in the ice bucket for perhaps thirty seconds then scurries away, seeming relieved to be off the stage.

The suited manager immediately steps up, loudly packing a box of Marlboros beside the table, peeling the cellophane, removing the foil, then pulling one cigarette an inch out of the pack, presenting the box to Don-zoca. Who ignores the manager but reaches for the extended cigarette. Lights it with a silver Zippo bearing the stencil of a Zapotec jaguar, leaving the disappointed manager hanging with his outstretched Bic. The manager then steps backward three small paces before turning away from the Don like a servant leaving the presence of a monarch. Immediately the first waiter appears tableside to open and pour the now even-colder wine, which the godfather tastes with grudging disapproval, as if he has no choice but to suffer ineptitude in service and poor quality in product. But Don-zoca's impatience belies a different concern, that for his new business. He is looking to go straight, is looking for help in extricating himself from his illegal enterprises. And he realizes with anxiety—for a man of his stature seldom requires it—that he needs help. He takes another sip of wine, looking toward the retreating waiter now almost sympathetically.

All this the widower—remember the widower?—watches from his formerly prime-corner now second-row table, finishing his enchilada and cerveza. Watching almost furtively, as do a trio of police officers speaking among themselves at the corner of the zocalo and Avenue de la Independencia. As do shopkeepers whose stores line the square; the newsstand operator in the northwest corner; the poor, homeless, the beggars; the young and elderly both slipping table to table at the cafes offering flowers and bead bracelets and hand embroidered clothing, carved wooden animals and black clay pots and replicas of prehispanic artifacts. All these, a cross-section of Oaxacan life, all looking for a few pesos, coexisting in the city square, notice the movements of the Don of the Zocalo. All except the smallest children, like the don and his shoe shiner once were, who run and beg and do stunts for the tourists and don't seem to mind if they're mixtec, Zapotec, Hispanic, or some mestizo combination; they're all just kids.

Something of this the young writer thinks, watching too, from a third-row table where he sits with his wife, stunned by the show the godfather has put on, the theatrics he has put the café staff through. It is then, while the don sips his wine quietly now, that the three American architecture students slip into the scene, entering the zocalo from the northwest corner, looking nervous, anxious, like they're up to something. And even more nervous when they see the threesome of police chatting near the newsstand operator. They look around, each a different direction then, as if they missed a street sign. One of the boys pulls out a map, turns it 45 degrees, nods to the other two. They head quickly toward the southwest corner of the square, near where Don-zoca's shoe shiner now sits in his own chair reading the newspaper the don had discarded.

So *los tres estudiantes de architectura* soon meet their ecstasy contact, eventually scoring six hits of the locally produced drug. Scoring something they've been looking to find in the courtyards of Oaxaca—and the zocalo is, after all, the largest and most central courtyard of the city—a "high," perhaps, something to lift their spirits to a higher plane, their senses to greater awareness.

Incidentally, the students need not to have worried about the police, since the dealing of pot and ecstasy goes on under their watchful eyes, with their blessing. The cops receive kickbacks on a per-deal basis, so to look for, seek out, and monitor the exchanges is in their best interest. The Don-zoca sees to it that the officers who are willing to serve him and protect his operations are rewarded. It's all a neat little system. Disturbing to the Dios-padre, however, is the greed of those police who have taken to stopping taxis and tour vans and demanding payments to allow them to pass. The small bribes of a hundred or two hundred pesos a stop have become so widespread that the *huelga*, the strike of the drivers, does not surprise the Don. Like his native ancestors, when pushed they will push back. But the strike remains an annoyance, dangerous too, since any indictment of the police force's activities could easily reveal other involvements in, say for example, the trafficking of ecstasy or marijuana. All the more reason, the godfather thinks, to move his capital interests to the marketing of cell phones and service, the moneymaker of the future in Oaxaca. His Spanish ancestors would be proud, he thinks, to see him uniting the needy people of the region in a new way of communicating.

* * *

Nearly 9 p.m. Thursday evening, on the rooftop of the hotel. The young writer is blocked, frustrated, is marking through several long passages in his notebook. Some noise rises up from the courtyard below, voices, commotion of some kind. Then the voice of the patrona calling up sweetly: "*Señor Viudo,*" literally "Mr. Widower."

The widower has been listening, but he has also been watching the young man at the far table drinking coffee and water and scribbling and stopping. His heart leaps at the voice, and his legs follow. But as he nearly trots to the stairs down, he calls across to the young writer who's been trying not to watch the excited old man. "Did you know, son, that Asimov used to work with two electric typewriters going at once?" The younger man looks up as if surprised. "When he got stuck on one plot-line, he'd just swivel his chair and work on the other!" And with that he is on the stairs.

The widower reaches the bottom step as the three ecstatic students bound toward him and into the stairwell. In front of him in the foyer, their professor spies them and calls out to them in a tone that demands response, as if their grades depend on it: "Is this a courtyard—Daniel, why or why not? Note the natural light here at 9 p.m., Kyle. Would you say this is meant to be at this hour a public or a private space?" A student, the first on the stairs, has almost made the landing, where he'd be out of the professor's searchlight scan. "And, oh, Mister Darren!" he pauses, watching as the legs on the stairs slide downward, become half a man, three-quarters visible, then the whole being. "So good of you to join us—and regarding the solar placement of this building, could you say it is on a north-south or east-west setting, and is it the properly situated?" Slight pause. "Oh, and …Why?" The professor's eyebrows are arched to an obscene degree, rounded and angular like fortune cookies. The low laugh the young students hear then does not come from their professor.

Meanwhile above, the husband of the student, the would-be Asimov, starts writing on the new blank sheet. On the open page of the other notebook are several paragraphs, one completely crossed out and another partly marked through; the last line ends mid-sentence with the three-dot ellipses of frustration. On the new sheet he begins, "The godfather of the zocalo stood in the doorway that opened to the courtyard of the Hotel Azucenas. He laughed, drawing the attention of the lovely plump patrona, the students of architecture, and their professor who seemed peeved to be interrupted from his off-hours lecture, his questionings of his students about courtyard function and purpose and design." These first words are written quickly, then there's a pause. Again he begins writing feverishly.

"It is, and it is not a courtyard, of course," Don-zoca cuts off his own laughter to speak in perfect English. He stands in the foyer, having entered off the street quietly and unnoticed. "Like the yin and the yang, this space that is at once a courtyard holds all the capacities of its opposite. At once inside and outside, light and shadow, even a place of both good and evil." He smiles while the students probably picture in their minds the end courtyard of the photography museum with its single tree, beautiful and dangerous as the apple tree in Genesis.

"But before you all get lost in the symbolic forest, remember that I speak literally as well." He pauses to eye the three ecstatic students individually, then the widower, then the patrona. "While some find their *apples* down by the zocalo," the godfather goes on, "others can bite from the ones much closer to home." To the three students, he means their drugs; to the widower, he speaks of the clear liquid in his water bottle. To the patrona, perhaps, he refers to the sumptuous Oaxacan chocolates at the reception desk and in tile bowls around her courtyard. Just then, a cell phone trills from inside Don-zoca's flawless Italian suit jacket. "*Perdoname*," he nods, turning ninety degrees away from his audience.

And the pen of the writer on the rooftop stops abruptly. *Shit!* He might be heard to say under his breath, under the bruised sky that reaches down to connect with the hotel's stucco walls. Orion and the dippers twinkle so near above his head that, had he a rake or a broom he could sweep them into a glistening pile that would confound astronomers for ages. The writer, in abject frustration, feeling an attack of anxiety, looks desperately from the new notebook page back to the old, the one with all the spurts and stops and mark-throughs. He looks, anguished at the last words written before the three-dot ellipses, as downstairs the cell phone rings again and the Dios-padre flicks it open, listens for a moment, his face growing dark. "Spanish bastards!" he hisses into the little Nokia microphone.

The godfather of the zocalo has come to the Hotel Azucenas to apologize—or, as his Catholic upbringing dictates, to confess transgressions. And to seek help in extricating himself from the old business so that he might begin anew and legit with his cell phone service providership. He knows that *los tres estudiantes* scored some ecstasy from one of his dealers on the street. He's found easily through his contacts where the boys are staying. A friend at the little tienda down the block offers information of the *viudo's* purchase of several liters of mescal. With alarm at first, and then some sort of faith in providence, he realizes his old childhood *amiga* happens to be the patrona of the hotel the students and the old man occupy.

While part Zapotec, the godfather has some Spanish blood in his veins, and he's a Catholic who for a long time considered himself devout. It is only recently, in the last few years, that he has begun to find something in the confessional—exactly, he realizes, what he's trying to accomplish in a fell swoop here at the Azucenas—lacking. Somehow the washing of sins merely by admitting them seems too easy. And to think for years he thought it was too hard, to speak of his transgressions.

But now, the phone call. One of his dealers telling him the police want his support against the striking drivers. They need his assurance before they will sanction any more deals. The hypocrisy of both of their positions he recognizes, of course. But for his part, he can assuage the feelings with simple rationalizations, repeated enough times that they become quite believable—he's a respected member of the community who gives large sums to church and charity; and, regarding the drug trade, as with alcohol or cigarettes, no one is forcing people to use his products, they do it by choice. But Don-zoca, despite appearance to the contrary, is not the sharpest tool in the shed, *no es la herramienta mas afilado en la caja de herramientas.* Or more accurately, perhaps, he is a man too-sharp of mind without enough soul, enough heart. But this imbalance, to give him credit, is precisely what he is here to rectify.

On the rooftop, the young writer pauses again. He sets down the pen onto the notebook page he can barely read now in the dim light angling out from the nearest hotel room's window. He gazes up to the stars again and then around the rooftop, searching for some inspiration. The phone call, he thinks. What next?

The writer then focuses his gaze on the table that the widower vacated. The old man's water bottle is left on the table, like the writer's own in front of him. With all the characters downstairs, he has the rooftop to himself. He picks up his water bottle and rises, walks quietly over to the widower's table, where he simply trades his third-full water bottle for the widower's. He returns then to his table, his notebooks. He raises the widower's plastic bottle to his lips and takes a substantial gulp. He sets the bottle down, reaches for his pen, and after a moment's pause begins scribbling again on the older notebook page.

The darkness of the Hotel Azucenas's downstairs courtyard is far from complete. There are lamps on the reception desk and in the office behind it; wall sconces surround the courtyard, evenly placed on the stucco walls; and from above, dim light from the upstairs rooms leaks down from above, though not enough to blot out the starry sky. The courtyard then, filled to near capacity by the patrona, the professor, the students, and the Don—a congregation like something out of Agatha Christie or a game of Clue—is both light and not-light, dark and not-dark at once. The crowded space has been deathly quiet since the phone rang and the well-dressed mestizo spoke the vehement two words, then listened, then in a harsh whisper in Spanish told the caller, "*Necesito pensar!*"

Even the students, whose language skills are sorely limited, understand the gist of his statement and can feel some gravity in the situation. Such seriousness, as well as the anxious crowd around them—including figures of authority—combine to form a powerful version of what on campus back home they call a buzz-kill.

Don-zoca flips his Nokia closed and repockets it. Don-zoca nods to his old friend the patrona, to the professor, to the widower and the students in turn. "*Mi amigos,*" he says gravely, "I ask to you, *ayudame, por favor.*" When no one seems to refuse him—which of course would have greatly surprised a man of such a powerful position—he nods toward the stairs. "*Quiza,* we could talk on the roof?"

The writer does not hear the procession of footsteps on the stone stairs right away. As he pauses momentarily to sip from the water bottle, pen still in hand, he's thinking how brilliant his wife is, how right she was that the Don-zoca should be made less stereotypically powerful and sharp. Much better, she had said, to give him maybe a little more humanity and a little less brains. He plunges back into work, scribbling furiously, pausing only again to sip the clear liquid from the water bottle.

The meeting of the *Ayudantes de Don-zoca*, as the helpers will call themselves, convenes on the rooftop. Present are the patrona, the widower, the students and their professor, and the don himself. Importantly, as they find as Don-zoca speaks so honestly to them, no one except those present knows of the don's plans to go straight, to get out of the drug trafficking business. For any plan to succeed, he tells them all, none in his drug network can suspect what will be *una picadura*, a sting. Having placed his trust and his heart in the hands and minds of those surrounding him on the hotel rooftop, the don seems relieved. He sighs loudly and leans back, content to remain silent now as his helpers hatch a plan. He does not quite understand why all seem so taken with the idea; he doesn't think the motivation of saving another human being could be so compelling. And certainly, he thinks, without any visible reward for their good deed.

As the conversation goes on, the young writer scribbles. He can see the outlines of the figures on the other side of the rooftop, can hear occasional words and phrases. He cannot make out, in the shadows of the far table, the widower, who has retrieved what he thinks is his water bottle full of the elixir, which he puts to his lips and then swallows with distinct disappointment.

The scribbler can make out the voice of the lawyer-widower, several times during the meeting humbly offering insights into aspects of law. The writer also hears a bit from the professor, a voice noted several times, he seemingly the moral and philosophical compass of the group. At one point early in the meeting, the scribbler hears the professor state in a vehement whisper, "You either must go straight, or not, but you cannot be both a drug dealer *and* a legitimate businessman." The professor's comments function to polarize the group. Later in the proceedings, the scribbler hears the professor again: "The police either protect and serve, or they are criminals, too; one cannot be both upholder and breaker of laws at once." The writer thinks he hears some chuckling after this last comment, from somewhere near Don-zoca though it could be from anyone.

After an hour at least, each group member has spoken, has put in something of value to the concoction that began like stone soup. What began as nothing but willingness has hardened into a detailed plan of definite action. (This action, of course, the scribbler envies most; he sips from the water bottle and wonders how they come up with such engaging, ambitious plots.) And just one side-note, one the don perhaps realizes, consciously or not: there are other motivations for the willingness of the participants, as is natural, perhaps, in the way that charitable contributions are tax deductible. The students have bought illegal drugs—this the don, the professor, the patrona know; the professor's study-abroad would be discontinued immediately for even an allegation of such misconduct. And the widower simply relishes the opportunity to be included, and especially to spend meaningful time with the patrona.

So then among the group members, hands are shaken, embraces exchanged. The writer overhears what is to be the meeting place the day after tomorrow. Saturday, at the *Alvarez Bravo Museo de Fotografía*. For his part, Don-zoca seems nearly overcome with gratitude, and holds the embrace of his childhood friend, the patrona, for a long moment. The widower, too, embraces the patrona afterwards, and the writer can't help but think that this hug, too, lasts longer than necessary. The meeting members then leave the rooftop, off to make their calls and arrange their connections. Much is to be done before the group reconvenes at the exhibit opening Saturday at noon.

* * *

On Saturday, mid-morning, on the hotel rooftop, the young writer is reading, scribbling, sipping. Knowing his wife is headed with her classmates to the photo exhibit opening, he finds a description of the site:

> *In the Alvarez Bravo Museum of Photography, a visitor finds three*
> *courtyards aligned on a north-south axis, with the gallery rooms*
> *flanking the stark middle area that is bathed in sunlight much of*
> *the day. The first courtyard features indigenous flora of seemingly*
> *impossible variation, and in the lush third courtyard the space is*
> *dominated by a central, perfectly shaped acacia tree. The middle*
> *courtyard features no plant life at all, only a central drainage*
> *canal two feet wide that stretches north to south and connects the*

visitor to the other courtyards. Arched central doorways create north-south flow and allow the visitor to see the museum's entire length, from the street entry 130 feet to the imposing acacia at the end . . .

The weary widower, so busy for the past 18 hours, rests at his roof-top table some fifty feet from the younger man. He's thinking of something the guide and driver described to him on their tour of prehispanic sites. Thinking, too, of the photography museum where he will head shortly. And, of course, thinking of the patrona, *my patrona* he says to himself now. He's not drinking this morning.

The patrona's brother, the guide, spoke of ancient Zapotecs and their belief in the life beyond death. Death was an honor—in their games, *juegos de pelota*, it was the winner who was rewarded with execution. But to pass into the afterlife, one first had to answer nine questions, completing a journey. Often there was a river to cross. The successful one arrived in paradise. The widower sees in the photography museum the first courtyard as the terrestrial, with all its plants and life; then the second courtyard as the kind of limbo, the intermediate place even containing a central river—the drainage canal—to ford before one advanced; and third courtyard with its central, idyllic acacia tree, a kind of Eden. The widower warms to the thought.

By ten a.m., sun has burned off much of the low cloud cover, and shadows cut distinct lines across the triple courtyards of the Alvarez Bravo as the caterers are completing their set-up work. Meanwhile, the students deliver the photographs to the museum, where the volunteer staff of currently out-of-work, striking cabbies and tour drivers use the frames provided to finish the presentations and hang the pictures in the gallery rooms off the middle courtyard. The students and the cabbies sigh relief when the finished products, twelve 8 x 10 black and whites, are in their places, randomly spaced among the 70 already hung on the walls of the six small viewing rooms. One of several unifying features of the dozen late-additions is the presence of an elderly man in the background of each; the touristy-looking, jeans and sweatshirt, baseball-capped guy holds up a newspaper, as if reading the paper on the sidewalk. The front page headline is discernable.

The students and the drivers are shortly joined by the Don of the

Zocalo, the lovely patrona, and finally, about 11, by the elderly man now famous because his image lurks in so many photos, the widower the students now call Hitchcock. He smiles and shakes the hands of the others, and moves swiftly with his own shaking hands to the table the caterers have set up offering bread, cheese, beer, bottled water, and tiny celebratory flutes of mescal.

The photography exhibit, *Arte y Vida*, simply art and life, contains 82 prints of everyday scenes from the city of Oaxaca, common images like the vendor juicing oranges on the street or the barker singing out his wares from the bed of the bottled water delivery truck. Simple capturing of light, shadow, texture. And like the courtyard they hang in, the photos possess some quality that cannot be seen but is only felt; beneath the visual splendor is something striking to the other senses and perhaps even more, striking some place inside the viewer indescribable but no less real. The presenters of the exhibition hope that this unnameable quality is the palpable link between *art* and *life*, something irresistibly present but wonderfully undefinable. As the pamphlet reads, "*arte es el misterio de la vida*," the mystery of life is this art. But none of this attempted analysis of what is perhaps un-analyzable can explain the impact of the 12 photographs added lastly to the exhibition by the unlikely team that had formed on the hotel rooftop two nights earlier. The impact is most profound on a small number of official invitees here, the police and the members of Don-zoca's drug trafficking network.

But as these luminaries enter the courtyard of the Alvarez Bravo *Museo Fotografia*, the young writer still sits above the courtyard of the Hotel Azucenas. He sips from his water bottle and, thinking of a gallery of pictures, scribbles:

Photographs seem distorted as our vision is—a distortion caused by limitation. The frame of the lens, even if 360 degrees, still leaves much out. Take the sky beyond the upper limit of the lens, for example, or the ground beneath. Imagine what you can't see, the burglar behind the door of the pictured building, the dog on the couch behind the drapes, the couple making love in the upstairs bedroom. Every photograph is a limited rendering, a clipped version. Just as our senses can provide only so much information, an excerpted version of all that is out there . . .

Pardoning the writer's interruption, now moments before noon, the police and the drug cartel workers arrive at the exhibit. The police, on duty of course, security for the exhibition opening, file through the entry courtyard and sample from the caterers' table before heading into the bright, stark second courtyard. They nod minor greetings to the cartel members present, as if they're neighbors and not business associates. Both groups step over the narrow drainage canal and move into the gallery rooms off the second courtyard, not certain but perhaps with an anxious feeling about what they will find hanging on the walls.

The settings vary, but the subject of the 12 photos is identical. Still, because each is placed randomly throughout the exhibit, the off-the-street observer might not realize the similarity right away. The pictures show regular street scenes, yes, but the action captured is clearly—in all 12, at least to a practiced eye—a drug deal. In some, bags of pot are passed to young, student-tourist looking folks; in others tiny packages or pills. In the background of each photo—again, not immediately obvious but readily apparent by repetition, an elderly tourist reads a newspaper. In some photos drugs and money can be seen to pass simultaneously. And always the guy in the background, his newspaper raised with the headline barely legible: *Huelga del Conductores Resolvado.*

It may be noted that the officials' anxiety is well-founded—in overseeing the drug deals, they had more than once noticed students taking pictures in which, given the photographers' line of sight, they could appear. Once they even gave chase, but the photographers dove into a conveniently waiting Volkswagen taxi. But now the police are relieved to find that while the hanging photographs depict the deals, their own presence is apparently not in the frame. As the police and the cartel members circulate through the small gallery rooms, they might murmur to one another or exchange a glance as another notices one of the twelve photos.

At an impeccably timed interlude, Don-zoca approaches and greets each of the official viewers, a large manila envelope conspicuous under his arm. While they chat, the don glances down toward the envelope he carries, more noticeably when he addresses the police officers. To them, he says something simple and pointed in whispered Spanish that the members of his team—the students, the professor, the patrona, the widower—already know. Under his arm, Don-zoca holds unedited, un-clipped photos; for each hanging photograph, there is a larger, more complete version in which the police are visible, overseeing the drug deal going down. Their complicity is indisputable, he tells them quietly. And if the strike of the drivers is not immediately resolved—as the head-line states, and including reimbursements of the extorted funds—the en-velope under his arm will be made available to the press. In addition, Don-zoca will explain his own plans for leaving the one enterprise and entering another, the legitimate cell phone business. Finally, the police, he tells them, are now officially out of the drug trafficking business, as well as, of course, out of the tour- and cab-driver extortion business.

So other hands are offered, begrudgingly, extended toward the don with some respect, anger and, in truth, some relief. These police, sworn to an oath, have been hypocrites for too long, taking money from the drivers and the drug runners both, perhaps buying with it jewelry for their wives and toys for their children; but these same children could soon be on the receiving end of the drug transfer. These police might now even ask themselves how they have slept through nights for so long. Same for the dealers, many whose faces are clear in the photos, who can either beg the don for legitimate work or move on; those closest to the don do not appear in the photos and already have positions in the Don-zoca Wireless Networks, Inc. In fact, when a cell phone rings in the courtyard where three old friends—Don-zoca, the shoe-shiner, and the patrona's brother, the driver—stand talking, all three reach for their pockets. Soon also there will be a D z Wireless phone in every cab.

Meanwhile in the third courtyard of the museum, where the edenic tree stands center and the sun beats down angling halfway across, the cool shade marks the other half like a giant symbol of yin and yang. In this courtyard shortly after noon, the hands have been shaken, the deals made, the agreements secured. The students and their professor sample the mescal, the food, the cervezas, savoring the findings of their fruitful study-abroad program. And the patrona, bougainvillea blossom behind her ear, takes the shaking hand of the widower, smiles at him. With her other hand she takes the demitasse glass of mescal from his other, looks into his eyes, into his soul he thinks, and turns it up. Smiles, sets the glass down and takes his other hand in hers. A glance toward the now empty mescal glass, she says to him in perfect English, "You need not use the drink to fill the place of her. She is not gone—she is here just as she is not here, always. At the same time. As I am here," she says.

And on the rooftop of the hotel not ten city blocks away, the young writer, stops scribbling. Sipping from the water bottle, he wishes for his wife's return from the photography exhibition. He looks down at his two notebooks, both open and full of his rantings. He thinks, then writes: the most unlikely of stories can be the most likely, if they actually happened. In this way, perhaps, the everyday art can be both beautiful and truthful. He looks out off the rooftop to the next rooftop, to the next roof beyond that, thinking of the things he can see, hoping to feel the things he cannot.

Clay Pigeons

Nash hasn't tied his work boots as he heads to his truck—their soles make sandpaper scuffing sounds across the smoothed pine boards of the porch and down three steps. And then on the gravel somewhere between porch and pickup, Nash passes through a cool pocket of air, noticeable because the rest is so warm, even already now in the early morning. The sensation is that of lake swimming in his boyhood, when he would paddle out toward the floating raft and he'd stroke through a colder patch of water, like there was something cool there but nothing was visible, as if it was the absence of something that left the small area noticeably colder than that water around it.

Nash recalls suddenly a sharp memory from his pot smoking days, getting high on the third tee of the local municipal golf course. Playing in his head an old song that surfaces seemingly from nowhere but it's the grass, he thinks, Brewer and Shipley in the where-are-they-now file, One Toke Over the Line, *sweet Jesus. Sittin' downtown at the railway station one toke over the line.*

Nash works as a bartender, which pays his bills, and Ruby's too if she'd let him, which she won't. He owns a few acres and a haybarn west of town where he works wood and makes furniture. He drives that direction now, almost eight on a Thursday morning in early September, in a small upstate New York farming town called Sanford. Nash isn't surprised by the cold spot, wouldn't have been surprised had it been a warm spot either. He is working on a theory about such things, pockets in space, and intends someday soon to tell Ruby about it, his theory, once it takes on a little more shape. Darius' death is a certain wrinkle, something he needs to crank in, to see where it fits. His palms on the Toyota pickup's wheel are still clammy, sweaty, and the nervous, unsettled feeling stuck in his stomach just the opposite of, say, pancakes, he thinks.

And earlier this morning, 6 a.m. or just after, Nash lying with ankles sweating beside Ruby, on his back stuck to the fitted sheet. She beside him, on her side, could feel the heat emanating off his body, believed she could see the waves like those that rise off the summer's tarred road.

Are you awake, she'd said.

I'm awake.

You're so hot—do you feel okay? And a moment later: *Do you re-member much of last night?*

No, not much. Should I be worried?

Then: Of course, he says, remembering hazily. The phone ringing, 3 a.m., his partner Simms at the bar trying to tell him of the death. Simms the lightning rod for bad news, relishing his role, his part in it all.

Geez, Sim, we hardly knew him.

You played golf with him that time. We've known him in the bars forever.

Nash then remembered the round a year or two back. A cool clear late-morning, a fall sky sharp as tin sheeting. Darius striding the fairway with a joint pinched between his lips, a sweet-smelling cloud around his exhalation.

Yeah, but, Nash says. *Get some sleep, Sim.*

He's up then while she lies motionless, eyes open like a corpse, thinking what she's thinking, and knowing him so well. He slides from bedroom to kitchen—in a four-room cabin it's a one-room swing—opens the refrigerator and reaches for the coffee can. His hand nearly, reflexive-ly, clutches a beer bottle on the top shelf, right, but then with conscious effort he resists. He retrieves from a cupboard shelf a coffee grinder probably fifty years old and still near-perfect functioning, clutches five-pound bag of beans then from the freezer, and pours a small mound into the chamber of the grinder. He hesitates then, thinking *one toke over the line* and how does it go, I always do this, what's the order of events here? He then pulls the dogfood container from a lower cabinet, measures out a morning serving, and heads to the porch where he dumps the cup's contents into a stainless steel bowl. The dog anxiously follows, looking from cup to bowl and back over the space in between having and not having, then uncomfortably digging in to the meal with Nash standing so close. Nash walks barefoot down the porch steps and a hundred feet to the road, where the morning paper lies dewy, bridging the drainage ditch beside the driveway. In his stomach the nervousness is funny almost, because it doesn't affect his outer demeanor, is unnoticeable unless one knows him very well, as she does.

His hands and feet still sweat, as he rotates the crank above the wooden box of coffee. Just as Darius might have, though probably didn't, every morning. Or his last morning, which was yesterday.

Are you thinking of him, Ruby asks, a hand on his shoulder suddenly then, watching out the window the sun growing from the light preceding to a sliver of an arc, then creeping over the line made jagged by the uneven growth of the hayfield, and apple trees, idyllic really she thinks. And her hand startling him. *Please don't think it's so close*, she adds, meaning Darius, she off then into the bathroom, the cabin's fifth room if you're not a realtor and want to include it. Seven hundred square feet, "near-fully renovated" the ad might read.

Darius was hardly a friend, was a deadbeat dad who had a house and some land out near Nash's barn, a guy who held down a space (always the same space; he'd mill around like a disquieted ghost if someone occupied the mahogany bar's corner where he'd stand, never sit) at the tavern where Nash poured drinks. Drinks that for some filled spaces inside.

But not for Darius, who in Nash's view was one of the laugh-at-your-back-with-his-football-teammates kind of high school asshole, one who'd swing a cat by its tail. Though of course Nash hadn't known Darius in high school, Darius a dozen or so years older than Nash. Darius had been 52.

Nash stands at the counter leaning over the morning paper, palms sweating so the newsprint curls like bark, wondering if it had hit Darius sometime last night. If it hit him he wasn't happy, maybe because of his immaturity or his mean streak. He pictures Darius and the realization hitting him, and him seeing there was nothing he could do to change, himself or any of it. Darius, seeing himself as a man with a decent human side that got insecure and overwhelmed by the other side, the high-school-prick side, and he somehow couldn't live with himself anymore, not one more minute. Was this how it went? Or maybe Darius had some longing, for a good woman, or some connection with his fifteen-year-old son. Nash tries to picture it and cannot.

He finishes grinding the next day's coffee while he and Ruby drink what is in the pot, his a short-pull of stronger and hers a milked down weaker version. After he takes a last slug and heads out, kissing her distractedly, knowing it is distracted and then stopping, pulling her to him and presses himself against her, kissing her differently but with still a blankness in his eyes, a blank space that is seeing, she thinks, a rope or a rifle Darius might have used. She would be only a single degree of separation more, from him, from Darius, she thinks, if that means anything. If *one* degree means anything even, she thinks. Another fine line, and she may be one toke over it, this a thought flickering in her unconscious. And then he's down the porch steps and across the driveway. Ruby notices his boots unlaced and dancing like a little boy's.

Nash drives up Boughton Hill and then turns right and back down it, where it becomes Maple Avenue as it nears the tracks. He crosses the tracks in his pickup, a Ford old but not-too, seventeen years (older than Darius' son), nothing for a tractor like a Farmall for example. Beyond the railroad crossing on the corner of Main the Exxon that had been an Esso long before and now featured a convenience store where he buys the beer to settle his stomach, the beer that the Darius-part of his mind had been focusing on since he woke and opened the refrigerator. It was 7:53 by the clock behind the counter.

You heard about Darius, the counter girl, Lou, daughter of an old classmate of Nash's at Sanford High, not really asking at all but assuming, said. Small town, no secrets. Plenty of folks listened to police scanners at night, like Simms and Lou's father did. He folded the bills of change while consciously *not-noticing* her missing pinky and second fingers that outreached, the space the fingers once occupied. Of course she doesn't acknowledge either, the fingers or much less the brother lost crossing the tracks not two hundred yards from this very spot, not even three years back. And while Nash has been through the Exxon dozens of times in the last year, he has never before felt how needy Lou is, how wanting for any connection of the human kind. Lou is probably twenty, pale and small and pretty in a plain farmgirl way.

To Nash, she is open enough with her family's opinion, that there really wasn't no cause for great grief regarding Darius. She says as much to him without needing many words.

Nash drives east out of town then on the old road that parallels the highway, still two lanes with bends and scenery. He passes the development that has sprung up on the land where his boyhood home had stood, now the site of two dozen homes but strangely none on the spot where their house had been, as if it was some Seneca burial ground or something, a reserved space Nash has thought. A half mile past he pulls off the road down a rutted path to an old gravel quarry he frequented as a boy. A place that had always been littered with shells and beer cans and shards of clay pigeons left by hunters practicing with their shotguns. He remembers when he was nine or ten finding a couple of unbroken clay pigeons among the gravel mounds. He wonders now, again, how unlikely such a find must've been—the discs flung from a thrower (Nash hears the deep yell *PULL* like a drill sergeant from a movie), missed by the hunters' rifleshots, then somehow coming back to earth unshattered. The odds must be astronomical.

He lights a cigarette and opens the beer, and sits watching the mounds of gravel in the silence only broken by a whir of insects, which begins to the west and moves like that wave fans do at ballparks, rippling across to the east and then dying out. And fifteen or thirty seconds later, a space of time but somehow linked to the earlier, Nash thinks, beginning again from the same source. Sips the beer and smokes, staring out the windshield above the dashboard on which the clock, not digital but actually with hands, reads almost half past eight. Listens to the wave begin to his left again, the insects, as if he were moving the balance dial on the stereo, all left then middle then all right speaker sound. And again, then, nothing.

Not three miles away, at the brick high school that was always there next to the grade school that was new just five years back next to the middle school that had been the elementary school until five years ago, a fifteen-year-old kid, Darius Winslow Jr., known as DJ, sits by the west window at the back of his first period English class. The teacher has assigned a ten-minute creativity exercise called freewriting, and the students are supposed to put pen to paper without regard to grammar or punctuation and just let words flow out of them. On his wide-ruled notebook page DJ has written *crazy feeling, nervous in my gut, cant do this cant write this way of experience I don't have. Nothing happens to me, has happened either nothing of importance only seventeen and feel like what is it I'm waiting, waiting for something of importance to happen to me. . .*

Nash, who is old enough, 41, to have a child in the high school but has no children, drives back this time to another convenience store and buys another beer. Pulls a 16-ounce Bud from the tilted tray in the reach-in cooler; nine in the morning yet two or three beers are missing from the row already. The cashier, greasy-haired and pimpled and scared of so much he's always looking for a fight, could be his son.

You got the gas on seven, he asks Nash. Like a challenge.

No, just the beer.

Kinda early, ain't it? A little smirk around his eyes and mouth edge.

Nash drives to his shop, the haybarn on some acreage he owns west of town, where he works with wood mostly and builds furniture and odd sculpture. He slides back the heavy barn door, stands in the opening. The morning sun immediately fills the space with dust-swirling rays, the large one from the doorway and smaller slices from the east window and through the gaps in the pine siding, and through the siding above and down gaps in the floorboards of the hayloft above. Nash sets his beer on the table saw, lights a cigarette under his no smoking sign by the door he put up when he was quitting. Flips on the little radio that immediately releases a tinny chorus, *come on people now, smile on your brother everybody get together try and love one another right now.* He wonders if the Young family still receives a few cents every time the song gets played. Could've been their one hit, Jesse Cullen Young and the Youngbloods. Lucky to have the one, Nash thinks. He sips and smokes and hopes they've gotten rich and happy, if both are possible. The carbonation and the cigarette burn together the back of his throat, and he relishes the feeling. Thinking again about the kid behind the counter, the attitude masking insecurities no doubt but still, annoying Nash and leaving him guilty feeling. What he does not think is that he in some way affected the insolent wiseass kid. Nash feels the nervous sweat again between his fingers, in his palms, and can't chase the thoughts of Darius, barely an acquaintance really, with his mean streak and his dirty jokes and the space at the bar that would be there from now on.

Dougie Drooz, 27, of 221 Maple Ave., apt. B, the phone book could tell you, excepting his age, which most who saw him would guess wrong, because his acned puffy face makes him seem a high-schooler ditching class; yet his little beer-gut points both ways, to the baby-pudginess of an idle teen, and to a 30-something prematurely staid loafer workingman. He works the counter at the BP station Fuel-Smart, gets high on his little one-hitter that's a steel straw painted like a cigarette, white with a brown filter end, the type that were everywhere fifteen years ago. Most of his off time is spent with pot, and with beers and magazines of girls he'll never date that he lifts from the store. He's a sad joke to those his own age still in town, rarely gets together with anyone he once was close to. He's got no idea, this Thursday morning at around nine, that an old local, Darius Winslow, has killed himself. He does notice that he's already sold a few more tall Bud cans than usual. He pulls open the glass cooler door, scans the shelves, and this puff of cold air hits him like the ophthalmologist's cataract test, an invisible pocket of cold that seems to come from the space where the beer cans were but are no longer. The weird feeling is of something hitting him but there's nothing there to see, to swing back at, except what he doesn't think about which is air. Or maybe the lack of, the hit of a space of void, of no-air, that hits him like a cold spot in the lake when he's swimming. Unsettling, and in his ill-feeling mood, leaves him irritated, dissatisfied with himself, which he doesn't face but turns outward toward his early morning patrons. *That's your gas on number seven. Little early for a beer, ain't it?* Laughing almost, smirking at least, at the poor middle aged sap. There but for you, his mother says, and Dougie thinks this when he doesn't even want to.

In the small cabin, Ruby Nash takes the morning *Democrat & Chronicle* and her coffee to the front porch and sits and watches the work traffic, just sporadic cars bunched together, tailgating one another and then huge gaps; and most of the vehicles she recognizes and knows their owners, their jobs. She watches them speed up Boughton Hill headed to the crest and then to town or, more likely, farther west then to the city, or north toward the mall and office park. She can't quite picture Darius Winslow as her husband does, can't quite see him with a shotgun and for this she's glad. But she can't shake the image of her husband staring into the refrigerator, not an hour ago, reaching for and almost grabbing a beer bottle at 7 a.m.

Once she'd taken the surname of her second husband, she thought her name sounded not like an architect's, which she was, but like a country singer's: Ruby Nash. And she had the nicotined fingers, the deceased parents, the off-the-wagon husband and still boyish, tom-catting ex-, even the late model pickup truck. But she favored classic rock though she hated the term. And she had never seen herself as much of a victim.

Ruby sits in the wicker chair near the hanging ferns and smokes and thinks, then focuses on a tiny spider in the air a couple feet from her and at eye-level. It scrambles up the strand it has spun out, vertical now but the slightest breeze, even her exhaled breath she thinks, will push the strand out across the porch to the porch rail or the swing or the fern, will push the strand of web toward horizontal. And the spider then can build on the strand, can web it out and widen it so that it hangs invisible in airspace that will be traveled by flies and other insects. An invisible and now-empty space where something once was and will be again. Ruby slips a pen from behind her ear and turns to the newspaper's crossword, still thinking about empty spaces like the crossword boxes, about spaces where something is or was or would be. She thinks now, sipping her coffee, of what she thinks of as longing, of the space she can't see or define in words, but a space Nash can be (but wasn't this morning). And isn't longing a way to describe that space? And strangely the way songs and lyrics sometimes slip into one's head for reasons she can't understand or will ever maybe know, she thinks of a young man's voice singing *I'm so dizzy my head is spinning, like a whirlpool it never ends, and it's you, girl, making it spin.* Tommy Roe, she thinks, and she was eight years old and a babysitter was playing that song over and over. Not then but years later she's thought of the babysitter, a girl Ruby can picture, teenager and so old and wise and cool then, probably in love or a version of that, with some boy at school. And the song encapsulated all that she was feeling, what she dreamed he might be feeling, while she was on a Friday night babysitting a bunch of kids whose parents had gone to dinner, she imagined, at the restaurant where he waited tables. And in the crossword the clue *fish eggs* and only three letters and she pens it in.

Three miles outside of town, the horse track rises like a modern sculpture, if the angular grandstand late-1960s architects composed could still be modern, which thirty years later it still seems to be since it's so notable and noticed, even if only by employees or designers like Ruby Nash or non bettors. Its configuration of Vees, angles impressive still today and visible from a mile at least, the Vees of the grandstands and the seats, roof-line and out to the paddock and track, where it's all impressive and traditional curves, the oval most classic and necessary, and the space in the middle, an oval, too, the grassy area empty but for the one stakes race every spring, mown crosscut at angles, vees again and greenspace gorgeous, lush grass around which the ponies must run a mile and a quarter and never to feast on it. Thinking this, on the Thursday morning of above mention, coming to work at the betting window at Finger Lakes Race Track, Dick Pole. His name a dizzy or oblivious parent's cruel joke no doubt, and probably a Richard Pole, Jr. who's humming the Surfaris' classic "Wipe Out" for no reason he could ever tell.

Dick Pole arrives at work at the track shortly after nine, though Post Time for the first race isn't until 2, arrives early because he gets ten extra hours a week sweeping and cleaning the grandstands, the restrooms, the concession areas which at this hour are entirely empty spaces, voids waiting to be filled by the race fans and bettors, most of course even waking now on the morning after the death of Darius Winslow with no idea of the suicide but that thought that today's the day my horse, my longshot, comes in. Forever optimistic, hoping eternal.

And Dick Pole sweeps the concrete concourse, pushing dust past the racing form and newspaper boxes, on the *Democrat & Chronicle* not section A but down in B in the Metro and obits section will be tomorrow lines about Winslow's suicide. And Pole won't look at this paper, nor will he remember that Darius Winslow was a guy he'd seen at the track occasionally, wearing aviator sunglasses and golf shirt and too-pressed slacks looking like he thought he was something. A guy who had come to Dick's window more than once ignoring the clearly worded sign above the opening that told him to state dollar amount betting, horse number, and expected finish, example "Five dollars on #7 to show," simple as that but most including Winslow and many for reasons other than that they were patronizing assholes, many would give the information all wrong and out of order like if he'd remember, Pole could recite the cocky Winslow saying *Howitzer, seventh race, twenty bucks if he wins or places*, that sort of thing. So Dick passes the newspaper, won't notice that he doesn't see Darius, who, Winslow, this afternoon. But does he feel a cool, moist, maybe clammy breeze or is he somehow different this Thursday in some way he cannot name? A cool pocket of air that spins his head in the direction of the turnstiles.

Ruby Nash comes in from the porch and sits at the kitchen table, where she finishes her coffee alone. Around her at the other five mismatched wood chairs are her parents, Libby and Gar, both more than a decade deceased, and her brother and sister who live in Los Angeles and Nashville, respectively. Across and right on opposite sides of the double sink, places they both often have sat, are her ex-husband Clay and Nash himself, who at this moment sits in his pickup at the quarry. While only her mind sees them physically, their presence as ever is felt, and she speaks to them like she does the cats, the dog. What are we to do about Nash—she smiles a kind of grade-school embarrassed smile—*what are we to do about you*, she looks at him then, *Nash*, she asks them all.

And it is Ruby's ex, Clay, who weighs in first on the issue, which surprises her because much of their dissolution came about from his lack of forthcoming-ness. The odds on a relationship making it, he says, not even a marriage because I know those are fifty-fifty at best, but a serious relationship gotta be somewhere in the thirties, maybe less.

Thanks for the encouraging news, Ruby says.

I'm not finished, Clay says, while the others, especially Libby and Gar, cut skeptical glances. You don't expect maturity from me, and you're no doubt right not to. But you and Nash have been better than most, for what, seven years?

Nash on the other drainboard side stares not at Clay but at a place in front of him, where Clay's words would be if they were visible. It's hard for Ruby to tell if he's listening even, as Clay continues.

It's easy for someone to say 'so he drinks or drugs, what's the big deal?' And it's no deal except when it affects what you've got. You could do worse I guess—Nash ain't a gambler. A lotta guys drop their paychecks at the horse track yonder.

Clay hits a nerve with this. Libby and Ruby both eye Gar, who shakes his head and lets escape a low groan. Thankfully, Clay still has the stage.

It's the same as if he obsessed on oral hygiene or mowing the lawn, Clay goes on. It's some longing he's got. So he reads the obits, figures his place in the lives of those who've died? No big thing—we're all six degrees, right, or usually a lot less really, from anybody on the planet. You've seen the movie.

Ruby sips her coffee then, feeling less than soothed. Nash of course and Clay, both, can tell this, can feel it. So, your point? She asks.

Take the Surfaris, Clay tells her. "Wipe Out," remember? It was a B-side, on the spot they just ad-libbed it, and it's the one everybody knows. Why? Who the fuck knows? Clay laughs. Or take "Dizzy," Tommy Roe remember, you were thinking it earlier. Ruby smiles slightly. A hit immediately, it's still played a good bit on oldies stations. But did Roe know what he had when he first played it. Probably not—least I'd be surprised. Hard to know what we got when we got it, that's my point. Take you and me, Clay tells Ruby. No, that's water over the bridge or under the dam, whatever, I know that now. So take you and Nash . . .

While across town at the track, Dick Pole continues to swipe the cool, smooth cement. The push broom is four feet across, and he maneuvers it with athletic grace, swiftly and accurately cutting back and forth across the main concourse the way the mowers do the infield grass outside. His eyes rarely rise from the invisible path before him, and other track workers, jockeys, trainers crossing the room know to give him wide berth. But on his seventh pass near the entry turnstiles he passes through what he can barely feel as a pocket of cool air, unnoticed by him except for the tiny prickling of the hairs on his forearms that shine with a thin layer of perspiration. Dick Pole slows his pushing imperceptibly, and his eyes leave the invisible path.

Diagonalling across the area is a trainer, a recent hire Dick knows, maybe three months at the track. Small enough to have jockeyed in his younger days, still lean, balding now at perhaps fifty. Always says *mornin'* as he passes, though Pole has never acknowledged this with more than a grunt, never met the man's eyes. But this Thursday in August, Pole slows his broom and responds.

Morning, he says. It's Joyner, isn't it? How you getting on?

Yes, the smaller man says, surprise raising his eyebrows into his sun-freckled forehead. Ed Joyner. He puts out his hand.

The two shake, exchange how 'bout this heat, this humidity's, and Dick Pole then resumes his sweeping with an imperceptibly crisper motion, smoother and more exact at the same time. Humming a song by the Strawberry Alarm Clock, a title he couldn't tell you but for some reason he remembers the band's name. He wonders what the members are doing now, hopes they're getting a few bucks a month for the sweat and the bit of good fortune that had them atop the charts for a tiny space of time, probably nearly thirty years ago.

In his English class, DJ lifts his pen, feels no movement in the already stagnant air and smells peppermint life-saver in the mouth of the girl beside him, probably pot and incense both wafting from the ridiculous wool overshirt of the boy on his other side. D.J's hands sweat so that his notebook page turns up at the edges and the paper doesn't take ink well. Fitting, he does not think, because he has no words for all this inside him, what he can't explain, reasons for things he doesn't even know yet, *longings* is the word he doesn't think. Just before the assistant principal enters the room, hands his teacher a note and they move their lips in grave silence passed back and forth, and the teacher moves toward DJ to summon him out of class, to tell him the news about his father. Just before the interruption, DJ is hearing in his mind a song, music he's composed that as yet has no lyrics, for the band he and two classmates play in. It's catchy, he's thought, this tune; he imagines what it might be like if the song stuck in others' minds, too, if it were to become something of a hit.

Now almost ten in the morning, Ruby Nash has heard all the advice her family and ex-husband have offered, what to do about Nash. For his part, Nash has remained on the counter, swinging his untied work boots slowly in tiny circles in the air, the laces rotating clockwise surrounding a small circular space the way a kid's sparkler does in summer night air. He's listened intently but has said nothing. Ruby has heard her parents and Clay voice concern, but their take has been positive, that there's much to be preserved. He's a good man, Nash is, her father has said more than once. For her own part, Ruby has no words. She has all these opinions in her head, sips coffee in the kitchen empty but for the dog and cats that she doesn't speak to now but looks at imploringly. Dizzy, she thinks, like a whirlpool it never ends.

If you asked him, Dougie Drooz, at 10 a.m. on this early September Thursday when business at the store has been busier than usual but now has slowed, if you asked him what he longed for, he'd look at you funny. Up yours, he'd probably say. Because he wants his skin to clear and he wants to quit smoking and he wants a girl, someone he can talk to who's not an air-brushed pin-up girl like the life-sized cardboard cutout holding the twelve-pack of Miller Lite and suggesting more than beer. Dougie's girl would have a tattoo on her shoulder, he thinks, that he'd move his fingers over as he looked into her dark eyes, noting too with satisfaction her thin, slightly crooked nose and her badly dyed hair, feeling some-thing better for noticing these things.

A guy in a pickup pumps supreme unleaded at #5, and no one is in the store. Dougie lights a smoke and moves to the tall coolers at the back, opens, and pulls out a 16-ounce Bud from a row with just two remaining. Again the cloud of cold air escapes the cooler, hanging close to Dougie as he shuts the glass door. Back behind the counter he pours the beer into a Styrofoam cup for large coffees, lids it, and tears the plastic along the perforations to form an opening. He takes a deep swallow, exhales smoke from the now-distant hit, missing it already as the guy on #5 en-ters the store. 'Sup, he says. Eleven seventy-one, Dougie says, taking another sip then, not meeting the eyes of the man opening his wallet in front of him.

Partially worked table leg in hand, Nash steps to the barn door and looks out in the direction of his cabin a few miles away. In the doorway he feels the warmth of the day, humid and sunny, and then he feels a puff of cooler air like he'd experience in the driveway earlier. He thinks about commercial pilots who tell passengers we're entering an area of turbu-lence; the plane is buffeted about, but looking out the window one sees nothing, no strong forces or visible pockets of pressure at all. He walks

Clay Pigeons   57

slowly back to the work table on top of which he has a black and white photograph of Ruby looking up from her design desk, glasses on her forehead, smiling quizzically as if, *what's that you said?*, looking up then as he snapped the photo. He hasn't noticed the photograph in weeks, until today. Nash thinks of the space between himself and the picture, a gap that opens and closes like the mouth of a fish. He thinks of the counter girl, Lou, and the pimpled gas station guy whose name he doesn't know, thinking they could save each other, thinking he has something both of them long for. He thinks of the odds against actual human connections. And he thinks he needs help with his theories about spaces and longings and losses.

Nash sets the wooden leg down beside Ruby's picture and heads back to the door, pulling it shut behind him. In his mind is the classic "Smoke of a Distant Fire." Bars long and languid, soothing, all drawn out. Sanford Townsend Band, he thinks, funny how theirs could be a group from this very—and very tiny—town, hoping inanely that somehow they make a few cents off his *thought* of the tune. His mind then turning with his body toward the pickup he could use to occupy, and lessen, the space between here and her.

Diagramming Wyatt

Circle 1: Watt

To Create Venn Diagram: Draw 3 connected (overlapping) circles
  —ask self 'what are 3 most imp. elements of this event, situation,
    people, etc.'
—label circles
—ask what characteristics do 3 elements have in common?
—what char. do elements <u>not</u> have in common?

From class notes of Sloan Rawlings,
North Greensboro H.S. (N.C.), September, 1997

In the late summer of 1937, a ten-year-old Ford pickup sputtered into the tiny central North Carolina town of Hopefield. An army-green canvas stretched over a steel ribbed frame across the bed, so that the truck resembled an old covered wagon. On the canvas were stenciled in large white paint the letters "A.I.C." Beneath the tarp, in addition to bedroll, coffee pot, rumpled clothing items, sat an 8 mm Eyemo movie camera and a couple dozen reels of film stacked in tins. While the arrival of the truck to Hopefield was not recorded, several hundred feet of its visit there were.

The truck bore a California license plate, strange and exotic enough to get attention almost anywhere, certainly from many of the 974 residents of Hopefield. But then in such a small place, most any stranger would draw attention. And the initials on the canvas intentionally conjured optimistic images—perhaps, the townspeople were supposed to think, part of the acronym craziness of the New Deal, this the first year of FDR's second term when jobs were still scarce but the horizon had certainly brightened. A.I.C., they would find (without disappointment), stood for "Adventures in Cinematics," the brainchild of a Richmond businessman with a penchant for motion pictures. His fleet of a dozen trucks, all featuring the California plates procured mail-order through a low but well-placed associate in Los Angeles, were currently covering the small towns of the southeast, taking pictures and possibly, though they made no promises, "star-searching" for the next Jean Harlow (who had died tragically that summer at the height of her fame). The profit in the business came from the consignment sale of the films, 30 to 45 minutes of silent "action" taken in the small towns. Theater-goers would pay a few extra cents to see twice—once before the feature and once after—scenes of themselves and their neighbors going through the daily motions of their lives. Some became quite star-struck.

After circling the town, a dark-haired, handsome man of perhaps twenty-seven stepped from the pickup he'd parked just across the tracks outside Johnson's Agway Seed & Feed. He wore a laundry-yellowed white cotton shirt; his suspenders held up wrinkled and not unstained slacks, the kind expected of a traveling salesman, which the townspeople at first assumed he was. But Watt Dawson moved immediately to the back of the pickup, pulled out his trusty Eyemo, and started filming. As townspeople began to gather around curiously. A gifted figure for his line of work, Dawson might have appeared more like someone who ought to be in front of the camera rather than behind it; but he exuded a quiet optimism, an energy almost irresistible, to the women young and old of Hopefield. And even to the men, the farmers who while they felt immediate protectiveness toward their wives and daughters in the face of such a man, still found themselves drawn to him, often buying him a beers at JJ's Bar after a long day of shooting. The women nearly always cooked for him, and Watt Dawson almost never ended up sleeping in his truckbed.

* * *

Some sixty years after the filming of Hopefield everyday life, in a Greensboro nursing home in 1997, one of "the next Jean Harlows," Etta Johnson, turned 77. This the same year her grandson, Wyatt, turned 17. As a present, Wyatt had ordered a video for his grandmother, procured from the Hopefield Historical Society. The video was a copy of the 1937 film, recently "discovered" by the town, actually sent to the historical society by an unnamed donor who it was presumed found the reel while cleaning out an attic. The newspaper ran a story about the town's history, offering to sell copies of the video, asking townspeople to try to identify the old residents. Wyatt thought his grandmother might relish the exercise of remembrance, and he himself bought a copy, deciding to make it part of his senior history project at North Greensboro High.

* * *

"*Scene:*" Wyatt tells Sloan Rawlings, his girlfriend and co-filmmaker, the two at work on their updated documentary "Hopefield: Then and Now," to be presented as their semester project for Mr. Burns' history class, due in six weeks, just before Christmas break. The two idle outside the west entrance of North Greensboro High School, Wyatt standing, absently flipping a football in the air, Sloan seated on the concrete steps studying from a spiral notebook open on her knees. Moments before the start of their last classes of the day. "*Scene:*" he says again. Sloane looks up from her notes, slightly annoyed.

Wyatt uses "scene" the way the urban cool used to say "*Word—*," a multi-definition term of several years ago. Such terms, like fashion, too, wend their ways slowly from the urban to the rural; the lag time, Wyatt guesses, being two to three years.

"*Scene:* The town ladies walking into Johnson's Variety, all dressed up like they probably never were regularly. Laughing and chatting, unconcerned about the Depression or Hitler and Mussolini's aggression in Europe, giggling and acting as if they don't notice they're being filmed. Flapper-type, what, Charleston music in background. Or would it be Swing? Anyway, they've got flirty winks to the camera and quick lookaways."

"That's all in the old film," Sloane interrupts Wyatt. "Nothing to impress Burns, D. there." That's what she calls their history teacher, Darrell Burns, just twenty-seven, in his second year at Greensboro and already with the majority of the female school population clamoring to get into his course, "the American Experience" he's named it, or "Amex" to the students (most of whom carry Visa). Sloane calls the teacher "D." to distinguish him from the documentary filmmaker, Ken Burns ("Burns, K.") who is Wyatt's hero.

"Okay, okay," he tells her. "But then *out* the Johnson's Variety door steps you and some of your friends, still black & white film of course, wearing your retro bell-bottoms and big clogs, bodies pierced, and it's the contrast of the ages. The building's the same, enduring, and the people are the same, too, in a way. What do you think?"

Sloane has been looking down at her notes again, but listening, and she looks up then to find Wyatt's bright incisive filmmaker's eyes trained on the third button of her men's oxford shirt, gazing at the shadowy wonders beneath the cloth-formed V. He's caught, and immediately turns away, deep in thought and studying the street in front of the school, his eyes following the street that, were they in Hopefield he knows, leads downtown to where Johnson's Variety still stands, as if he can see the store by intense concentration.

"Burns, D. does that sometimes," she tells Wyatt because she knows it drives him crazy. "When I lean over his desk to ask a question or point something out." She says this in a way that makes him think *premeditated*, which *does* drive him crazy with conjecture, with picturing the scene. "But it's not like there's much to see." She grins at him then. "You know?" Her eyes are back on her notebook, as Wyatt pauses to think, to visualize.

"*Word*—" says Wyatt Johnson to Sloane Rawlings, as she is rising from her seat on the steps, is closing her notebook and turning toward the side doors, through which and down the main hall and in the fifth room on the left, she's got an exam in the course she both loves and hates called Senior Logic, a test on Venn Diagrams.

"I mean, Scene:" says Wyatt, with some urgency now. "Extreme close-up of Watt Dawson, hold on the rugged, handsome face, the eyes looking off toward the fields, toward some future he's imagining that no one but him can see—" Sloane pauses for a moment, her hand on the huge brass doorhandle. Probably thinking *he*, "some future no one but *he* can see." But she's in a hurry, Wyatt knows, and won't waste the time to correct him.

"I gotta go," she says. "I'm late for this test." She slips through the door he now holds, begins a run down the hallway, her notebook hugged to her chest causing some side to side motion in her body, an inefficient twist Wyatt notes, admiringly, as she recedes.

"—and slowly pull away," he's yelling now at her back, "pull back from the still just like Burns does, taking in more and more, the road, the workers silhouetted. And he's gazing at—you realize slowly—he's looking at *her*, at Etta, fifty feet from him and her face turned away. Gazing at her back—"

Wyatt lets the door close then, Sloane's figure out of sight and into a classroom. He'll cut Chemistry again, his last class of the day, to spend some extra time on the movie. He's got so many ideas for it, and for himself and Sloane.

He breaks into a jog along the back side of the school building, behind the bleachers of the soccer practice fields, gets to the fifth set of classroom windows, and thinks about jumping for the sill, chinning himself up to see into Sloane's room as he sometimes does. Thinks better of it, keeps flipping the football up and catching it as he runs past. And this, the leather ball spinning on its axis and paraboling up and down the row of windows, moving but dissociated from any "mover," is what Sloane sees as she looks up from her test full of Venn Diagrams. She doesn't think anyone else notices, this time, and smiles.

Circle 2: Etta

It's fairly easy to put labels on each of the three circles, but it's the overlap areas that stimulate the person. The overlap areas are even more powerful than the circles themselves. Life occurs in the overlap areas; that's where the 'truth' is. So, one uses Venn Diagrams to identify or present truth.

from the notes of Sloane Rawlings,
quoted from class lecture, Sept 1997

That the 1937 film centers on the people of Hopefield has been noted. And in his two dozen or so viewings of the video, Wyatt Johnson has been struck by other details, which he has jotted on a yellow legal pad later to be arranged and hopefully made sense of. The speed of the film, quick and jerky and Chaplinesque, enchants him. The film shows only the outsides of buildings, storefronts, houses, barns, the Esso station and school, and this disturbs him. With only a handful of exceptions, all the more than two hundred people shown are white, also disturbing. (There's a black man with a broom at the gas station, and a few field workers picking berries, some distance from the road.) The lack of sound in the video also disturbs Wyatt. And while he is almost certain he can identify his grandmother, Etta (Johnson, but then—Hotchkiss), in the background of one of the downtown scenes, she has mentioned nothing to him about her appearance. And while Wyatt can imagine explanations for most of his questioning notes—the Eyemo camera was spring-wound, so recording speed was difficult to control; lighting was unsophisticated in 1937, so outside shots developed better images; whites were likely the paying audience, so the filmed scenes would include more of them as an economic decision at least; cameras in 1937 were of course not fitted with microphones, so recording sound was a separate (and more expensive) undertaking—all these possible answers, yet Wyatt still finds himself unsettled.

He'd hoped for fact, but the film was made by a subjective person, just as the articles of the time in the Hopefield News were written by reporters trying to sell papers. He thinks of Sloane's Venn Diagrams: these, too, present a moment in time that gives no real explanation of cause and effect, only what appears to be so in numbers. Wyatt feels somehow that an entire dimension has been left out.

Wyatt has only the film, an unreliable "center," he thinks; and around it the accounts of his grandmother (the only one present then, and still now), and newspapers and history books. (The Hindenburg crashed that summer, 1937, and Amelia Earhart disappeared.) And Wyatt knows it's all more than a school project he's working on; he feels the pull of his personal history. What is "Wyatt," he thinks, is there somewhere, between the accounts. On a Sunday afternoon, he and Sloane visit Etta at the nursing home.

* * *

You'll understand, I think, when I finish, why I haven't properly thanked you for the film you sent, Wyatt. She looks at him with a kind but piercing stare; he thinks of a bird of prey, a Coopers Hawk with grayish head and determined, purposeful eyes. You're fond of scenes, Etta goes on—how does she know this, Wyatt wonders, glances to Sloane who won't tip her hand if she has one—so I'll give you, let's say, three.

A barn on the old Johnson property—you'll remember seeing it in the background of a scene in the video. The one that seems to me out of place since it's taken from the road and shows few people, some field workers picking strawberries, a house in the distance, and the old hay barn. I filmed those scenes, Etta tells them. She breathes audibly then, giving the two time to think about her revelation. Unseasonably warm for November, the air carries parts of apples and rotting pumpkins. And something being fried inside the nursing home, maybe okra and chicken for the residents' Sunday dinner. Etta sits in a worn rocker that creaks so slightly as she speaks it could be the wind or part of her voice, her inflection.

We became friends, Watt Dawson and I, she says. *Friends* seems a funny word—we were lovers, too—but I favor it. If he had lived long, I think we'd be friends today. But anyway, the barn. I filmed it out the window of his old truck, and he left the frames in the final movie out of some sentiment, I'm sure, because they don't really fit in, otherwise, with the rest of the piece. We lay together on the straw of that barn. Wyatt and Sloane exchange a quick glance of surprise. Now your next scene, she says.

On the Monday following the Sunday they'd sat on the porch re-counting his grandmother's tale, when Sloane had been oddly serious, taking down the story but offering little comment, and only half-hearted chuckles at his jokes, Wyatt met her at her locker between first and second periods. The day had dawned with skies the gray of southern porch-es, and the rain came steady soon afterward, giving the school halls a de-pressing wintry light, a moldy, dusty smell. The weekend-buffed floors were already slick before the wet shoes hit them, and a freshman wipes out just past Sloane and Wyatt, his three-ring binder exploding on impact. In the crowded hall, some laugh, some sadly shake their heads and walk on, a couple stopping to pick up the rapidly separating papers that are floating up and out like windswept leaves before landing and sticking to the wet floor. Wyatt watches the tragedy, still part of his mind in his grandmother's 1937 world, chuckles to Sloane: "Oh, the humanity!"

Again no reaction from her. He shrugs, turns toward the now kneel-ing boy sweeping all in arm's reach toward the folder poised like a dust-pan. Wyatt, just a few feet from the boy, starts toward him to aid in the cleanup. Sloane grabs his arm as he turns, rotates him back to face her. She's flushed, her eyes reddened like she's been crying or is about to. "Wyatt, wait," she says. "We need to talk. I'm late."

Idiotically, he scans the hall for a clock, thinking *we've got plenty of time, the first bell hasn't even rung yet.* Wyatt doesn't wear a watch and is a few minutes late for everything, which Sloane hasn't seemed to be bothered by. It's been a joke between them. But then it hits him, a slow realization she can see cross his face like a heavy cloud eclipsing the afternoon sun.

"Ohh," he says. "Okay." His face now shows, he'll think later, like a boxscore, all the information registering: shock and fear; pride, hope, love for her; maybe panic, too, in the slots for at-bats, runs, hits, batted-in, left on base numbers. "Okay. After third period, the west side steps. I'll see you then." He leans forward and kisses her cheek, not sure later whether her reaction is receptive or much less, she turning away quickly then in one motion closing her locker and wheeling off down the dark, slick hall.

* * *

A breeze has altered the feel of the nursing home porch as a breeze carrying the smell of winter passes over Wyatt, Sloane, and Etta. I've given you the barn. Okay, scene two, Etta says. Warm, humid late-summer day. A picnic, just Watt Dawson and me, on the outskirts of the Johnson land, the family and the land that I'd marry into, as you know. I sat on an old army blanket, beside me a basket of fried chicken and potato salad and everything else you'd expect. Me alone on the blanket, he under the engine flap of that pickup, adjusting the belt that had been singing since we'd left town. He's whistling in the background of my thoughts, wrenching and tightening and testing; God, how he loved that truck. And how I loved him at that moment.

But I sat on that blanket and knew two things. And given those two, I laid my options out in front of me like cards in a game of solitaire.

Etta speaks out to the surroundings, knowing her words are felt by her grandson and his girlfriend, but she does not look directly at Wyatt. She will glance at Sloane more than once.

First, I knew I was with child. Had known it, somehow like women the world over will tell you, from the moment. For me, the time in the hayloft. And second, I knew that Watt Dawson, a wonderful man, would be leaving town in a day or two or five, when his filming was finished. He loved me, I'm sure of it, and would have taken me and our coming child from town to town on his movie-making tour. He'd have loved it, I think. But I'd also seen the way he'd pulled into town, and his dashing good looks, and even as he said them to me I'd known that the phrases were exactly what he'd said to others, how many I don't want to know, and would again. What's that Willie Nelson song about all those he's loved? I believe Watt to this day.

Amelia Earhart disappeared that summer, 1937. She was a hero not just to me but millions of girls. But I was seventeen and like all seventeen year olds saw myself as different, as more thoughtful and worrisome and stronger than any girl my age then or since. On that blanket I thought I'm her, and Watt was my co-pilot Noonan. And all that summer I remember expecting to see her stride out of the woods by our house, like Dr. Livingstone, because she was a survivor, a fighter. And when Watt turned to me, wrench in hand, I could tell he wasn't my Noonan. But he sure was something.

So you can imagine my options. The 'road show,' soon with baby, and I could imagine the sad playing out of that. Abortion, common though whispered in our day, and there were kind and safe doctors and nurses I could have found. Or disappear for nine months, a couple I knew did that; and returned to Hopefield with a child, and if they were attractive they still found husbands. I sat on that blanket and he started the truck. And he turned to me so self-satisfied and boyish and still beautiful, the Model T engine clicking smooth behind him like that pendulum they sit on a piano. I chose to keep the child and let him go. And he strode back to the blanket the conquering hero, and we made love there and I decided that was the time I'd call the conception of my first, your father, Wyatt, Will Johnson.

The rain has subsided by ten-thirty when the bell ends third period and Wyatt walks numbly to the east steps, where he'd filmed Sloane-as-Etta a few days before. A humid moldy muddy smell hangs in the outside air, and there's a steady, metronomic pinging from a leaking gutter above, drips leaving the roof and striking the downspout as it bends outward beside the cement stairs. Wyatt waits for Sloane, listens to the first bell, continues waiting but moves down the steps so as to be out of sight of faculty scanning the halls. The second bell—the "late" bell—then blasts. Wyatt is now late for geometry, Sloane for only a study hall. He paces now on the grass outside the brick building. Lights a cigarette. Thinks about Etta and Watt and 1937 when things seemed so much simpler.

Wyatt looks back toward the building to see Sloane's face in the steel door's window, and a second later she pushes it open and descends the steps. He flips his cigarette away and meets her, grips her upper arms so she faces him. Wyatt looks straight into puffy eyes, holds them a moment, then kisses her. Quick, close-lipped, firmly. He can taste the bite of nicotine on his tongue, can smell her skin moist and sweet like an infant's. "Okay?" he not quite asks, not quite tells her. She's still a moment before rolling her eyes undecidedly, then nodding. "Let's walk," he says, taking her hand.

Wyatt and Sloane walk across the now soggy, sun-browned school lawn to the woods west of the school where the cross country team has their meets, where Wyatt's football team, too, runs loops. The muddied path is pocked with cleat marks, the air a post-rain misty, and they smell pine and mud, somehow clean in combination. "We have options," Wyatt says once they're out of sight of school, in a different world somehow. He wants it to be simple like 1937.

"This is *ours*," Sloane says—he's not sure she means the baby, or the predicament. "What do *you* want to do?"

Wyatt steps silently over the pine straw softening the path. "I want what you want," he says lamely.

"We're so young," she says. "I love you, I do, but we're so young. I don't think I'm ready for this."

They don't talk about mistakes, about sex without protection that only happened once that he can remember, a stunning time in the barn of his father's family property a few weeks before. There is no blaming.

"The toughest part, then," Wyatt says softly, understanding her drift, "is yours. You're seventeen, so you'd have to get permission. Your parents would have to know. You'd get counseling and lectured to, they'd try to humiliate you I think." He wants to be strong and understanding both, and yet the overheard "facts" of teenage abortion come together in a too-bleak picture. He's upset her. He can tell she's silently crying now, looking down at the path ahead, her eyes focused maybe ten feet in front but not really seeing. Wyatt squeezes her hand but she doesn't grip back. And suddenly they both feel a presence, something warm near them, and look up to see an eight-point buck on the path in front of them not twenty feet ahead.

Though sporting the beautiful rack, he's not large, maybe eighty pounds. Motionless—and they've stopped short, too, now—he stares at them through huge brown eyes. Curious, not exactly fearful, his nose twitching slightly. The area, the state and more, has become so overpopulated with deer that they don't grow to nearly the size they did decades before. Wyatt remembers seeing an old county newspaper in the library from around 1910, a local article that mentioned hunters bagging deer of over a hundred and fifty pounds, not uncommon then. But now, they're smaller and everywhere—here around the school so accustomed to people as to be almost tame—and in the winters they starve to death by the hundreds. Or meet violent death hit by vehicles on the roads. Wyatt doesn't hunt, but he doesn't protest the practice—starvation especially seems a most awful alternative.

The three stare at one another, motionless, for perhaps ten seconds. And with a calmness then, the buck steps off the path, taking a few steps into the woods before breaking into a high-bounding gallop. Wyatt and Sloane hear other sounds in the woods then, more deer in flight, but they see none. Sloane then squeezes Wyatt's hand back.

* * *

The third scene I'll give you, and then I've got to get inside. It's getting cold out here and I've got Sunday dinner at five, no reheats if you miss it. You'll like this, Wyatt, because it's a movie.

Wyatt and Sloane pass a glance back and forth, like after two hours of *Apocalypse Now*, he thinks, as if to say they've had too much but they know there's more. Like in a French restaurant when you've ordered the full menu, and you know there are two courses left but you're stuffed.

The short version, Etta says, because I've got supper near on the table. I'd decided to keep the baby; and Watt moved on, never knowing. Walter Johnson of the Johnsons of Hopefield, perhaps green with the rumors of my connection with the filmmaker—Walt had always shone for me; I was pretty then, yes?—proposed not two weeks after the pickup pulled out of town. We were married Christmas, 1937, and Will was born the spring of the next year. I slept with Walt—named for 'The Big Train' the Hall of Famer, you knew that, Wyatt—the day he proposed but not again until the wedding. Needlesome folks who did the math figured premarital ardor, but our two later children together silenced most of the gossip. Etta pauses, to catch her breath, to think perhaps.

So to the movies, right? Sitting in the Spring Garden Cinema, 1946, little Will, eight years old, and I, were set to see *The Best Years of Our Lives*, a big hit that year. The twins, Nathan and Estelle, were with their grandparents, the Johnsons. Walter had been killed in France the year before, shot in a friendly fire incident just after VE day. I was saddened— I'd grown to love him when we were first married—but he had changed so much. Until the war gave him some purpose, he'd become lazy, collecting money for his father, and mean, especially to Will. I think if he didn't know who Will's real father was, he felt it anyway. And he grew to hate himself, partly for all his wealth, his soft hands, when folks around us had calloused, cracked hands and not a dime in them. But that's all another part of the story. I feel I'm talking in circles a bit here. But that's part of the way time works on an old gray head.

So the movie-house, remember? Will and I sat munching candy watching the newsreel before the picture. And there's scenes from the Pacific Theater, that's what it was called, you know. Incredible moving pictures of Okinawa, troops engaged and gunfire all around. The announcer says the photographer had been killed there and had been a journalist decorated posthumously by President Truman. The photographer's name was listed as Watt Dawson. And I knew it was my Watt. And your Watt, too, Wyatt. Your grandfather. I asked your mother not to tell you, to let me when I was ready. But if you'd have grown up in Hopefield, the truth would've come around to you, I guarantee. Well, I've got to get in, I'm about to freeze out here now, and I don't want to miss my supper. 'Sides, I've dropped enough bombs for one day, yes?

That night after dinner, after his football practice and her homework, after both Wyatt and Sloane had been thinking of nothing else all day, they met in Greensboro, just ten miles and a world away from home, two worlds from Hopefield. Wyatt had bought a six-pack with a fake ID from a convenience store where the clerk was the older brother of his teammate, a wide receiver of talent, of awesome speed Wyatt had always thought, but a guy whose number never seemed to get called. There were cases like that, Wyatt already knew, and reasons behind them, too. Wyatt was embarrassed to bring just Bud Light to the counter so he added a 40-ounce Bull to give the deal some respect, so Larry's big brother Charles wouldn't nix it. Luckily, and as always since the QB threw toward Larry twice as much as Wyatt, Charles green-lighted the deal. Wyatt headed to the 24-hour Wal-mart (why had Sloane chosen this awful strip mall), parked in the dark. Twisted open the malt liquor and slugged hugely. He didn't know whether he wanted to be a father or not. Part of him was excited about the idea. Another, scared shitless. But he on his own would lean against, fatherhood, and he thought Sloane was wavering toward at least delayed motherhood.

He met Sloane in the parking lot, she a half-hour late and apologetic, on a cooling night when he'd run the A/C in the truck the whole way over, he couldn't tell you why. They hugged in a kind of desperate way, and he could smell moth balls in the collar of her suede jacket—maybe the first pulled out for winter—and also blacktop and motor oil, from the heat of the day and the many that changed their oil where they bought their four quarts and filters, reasoning that it's just more convenient if you gotta take something back, and why should I get spilled oil all over my own driveway.

They sit in Wyatt's pickup, and Sloane opens a beer. He lights her cigarette. "If I was going to have it, I shouldn't be doing either one of these," she says, tipping her vice-filled hands and looking at Wyatt.

"I'd marry you, you know that," he looks straight at her. "You know that." Wyatt lights a cigarette now, too. Slugs from his 40-ounce bottle that has rapidly warmed on the seat, between his legs. The night is still warm, humid, and even with the windows open the smoke hangs in the cab, needing a human breath to push it out. Wet-dog and Marlboro Light meet tar and motor oil smells. Wal-mart is doing good business for ten on a Tuesday evening.

"I do know," Sloane says back, meeting his gaze. And after another sip and a silent moment, she goes on. "I'll tell my parents, and you, yours. We'll do what's safe and best for us, for now. We can marry and have a family later, if we choose, but not now, not when we're seventeen. That's not fair to a child, either."

Wyatt nods, and he can't tell what he's feeling, the factors too many and too hazy to delineate or assess their weights. In the Venn Diagram of emotions, he suspects Sloane carries a handful he can't begin to comprehend; and he, too, must feel things she does not. A police car pulls slowly into the parking lot. Unspoken understanding then, and Sloane kisses him long and firm and soft-lipped, gets out and into her Toyota. They pull slowly out, Wyatt following her all the way home, where she waves. She parks and gets out and he asks out the window, low, "Can I come in with you?" She shakes her head, kindly, "Not yet," she says. And he thinks her face looks very old, thinks that she'll be perhaps more beautiful at forty, fifty, sixty. And pulls off slowly down the quiet suburban street where, the eleven o'clock news over, people are turning out lights and going to sleep.

I don't know if I was more shocked by finding out of his death or remembering sitting in the Hopefield movie house with little Will, realizing we'd been watching his real father's work. I'd never forgotten him, of course, and I'd been planning to try to find him then, after the war. Not that he'd have changed or would be ready to settle down, but when Walter died I couldn't help thinking of him. But that was all very long ago now, and you two have your story, don't you. I was planning on trying to explain why the videotape you sent affected me so strongly. But I think now you understand some of it.

The rain had begun again off the porch, and Etta rose and hugged her grandson and his girlfriend. She headed inside for supper, and the two teenagers stepped off the porch into the soft, steady drops.

Circle 3: Will

28 Country & Western songs on WCWG surveyed as to content, regarding the themes Truckers, Love, and Prison. Let the three circles be T, L, P. Note the following facts: 2 songs were about imprisoned trucker who was in love; 7 songs about truckers who were in love; 9 songs about lovers not in prison; 11 songs about truckers not in prison; 22 songs not about prison; 16 songs not about love; 16 songs about truckers. Answer the following:

1. *How many songs were about prison?*
2. *How many songs were about truckers who were not in love?*
3. *How many songs were not about truckers?*

From Senior Logic Test 1, paper of Sloane Rawlings, North Greensboro H.S. Sept 1997

Eleven months after Wyatt and Sloane present their history project, "Hopefield: Then and Now," Wyatt will be in his first semester at Appalachian State and Sloane will be at the University in Chapel Hill. Both will have received academic scholarships, and Wyatt will have nearly made the football team as a walk-on. Wyatt's grandmother, Etta Johnson, will have died, unexpectedly, peacefully, the previous spring. And in the late summer, Wyatt's mother will call him at his dorm to tell him that his father, too, has died, accidentally shot by deer hunters while cutting firewood near, surprisingly, Hopefield, North Carolina.

Wyatt will call Sloane and they'll arrange a trip back to Hopefield during their fall break from classes. The October, 1998 day will be warm, Indian summer, when they put sandwiches together at Wyatt's mother's house in Greensboro, lift a six pack from the refrigerator, making themselves a picnic lunch before piling into Wyatt's pickup and heading thirty miles northwest.

"I had no idea he'd been living there," Wyatt's mother says again. Meaning Will, Wyatt's father; meaning Hopefield. "The child support checks always came from a bank in New Jersey." Wyatt hadn't seen his father in seven years, since he was eleven. As he had said in the history presentation of a year ago, he didn't know what he did or where he'd gone. In a way like his father's own father, he'd said, as the screen behind him and Sloane filled with silent, black and white images of the people of Hopefield in 1937.

"Apparently he'd been living on his family land for years, when all the time I'd thought he was up north," Wyatt's mother went on, again. When Etta died I don't know if he didn't find out, or if he chose not to show up. But he loved *you*, Wyatt, always did. I think he just didn't know how to be a father. He never really had one, either," she tells Wyatt what she'd told him since he was very young. "He *provided*, albeit long distance" (his mother could always get away with words like albeit), "you got to give him that," she says.

Remember, if you find the place, take whatever you want to, she tells Wyatt. The will said anything and everything. You've got that key? Wyatt nods, feeling it seeming sharp and cold in his jeans pocket. The real estate office can give you directions if you get lost, his mother goes on. Lord knows that was a big piece of property even if he sold most of it.

Wyatt hugs his mother, who is on her way to work. It is a Thursday morning. "Thanks for the sandwiches, Mrs. Johnson," Sloane tells her and hugs her also. And they will climb into Wyatt's truck and pull slowly away.

They'll be silent most of the trip, sitting close, her hand on his thigh, not even the radio on. Remember the last time we came here, he'll ask, knowing that's what she's thinking, too. The research trip for the presentation, the "Hopefield Today" portion that they'd tacked on to the beginning and end of the video, the camera panning across the fields and then to the old school, now a day-care that they were passing. A few more miles then, and into very rural areas, farmland. Somewhere around here is where the Johnson land starts, or at least *started*, Wyatt tells Sloane what she remembers from before, too. Wyatt will slow as they pass the old Johnson family home which in the '30s had to have been a mansion, now in slight disrepair, the worn-grass side yard covered with brightly colored plastic kids' contraptions, a slide, a sandbox, a couple of small bicycles. And down the road another mile, with just tobacco on one side and corn on the other, woods ahead, and a single mailbox on the left. Wyatt slows the truck. Beside the mailbox runs a dirt path, a pair of tire tracks between woods and cornfield. In small, neat square letters in white paint on the gray aluminum mailbox: "Dawson."

Do you think— Wyatt asks. I don't know how we didn't notice it last year when we were passing right here. Sloane shakes her head, too, almost smiling. Wyatt turns onto the rutted path.

The driveway is pot-holed, some holding the muddy water of recent rain. New tire tracks imprint the mud of the path that is overgrown and clearly little-used. I love a path like this, with two tracks and grass in the middle, says Wyatt. Is there a word for that? There ought to be. They bounce slowly along between light woods and cornfield. About a quarter mile off the main road, the path bends down an incline away from the cornfield. Down into the woods, then back up and into a wide clearing where they see the cabin.

A hard freeze a week before will have snuffed most insect life, so beyond the sound of the tires on dirt there is silence. The Indian-summer warmth will bring up moist, sweet smells of earth and grass, and distantly perhaps tobacco, corn, woodsmoke. Wyatt will stop at the mouth of the clearing and cut the engine. *Whoa, Scene:* he'll say, as they take in what's before them.

The cabin is small, unpainted pine board and batten, with a rusting tin roof that overhangs a narrow front porch. The place looks familiar to Wyatt and Sloane as something from the Depression-era photographs of Margaret Bourke-White and others. Like something from the Hopefield newsreel. And parked beside the cabin is a pickup Wyatt and Sloane have never seen but recognize immediately, a 1927 Ford with an unreadably faded California plate and a canvas covering the bed on which are stenciled the initials "A.I.C." Holy shit, Wyatt says, but he's not really surprised. And neither is Sloane, as they look from one another back to the scene before them. On the far other side of the cabin is another pickup, a rusting yellow Toyota maybe a dozen years old, that old Dawson probably used for his trips into town. The real estate agent said they'd see him around sometimes, but he rarely spoke to anyone, kept to himself. Was seen periodically at the Kroger grocery and the liquor store; not unfriendly at all, just quiet.

Wyatt and Sloane will use the realtor's key to open the shiny anachronism of a Master lock on the front door, and find inside, strangely, nothing unexpected really either, although they will have never seen the things before. On a handmade tressel table stacked steel film canisters bearing names of many small towns in the area, in South Carolina and Virginia, too; beside them, an 8 mm Eyemo movie camera; on the walls framed photographs, yellowed newspaper shots, of Walter Johnson in front of the town hall and Watt Dawson in an army uniform, crew-cutted and smiling. In the smile of Dawson is something of Wyatt, Sloane will remark, and it's certainly there, in the slightly squinted eyes, the grin somehow boyish and too-old at once. And countless other old items, so that Wyatt and Sloane will feel as if they've entered a museum. But for the gas generator in the kitchen, which presumably ran the lights and the water pump, the place was timeless. A woodstove in one corner, a very comfortable looking well-worn blue sofa angled in front of it, crumpled army blankets across it as if a napper awoke only moments ago. Just one large, rectangular room furnished sparsely but with a rustic functionality to it. I could live here easily, Wyatt says.

After a long, silent tour of the inside of the cabin, he and Sloane walk back to Wyatt's pickup and get their lunch. Beneath a pecan tree in the front yard, they'll munch tuna sandwiches and sip now-warm beer from sweating brown bottles. After eating, Sloane will lie back on the army blanket they pulled from the couch inside, and Wyatt will walk across the yard to the old Ford. He'll inspect it, raising the engine cover flaps, and Sloane will watch him from the picnic spot. He'll return to her, reporting the truck in seemingly good repair. And they'll lie back together and they'll kiss. Wyatt will slowly unbutton Sloane's faded oxford shirt, his eyes never leaving hers.

And later when it seems to them time to go, Wyatt will be thinking things he might want to take with him, to keep. The Eyemo camera perhaps, the film tins which he could return to the towns they hold pictures of, maybe, and a handful of photographs. But for the army blanket, they will have left the cabin completely undisturbed. Finally, they'll walk around to the back of the cabin to survey Watt Dawson's south view, and find a mammoth woodpile, a chopping stump, a maul and sledge laid next to the stump as if the wood splitter, mid-job, had just decided to take a moment's break. And then there at a little pine table on a small back half-porch, a manual Underwood typewriter with a page in the carriage, a manilla folder stacked full of typed pages beside it. And Wyatt will open the folder and flip it over to see the beginning, and read the now yellowed edge page, "In the late summer of 1937, a ten year old Ford pickup sputtered into Hopefield, North Carolina...." In the end, Wyatt will take only the army blanket and the unfinished manuscript. Will he pass the ten-gallon gas can beside the generator and think about using it, spreading gas around the little place and pulling away as it all goes up? Of course, yes. He'll go so far as lifting the handle and shaking the can that will be near half full.

But he'll shake his head then and replace the lock on the front door, and slide the key onto his ring that holds the keys to his truck, the key to his mother's house, and the key to his post box at school. And he and Sloane will pull quietly back down the long path to the main road. Driving home, thinking their thoughts. And Wyatt will think that Sloane, her hand on his thigh, is thinking some of the same thoughts he is, and some completely different and all her own. But in the sets of their thoughts, Wyatt thinks, there is certainly some overlap, some perhaps tiny shaded area in which are the ideas of both of them. A small subset where their thoughts are the same.

Have You Seen Me?

He is nothing like she remembers. She thinks the word husk when she first sees him, pictures a dried cornstalk barely upright in a muddy winter field. No matter how much her conscious head knows that all will be completely different after thirty years, there's that muscle of memory that regurgitates the way it was then, flashes it like an ID except it's not. She knows that the man she sees will not be the one of thirty years past. But neither, she thinks, is he like the image on the junk mail card, the have-you-seen-me kid lost years before, the photo a computer projection of what he'd look like today. The flipside of the card that reads "carpet cleaning $6.95 a room*," the asterisk referring to a paragraph of exceptions. No, he's nothing like she remembers.

"Do I have any idea?" he repeats her question, like a child although he's 66. Far into adulthood, in fact, at the sickly sad end of life. He sits in a VA hospital—the building and all in it yellowed with age—his bony legs covered by a plaid, not-even-real-wool blanket, his disease-wracked body covered by the government for his post-Korean War service in the Navy.

She remembers his smoking. She pictures the Marlboro box, sees the cowboys in the old television advertisements. In her mind hears the inspiring Copland theme song. Her first cigarettes were slipped from his boxes. He knew it, asked her to smoke with him, but she never did. Even today, she smokes like she drinks, mostly alone.

"I don't have any idea, probably. You may be right," he tells her, seeming lucid, and his eyes go milky. They sit in silence for perhaps three minutes, thinking their own thoughts, looking forward at nothing like people on a city bus. She's seeing him then, more than thirty years ago, strong and tan and, while nearly the same age as her own father, nothing like him. And with a grip on her held for all those years.

"It hurt, too, of course you know," she says. Here a little leak of bitterness, a roofing nail in a tire, she might think, having worked construction and having proven herself an equal to the men she sweated beside. "Knew, I mean. Then." She stammers, "That it hurt, I mean." She winces, hearing her voice like a nervous kid, like she was then, at thirteen babysitting for the neighbors. But also eased somehow admitting this, as it seems to loosen his grip on her by some small degree.

He turns to her then but shows no sign of remorse or even understanding. She's spent more than thirty years remembering him, and in twenty minutes on the computer, tapping a series of keys she'd started hitting many times before, she had found him. A phone call then, and while they could not divulge his condition, she is certain he's dying. And if you were to ask her why she's chosen to visit now, after thirty years—is it to confront him before he dies; to face him with anger or with forgiveness; to appreciate him rendered impotent; to see him suffering?—she would answer only yes.

So she'd garnered the strength and driven the hundred-forty miles to the hospital where he's sits gray before her, wasting to cancer. He needs a shave. And to wash his hair. Or someone should do it for him. She thinks he'd probably feel so much better, cleaner to be shaved and groomed. He'd be no trouble, now—he seems gentle as a child.

"Where's your room?" she asks him, and he points down a long corridor of highly buffed green asbestos tile. His kitchen all those years ago had had the same, although that was years before the lawsuits.

She grips the handles of his wheelchair—red plastic covers over steel, they're like handlebars of bikes she grew up riding, with colored streamers dancing from their ends—and pushes him in the direction he'd pointed. Someone, an orderly perhaps or he himself, had set him near the main entrance where he could see her drive up, even park, and come in. Now they approach an intersection of four hallways.

The northwest corner—assuming she's pushing him north, and she knows this since the hospital's main side is a southern exposure, notes it because she's the daughter of an architect—is where the nurses' station sits. Opposite this counter—southwest corner, where the Esso gas station was in her home town, *their* home downtown where Maple met Main— sits a glassed-in corner office. Hanging on the inside of the window from little suction cup hooks, a white plastic sign block printed in red:

Have You Seen Me?

"BARBERSHOP TODAY." There's a bright icon beside the words, the red, white, blue candy-cane stripes, the barber pole that she remembers suspended outside two storefronts in their town. She has no idea what the room is for days not "today," but she slows his chair as they approach.

Through the large office window they can see a shiny steel barber's chair with a brown vinyl seat that an old man is just rising up out of. He has just a child's soft thin hair, but the fresh cut has made what little he has orderly, combed back, an elderly deacon in church. The barber, a dough-faced man of mid-forties with oily black hair and blotchy skin, tells the man leaving to come back and see him next week. The deacon nods at the woman holding the wheelchair and then looks at the man in it without expression. She thinks that the deacon has a daughter he rarely sees. He steps slowly out of the glassed-in room and shuffles down the hall.

The barber then looks out through one picture window at her holding the wheelchair and him in it. She looks back, while from the chair he stares ahead in silence. The nurse had told her coming in that his mind was affected, that he sometimes didn't speak for long periods and his words then were sometimes indistinct mumbles.

"What about a shave and a haircut," her words directed at the top of his head, the face turned away down the corridor where the grandfather is still well within sight. She doesn't think he's heard.

The barber has, nods and shows a slight cool smile, motions with palms up and fingers flexing as in *bring it on*. "Sure, no appointment needed," he says to them.

From the wheelchair he turns toward the barber and almost imperceptibly shakes his head. His cloudy eyes show what might be pain behind them, or might be fear.

"Come on," she says. "It'll make you feel better."

She guides the wheels through the wide doorway, parks him beside the recliner chair, and she and the barber take elbows, help him stand and shift from one seat to the other. His eyes now show resistance but his body does not respond. She takes a folding chair in front of him but does not pick up the copy of *Time* magazine left on the floor beside. The barber, like a strangler from behind, loops a light blue apron over her old neighbor's head and ties it behind his neck. He combs and cuts the hair, the scissors clicking in some precise meter she can't quite recall from a poetry class—*comb, clip-clip, comb, clip-clip*. The barber lathers his face and neck with a little round-handled brush like her grandfather used, and then he unhinges a straight razor like a prop from a western movie. She watches her old neighbor as his eyes grow wide with fear, but he makes no sound. She watches his face for emotions, and she sees this fear, this will to resist, but also something else she thinks may be almost enjoyment, the sensual pleasure perhaps of someone touching one's skin, one's hair. Then fear seems to override and he looks to her, a moment staring straight at her, with a painful imploring she can only translate to mean *please make him stop*.

But the barber shaves him, the blade scraping smoothly up to his chin where the mouth opens slightly, involuntarily, the movement causing the barber to falter, a tiny cut appearing as a thin red hairline not even bleeding. She's not sure whether he is unable to move, to resist, or simply does not, simply gives in. She lets her eyes for not a single moment leave his, and she thinks at one point she sees something like recognition.

Schrödinger's Cat for Inmates and Baristas

1: Mabe

During the period Cal Mabe was corresponding with the prisoner on death row, he was also editing textbooks. He'd done myriad jobs involving brawn and brain, had taught school, for example, and both built and moved furniture—turned a lathe for a time, and for another pad-wrapped and loaded chairs and tables and drove a semi over the road for a company everybody's heard of. But now he read books, mostly high school science, currently one involving quantum physics. The publisher had sent him a promotional t-shirt printed with a concept from the latest text, a shirt Mabe had agreed to himself that he wouldn't wear until he had at least a rudimentary understanding of its concept. On the front it read: Schrödinger's Cat is Alive. On the back: Schrödinger's Cat is Dead.

At 61, Mabe was a quiet man, a widower of a dozen years. Most of his family, and his wife's family, lived far away in Indiana, where he and his wife had lived their entire married lives. After her death, Mabe had returned to South Carolina where he had grown up. He'd bought a small house with some history in a university town in the county next to where his father's farm had been. His father had used to take him to the college football games on Saturdays in the fall, so he'd had fond memories of the town where he now lived. Still, he was introverted and somewhat awkward socially, so he had few friends. Mabe sometimes thought his solitude was due to his judgmental nature; that is, he tended to see himself and others as wonderful or devilish, blessed or cursed, brilliant or slow, or one of any other numerous dichotomies.

As far as he himself was concerned, he tended to view himself in terms of a theory a therapist had shared with him decades before. The therapist's rather crass personal theory was that Mabe viewed himself as either "God's Gift" or "a Piece of Shit"; in other words, Mabe saw himself at times as smart and valuable, and at others as unredeemable, worthless. There was no middle ground.

When not editing, Mabe walked his hundred pounds of nearsighted canine.

A constantly shedding mix of breeds the shelter couldn't elucidate, Magoo allowed opportunity for Mabe to practice social skills with passersby, most of whom seemed to know exactly the dog's unique DNA. When Mabe and Magoo tromped about town, they would often stop for a mug of black coffee and a bowl of water at the Grounds Crew, a café at the north edge of the three-block downtown.

Mabe also worked on his correspondence with the death-row prisoner who was his pen-pal. Months before, when they'd begun their letter writing, Mabe had searched for information about the man and his case. He had found a 277-page appellate brief outlining the situation for which the man had been sentenced to death. The details of the mishandling and injustice disturbed and sometimes enraged Mabe, even more so as they corresponded because he came to see the prisoner as entirely sympathetic, thoughtful and sensitive, and a victim of the cold, flawed system.

2: Eva

One of Mabe's few in-town acquaintances was the waitress at the Grounds Crew, a *barista* was what her boss preferred to call her. Preferred to call her instead of paying her a living wage, she told Mabe, as if the title alone was currency. "Not in dollars, but in respect," he'd told her, and so she'd asked him if she could have that respect cooked medium well, with a side of okra. She worked six days at the coffeehouse Mabe frequented.

Eva, whose last name Mabe didn't know, had shared little bits about herself with Mabe over the months he'd been coming in. She was 21 and had a little boy she'd shown Mabe pictures of, an inquisitive-eyed, mussed-blond-haired kid of perhaps three years old. Like Mabe, Eva came from the country. However, unlike Mabe's bucolic upbringing by caring and mostly committed parents, Eva's growth came in a single-wide raised by an alcoholic mother and an often absent, otherwise abusive father. For her hardships and determination, she earned Mabe's thumbs-up rating almost immediately.

What he didn't see, Eva has sensed, is her powerful self-serving streak, and her aggression. From her earliest days she learned she could wield some valuable power over men. At the same time, the girls, and other women, their eyes bore right into her heart, making her want to cringe behind a dumpster or slap them, or both. Because, in part, she knew, what negative they thought of her was true. But also because she was angry—they didn't know her, didn't understand anything about her even if they thought they did. But the boys, and the men, they made it so easy. So easy she felt guilty sometimes then, at seventeen, and even now four years later with a baby at her aunt's and a dirt-paying job, and she knew it when she talked to the college boys who'd try to hit on her, or to Mabe, the old professor or whatever he was.

3. Granger

He has an hour every day outside, which he spends either playing ball or lifting weights. He prefers the solitude of the weights, but for a skinny Hispanic kid who is only 22, on Death Row since 18, he has some quickness, a few moves. And he doesn't take any from the others who play—or, more honestly, he *does* take it, the elbows, the flagrant fouls, has the bruises and bloodier wounds to prove it. And he gives it back when he gets a chance, fighting through (what they still call, in here) picks, holding position on a box-out, bumping and leaning down low. But what he thinks some may respect him for, what they'd never admit, he guesses, is that he can *pass*.

For this reason he's first chosen for pick-up games. Because when he feeds Candy for an alley-oop slam, or drives and kicks it out to Blades for an open-look three, Granger makes his teammates look good. And he's fine with them getting the credit, the glory (such as it is, on The Row); Granger's had plenty of credit, if you mean by that, responsibility. So whenever he gets the chance, he passes. A high school coach's dream, this kid.

Except that he never really had the chance. Seems like another life-time ago. Longer than his lifetime ago, anyway. Partly, too, he thinks, because every day is the same here. In that way he's exactly not like the dogs, the pit bulls he adored as a kid, who love the routine and to have every day so perfectly like the last. Routine: that's what those dogs loved, and what Granger now hates. Although he can't really say hates, because that implies a level of emotion one in his position isn't allowed to feel. Because he's denied all rights, most of all that right to feel. He can *think* it, but he'd never be able to write it down—for example, to put it into words to his pen-pal on the outside—because in the constant cell searches the guards would find his written thoughts, feelings. And with such sensitive information, they'd make his life very difficult.

But call it feeling, anyway, because the routine is difficult. The same conversations with the same people about the same issues that are personal and repetitive and are for the most part never to be resolved. Because Granger and the other sixty-three on the row will, odds are, never see the street again, never get the chance to explain or apologize or make amends. Except with The Maker, that's what Blades tells Granger since he's seen the light. Granger suspects Blades just likes to hear himself preach, and likes Granger most because he'll give up the ball in the yard, will feed Blades down low rather than pull up for the outside shot every time. Like they tally *assists* in here, Blades laughs at Granger, who tells him back that his points don't count for much in here either.

So about Granger, the coach's dream as a high schooler. He wasn't really there but for about a year total, but his teammates will never forget the kid who loved to pass. Yet during much of the high school period Granger was angry or absent, was often in trouble and for a year in jail. Then he was out and stable and remarkably, by everyone's reckoning, a model youth. He was stable on bipolar medications, was playing varsity ball and leading church group activities. But then he was jerked off medications by a seldom present but violent Marine father with an *any son of mine* attitude. Then Granger was back in trouble, this time with a girlfriend everyone said was manipulative but Granger was so stuck on, who was now going to have his baby. But who had ordered Granger, "You gotta kill her—she seen my face" of the 61-year-old woman of the house they were robbing, "for our baby, you gotta do it, for us." Days later Granger and his girl Ella and her homeboy Raymond Howard, who was as spellbound by Ella as Granger was, get picked up. And then Ella and Howard meet and talk and then talk to the detectives. They sell out Granger completely and end up walking without so much as an asterisk on their records.

Granger sometimes lies back on the bench and presses the heavy bar toward a vision of Ella on the water-stained gray ceiling of the weight room, sees her face and for the goddamn life of him can't hate her. He thinks of his son—he knows it must've been a son—and wishes they could meet. Wonders if he looks like his mother—that's how he pictures the boy at four, a beautiful little blonde like his mother. The boy's mother, the then-17-year-old girl whom he would've done anything for. And in fact had.

4: Mabe and Eva

"Hey, Mabe?" the café barista starts to ask, pronouncing his name correctly, "maybe," and not like rhymes with short-for-Gabriel, which his schoolteachers always had. She's behind him wiping a table, and he can feel without turning that she's reading the back of his tee shirt. It's the promotional item sent to Mabe by the publisher of textbooks he edits, currently one on Quantum Physics. Schrödinger's Cat, in block letters, alive on the front and dead on the back.

"Let me buy you a beer and explain to you about this Austrian physicist and his cat," Mabe says over his shoulder. "Or maybe you can explain it to me."

"It's ten in the morning. And this is a coffee shop, Mabe." She gives him a little tired smile. She's only twenty-one, but could be forty, he thinks. Wispy blond hair, freckles and wrinkles both around nose and eyes. No, she could be forty looking like twenty-one. Older face, tired, often sad. Her eyes are green and marbled, like a cat's. Mabe's got four decades on her. So it's back to the shirt.

Eva looks around the small shop. The only other patron is engrossed in his laptop and will be for hours more, she knows. She pulls up the iron chair to Mabe's table. "So what about this cat, and how can it be both dead and alive? Tell me it's alive, will you?"

"Schrödinger's Cat is an experiment," Mabe tells her, what he's only just learned himself. "It's designed to illustrate probabilities in quantum physics," he sips and pauses. "What they call quarks and gluons, they're 100 million times smaller than an atom, and they're trying to figure out how these tiny things act." He pauses for emphasis. "They don't act like big things, like you or me, I mean."

"So where does the cat come in?"

"I was getting to that," Mabe says. "See it's what they call a 'Thought Experiment,' which means you just have to imagine it. The cat's in a box together with a radioactive element. The radioactive substance has a 50-50 chance of decaying within an hour. If it decays, gas will be released that will kill the cat."

"Does the cat have a name?" she wants to know. "What kind of cat?"

"See, I told you that it's a thought experiment. You just have to imagine it in your head."

"Can it breathe in there? Why not have a window in the box. Then we could watch."

"Thought experiment," Mabe says. Pauses a moment. "But you make a good point, *the* point as a matter of fact. If there was a window, we could look in and see, at any moment, whether the cat was alive or not." He can't tell if she gets it, or really even if *he* does anymore.

"But it's because you can't see, see, that the cat's both. And they try to say it's everything in between, at varying probabilities," Mabe goes on, then stops, suddenly unsure. "Or something, damn, I don't know."

Eva may have lost interest because she's the one who gets it, Mabe thinks. She watches him sip his coffee, maybe just enjoying the break. She sighs.

"Mabe, I got to get back to work," she stands. "But I do like that shirt."

5. *Mabe and Granger*

They correspond, letters, delivered back and forth by US Mail, the way people used to before blogs and texts and tweets. Mabe's letters are addressed to Granger as #0703526, and he knows that each is opened and read and analyzed for content; anything deemed inappropriate Granger will never see.

Same for Granger's letters to Mabe: read, analyzed; anything for any reason not appropriate will never reach the outgoing pile. From the state's standpoint, it's not so much secret messages or subversion, the cake with a file baked in. They're mostly concerned with contraband, especially drugs. Granger has to buy stamps, for example, since any sent in to him might be laced with acid he could lick and get high, lick and commit suicide. It wouldn't be the first time.

So in the letters they discuss their families, their beliefs, politics, dogs. The incident for which Granger is where he is does not come up, is not addressed by either party. But what strikes Mabe when he thinks of Granger, pictures him going through his day, his meals and hour of recreation, his reading and sleep in his cell, his crosswords and Scrabble games, his monotony and his appeal that sits in the cue before the state supreme court, what strikes Mabe as he edits the textbook and grapples with quantum physics: that he doesn't really understand how Schrödinger's Cat can be simultaneously alive and dead, but he can see how Granger is. Sentenced to death but the sentence yet to be carried out, Granger is living, breathing, eating, lifting weights, sleeping. And dead at the same time. Mabe's chest aches when he considers this, and he wonders how he can help this man when his only weapon really is the pen. He feels somehow strongly that he can't express his own feelings, these ideas to Granger. He has never even written to Granger that he's read the appeal and knows the facts of his case. To Granger, Mabe is only his words on a page. And very limited, edited words, chosen to convey as much information and emotion as possible while still passing security. Just as to Mabe, Granger is only those bits of information he's printed on his white, blue-lined notebook paper.

There's a gap between the writers, big as the spread between life and death. It can be measured in miles—very few, in this case, less than fifty between Mabe in the small town and Granger in the prison outside Columbia. In years, it's nearly forty, with Granger the kid who's ironically much closer to death than the much older man Mabe. There's a gap between their beliefs, their rights and freedoms, their concerns. Mabe, for example, could lift weights or play ball all day if he wanted, but he's got water and electric bills to pay, and dog food to buy.

And also in the gaping difference between them is Hasty, the woman strangled; there's the girlfriend, Ella Ames, and perhaps the child she was pregnant with at the time of the robbery; there's Ella's buddy, Raymond Howard, and Hasty's grandson, Reggie; there's judge and jury and family and friends of all of them. There's all this between Granger and Mabe that they never discuss, never write about in their letters.

6. Ella and Granger

Approximately 10:15 a.m. Thursday, May 17, 2002. Late spring, really more summer in South Carolina. Skies cloudy, hazy, the temperature already in the 80s. Ella Valerie Ames, 17, Carlos Granger, 18, and Raymond Howard, 18, arrive at 3007 Lees Cross Road, the house of Jerrilyn Hasty, 61. Granger driving, Ames giving directions. Ames' stepfather testified that the night before Ames had asked him the location of Lees Cross Road, and he had told her. Ames is at the time fifteen weeks pregnant.

The three arrive at Hasty's home, and Ames and Granger go to the door. When Hasty opens it, Ames asks for Reggie, Hasty's grandson and a friend of Ames. Granger and Ames are allowed into the house. At gunpoint, Hasty is led to the back bedroom and told to lie face down on the floor. Granger holds the gun on Hasty while Ames goes to the front door and signals Howard in. At some point Ames gives Howard and Granger surgical gloves and puts on a pair herself. Ames tells Howard to go through the house for things of value. She returns to the bedroom and locates some jewelry and a large jar of change there. Ames dumps Hasty's purse onto the floor, takes a wallet and removes a debit card and several dollars in cash. Demands Hasty give them the PIN for the card. Hasty says they can have anything, just don't kill me. She gives them the PIN.

Howard loads a small television and a VCR into the trunk of the car. He is in the kitchen going through drawers when he overhears Ames tell Granger: "You've got to kill her. She seen my face." Granger must have hesitated, because Ames urges again. "For us, for our baby, Granger. You got to do it, now!" After approximately five minutes of indecision, during which Ames continues exhorting him, Granger takes an electrical extension cord that was attached to a box fan in the window. He ties one end around the bedpost—a clumsy effort, authorities believe, to make the death look like a suicide—and wraps the other end around Hasty's neck, strangling her. Later the medical examiner cannot determine whether the ligature cut off blood supply—called strangulation, causing victim to lose consciousness in ten to fifteen seconds—or oxygen supply, where the victim suffers oxygen hunger before losing consciousness. Ames and Granger then exit the house together. Howard is already in the car.

Bank ATM surveillance tapes will confirm that over the next two days, Hasty's bank card will be used numerous times to withdraw a total of $1790. Howard will testify that he used his share, approximately $320 total, for a tattoo, for clothing, and food. Reggie Hasty, the victim's grandson, will discover the body the next morning, Friday, May 18. He will be a suspect initially, a habitual drug user who admittedly had stolen from his grandmother before. A past boyfriend of Ella Ames, Reggie has never met Carlos Granger but knows his name as the person Ames was dating at the time of the incident. Ames, Granger, and Howard will be arrested on May 21 and charged with the murder of Jerrilyn Hasty. Ames and Howard, for their testimony against Granger, will have abetting and robbery and conspiracy charges dropped or downgraded, and will be freed on two years probation. Granger alone will face capital charges, and will be convicted nearly two years after the incident, on March 11, 2004.

7. Mabe

Frustrated after a near full day's editing and barely scratching the surface of the meaning of Schrödinger's cat (the *fur* of it, he thinks), Mabe turns to the massive 277-page appeal filed for Granger to the state supreme court. Mabe's work desk sits before a window that he opens to cross ventilate the upstairs. A little breeze blowing in what they say will be a fall storm overnight. Mabe has read most of this that they call a brief three and four times, but opens at random and reads from the section describing the Granger's background and upbringing:

> The defendant's father, a U.S.Marine, was physically and verbally abusive toward defendant's mentally ill mother and his older sister as well as toward defendant. The father was violent, unemotional, obsessed with order and that his son be "a man" and not "a sissy." The defendant was not allowed to play with friends but instead made to do chores and exercise alone. Once when defendant was seven, he was made to stand outside naked in the rain for two hours for disobedience. Defendant's sister testified that when punished, defendant "was not spanked, he was punched."

Mabe shudders at the description. He reads on about the family starving, in ragged clothes, while the father was in the service or driving a truck, and the mother was bipolar and also suffering from stomach cancer. During a period in jail for robbery, Granger was diagnosed as bipolar and given anti-psychotic drugs. Once out, Granger became active in church and school, played ball, held a parttime job. Then his father discovered the medicine and pulled the "be a man" and "no son of mine needs pills" and forbade him to take them. Soon after, Granger began running with a different crowd, left school and church. And he met Ella Ames.

Mabe feels hot, feels burning injustice. Yet as he flips pages forward, he comes to the description of the murder. And it's such a brutal act. A senseless, violent act by the same man who writes the sensitive letters to Mabe about the sister he's so proud of, about the pit bulls he trained and loved as a kid, about memories of working on cars with his dad. About reggae music and history books. How could the same person be both these characters? A line of thought that was not a line at all but a circle, one curling its way back around somehow to Schrodinger and his box. With a cat inside that was somehow both alive and dead.

Mabe flips forward to the section of the brief on sentencing. Where the one who planned the crime, Ames, and her friend, Howard, had walked from the courtroom free with only probation and no records. Mabe wonders what he might do if he were to meet the manipulative bitch who had taken such advantage of Granger, who'd adored her unconditionally. Granger, who according to defense doctors' analysis had a mental/emotional age of ten at the time of the incident.

Mabe knows he needs some air, feeling enraged as he does about the injustice here. Manipulative bitch, who throughout the brief had used Granger's adoration for her to get what she wanted. Her idea to rob the woman, her command that Granger kill her. While Mabe's friend, the sensitive and now remarkably mature Granger, is nothing but a victim, a sympathetic character like Mabe's coffeehouse server, Eva. Much like Eva, Mabe thinks, what with the physical and emotional abuse as youths and the struggles, so different from his own background. For Granger in his cell, or even Eva in her barista's apron, something as ordinary as walking down the sidewalk on a warm fall afternoon, window shopping, stopping to sit outside for a coffee, such activities were impossible or at the least unheard of. He imagines Granger, on "the Row" with no rights at all, and Eva, in a sense free but with so many decisions made for her.

Mabe knows of her little boy, now four and living with Eva's aunt. She's shown him photos.

Mabe exercises his guilty freedom and heads down the street for a coffee. Only one other customer sits outside, and Eva greets him but distractedly. It's a Friday, and Mabe guesses that business should be better.

"Payday," she says, setting his mug down on the steel mesh tabletop. "Joy." Eva pulls her check stub out of her apron pocket and points out for Mabe her hourly wage and tip declaration. Because of tips, her hourly wage is the least allowed by law, just over three dollars. And since she's taxed on wage and tips totaled, her paycheck is docked to nearly nothing. Mabe frowns, scanning the rest of the stub. At the top is printed: "E. V. Ames."

"You've never told me your last name," he says. "Ames, that's nice." He stares at the printing, putting her initials together. That's where she gets "Eva," he thinks.

"My real name's Ella," she says. "But that sounds like I weigh two hundred pounds. Eva just sounded so pretty and different. I wanted a new life when I moved here."

And in Mabe's ears is a high-pitched whirring. He'll think later that it sounded like a huge mill saw, the kind that slices redwoods into quarter round. He'll think later that Eva's lips were moving but he heard nothing more. He won't remember rising and walking quite mechanically back up the street toward his home, where the massive appeal's pages ruffle beneath the open window over his desk.

Wake

Tad Cody, 11, eases quietly unnoticed out of the main visiting room, into the hall of the old house, floor creaking beneath oriental rug. He slips to the back of the house, and out the screen door (the hinge squeaking slightly), holding the handle and closing slowly so as not to let it spring back and slam. He wears an overlarge gray suit that smells of moth balls, a hand-down from a cousin now fifteen and wrestling varsity. The legs of the slacks are six inches longer than Tad's own. He wears tight, undersized brown dress shoes. On the back steps, the cuff of his right pantsleg catches on his heel and he lays out, skinning his palms on the concrete of the walk, absolutely silent with his pain. He glances quickly behind, but no one has followed.

Tad climbs to his feet. A tin bucket full of sand, a makeshift ashtray, rests beside the bottom step, butts poking up at different angles and heights, like fenceposts on a storm swept beach. He quickly locates the longest, non-menthol cigarette end, a Marlboro Light, cups it in his hand, and walks slowly out into the gravel parking lot, his free hand reaching into the enormous suitcoat for the matches he'd deposited there earlier in the afternoon. It's now after six, though the August heat still seems oppressive. His shirt-collar scratches his sweaty neck. Tad slips the matches into the shirt pocket and removes the suit-coat, laying it over the tailgate of a faded Ford pickup parked at the edge of the lot.

Fifty paces on, the funeral home's parking lot gives way to a small unmowed field, some scrub oaks and maples shooting up, young and wild, like the field hasn't been planted or plowed in a dozen years. A low stockade fence divides the lot from the neighbors' backyard. The funeral home, built in the 1880s, had been home to two prominent families. The second, undertakers by the name of Quinn, had made the homestead a place for Catholic wakes, starting back in 1953. Its creaky floors and Persian rugs have made the Irish residents of this small town north of Boston to feel comforted and comfortable. Tad doesn't think these things, not consciously at least. He reaches the edge of the field and lights the cigarette.

Inhaling, then coughing, then inhaling again, less of a pull this time, letting the smoke leak out his nose in a way he's practiced. He turns back toward the old house and thinks of Pappy O'Meara, the man who lay waxy and peaceful, napping in the coffin in the main room. Tad's great uncle, or grand uncle, or something like, his father's mother's brother is what he is, was. *A son of a bitch*, he'd heard whispered inside at the wake, *drank himself to death like the rest of his people.* Tad remembered Pappy had smelled not of booze but of stale cigarettes and coffee-flavored hard candy. And he'd heard the hardship stories of the migration from Ireland, had heard survivors like Pappy say they'd *better off to have died.* And Tad thinks it's like inside, where the flowers around the coffin seem to have canceled the smells of coffee and smoke, leaving nothing. The son-of-a-bitch Pappy, the tough immigrant and gruff father, lying in a roomful of genuine tears and grieving, leaving Tad with a feeling he can't name, gray like the ocean.

He's staring at the stockade fence then realizes he's seeing movement, a trembling like from a video on "pause." An injured rabbit the size of a junior football crouches parallel to the fence perhaps fifteen feet from Tad, its backside scraped raw and bloody. Beside it in the scrub grass are tufts of brown fur and a small white ball that Tad realizes may be the animal's tail. Tad does not hear or see his uncle come up beside him. It is this man's father that lies odorlessly and serene inside.

His uncle wears a suitcoat, pulls from the inside breast pocket a pack of cigarettes, from another pocket a chrome lighter. He flips the top, lights a Marlboro. He notices Tad's scavenged cigarette has gone out, hands the lighter to his nephew, still without a word. And then they're both puffing, watching the rabbit. The silence has been interrupted only by the metallic clicks, the open-close of the lighter, the top hinged and shutting firmly sealed. To Tad, his uncle has always seemed somewhat sad and distant, in a way that strangely has caused Tad to feel closer to him.

Tad's been thinking of the word *wake*—wanting to ask someone about it, why it's used for this ceremony, what it means in this context (*context* a word from his reading class at school)—but the injured rabbit has chased these thoughts. Tad wonders if it was a cat that did the damage, having seen his barn tabbies playing, cruelly he thinks, with injured mice.

"Probably a cat," Tad's uncle says, exhaling smoke.

Tad field-strips his own cigarette and pockets the butt, sensing his uncle watching, not wanting to appear disrespectful, or to litter. A moment later, his uncle does the same with his own.

The rabbit has felt their movements, long ears twitching, but it waits before fleeing. Tad wonders if the rabbit is too hurt to move, if its legs are injured, but it suddenly hops off ten yards into the higher grass, disappears. Its cottontail, held by a strip of loose skin, dragging behind the leaping body. Tad wants to ask if his uncle thinks the tail can reattach itself, if the rabbit will survive injured and bloody. His uncle says something then, that Tad will only recall later. More than ten years later when it will come flooding back, triggered perhaps by the environment, same town, same street even though a different funeral home.

Quinn's will refuse to host the wake of Mike O'Meara eleven years later, on Catholic principle since he sinned in choosing his own death. Tad, a year out of college and living then in Baltimore, himself not a church-goer, will return to Massachusetts for the service. He'll stand before the placid sleeping body, its skin dull-glossed like wax fruit. He'll nod to his uncle and then step outside for a cigarette.

Tad will think of the word *wake* again then, remembering the definition he'd favored before, that of *arousing, as from sleep*, as if his great-uncle Pappy O'Meara could have awakened on that long ago afternoon. And the other, the *watch kept over the dead*, which fit the context of course but somehow had never worked for Tad. And he'll think somehow his Uncle Mike would have favored the third usage, the *trail left by an object over liquid, as a ship over water*. Somehow Tad will understand this best, the trail that might connect a body to all others, that ripples then fades to memory. Tad remembers what his uncle had said that evening long ago, as they watched the injured rabbit drag its bloody tail into the brush: *maybe it's harder, sometimes, to live.*

*Resemblances to real persons living or dead, especially Dante
Alighieri (1265-1321) or Beatrice Portinari (1266-1285) are
purely coincidental.*

Mendacity

In the best-selling novels of Verdadi, the characters based on Beatrice Ricci always are outwardly stunningly beautiful, but they are also described as possessing an inner beauty and an accompanying quiet sadness that seems almost nun-like. Thinking back, I'd say these characteristics fit generally well for the most part, describing this girl who was no more than an acquaintance of mine in high school. If words can describe such a look, which I doubt.

But nurses and staff agreed that Beatrice Ricci was the most beautiful baby ever delivered at Johns Hopkins. She grew up less than two miles from the hospital, in the area of restaurants and row houses near the harbor called Little Italy. She was long black-haired and olive skinned, so stunningly gorgeous as a little girl and an adolescent, so that boys as young as nine would call to her not Bea but Beaut, short for beauty, pronounced like the city in Montana. One such boy, nine when Bea was eight, was Dante Verdadi, the prize-winning novelist, a high school friend of mine whom, had I not over the years seen the name and read the books, I'd have lost even memory of like so many in that time of my life. Maybe that's not entirely true. But this isn't a story about me.

Now as I think of her, it's Sunday morning, late morning, and my wife and I scan *The Sun* and drink coffee, the Ravens' game still a couple hours off. I'm just back from running the dogs up to Patterson Park, tied them outside Crabber's where I had a quick bloody mary with a couple Fell's Point locals who'd been at the serious business of drinking long before I showed up. I walk back into our row house, up the marble steps in serious need of a stoop-scrub, and she's there on the couch with the Arts section open and one of Dante's books, a hardback got to be $24.95

if a buck, beside her knees bent Indian-style. At least there was a time you could call it that. Anyway, the book is upside down so the bottom's showing, the dust-jacket photo of the Pulitzer winner himself, dark, handsome, sensitive looking at the camera as if to say *I've felt it all.*

"That poor, beautiful man," she says to me, first thing, the hounds prancing around her, slobbering. She whisks up the book and slides a pajama sleeve cuff over the photo as if smoothing out wrinkles from the inwardly glowing face. "Didn't you say he was a friend of yours in high school?"

"Yeah," I say, "we played some ball." I chuckle a little, reminding her that I was JV and warming the bench while Dante was the good-looking Italian kid with moves and quickness, starting varsity by the end of his freshman year. And we knew each other, sure, and our teams sometimes scrimmaged one another. Of course I'd see him in the locker room or walking home with teammates vying for his attention, or later on with that cheerleader who wasn't Bea and, while pretty and sexy and smart, never touched Beaut in any real way. But I get ahead of myself. The thinking's always faster than the telling of a story, isn't it? But is one more accurate, more honest, less subjective?

So I'm remembering my sophomore year, playing in the JV games early, then riding the pine bench later for the varsity nightcaps. This Friday night in early December, bitter cold outside, too cold even to snow. The air so dry and sharp, it used to freeze on our showered hair, stiffening the strands like soda straws as we'd sneak out for a smoke after our 4:30 game and before the real team took the court at 6:30, theirs before a real crowd, too, and not the parents and little brothers and freshmen doing homework in the stands who made it to ours. Baltimore's a good high school basketball town, it's pretty big time, with of course Dunbar getting most of the attention but we've sent our share to college notoriety if not the NBA. And our varsity wasn't bad that year, over .500 anyway, thanks to Dante's outside jumpers and the low-post play of a gawky 6'10" senior named Petroski—we were almost all Poles or Italians.

So the JV smokers, Danny and Mike and Lucas and me, we'd just gotten waxed by Patterson, I think, lost by upwards of twenty points which was not uncommon and funny, really, at least to some of us who didn't take the winning and losing as life and death. We showered and put on street clothes and slipped out the exit to burn one between games, propping the door with a sweat sock or towel so we could slip back in, of course stinking of Marlboros and fooling no one. Outside, while our hair froze, we swore brazenly about the cold, *fuckin'* this and that, laughing, talking about girls, too. Luke saw himself a real romeo and if you believed him, got himself plenty though most of us knew it was just magazine and a handful of his own self. But his stories always made us laugh, and they never hurt anybody that I knew of.

Anyway, we ditched our butts and stepped back into the humid locker room. It smelled like the greenhouse my mother worked in part-time—tropical and a little rank. I told her that once and she said probably because of all the green things growing in there. Inside, Danny's glasses fogged up like always and he did the blind-corpse walk from "Night of the Living Dead." I knew it pissed him off, though, the thick glasses and the acne on his face. Yet when I saw him at a twenty year reunion last year he looked the best of all of us, fit and just a little gray at the temples, had his own marketing firm and pulled down high six-figures. Anyway, we all chewed a couple tic-tacs and splashed a little of Mikey's *Aqua-velva* on our faces, like any of us had needed a shave. And we headed back to courtside, where we sat on the far end of the bench. The varsity game had just started, and I remember as we sat down Dante beat his man baseline and laid it in, smooth as Isiah Thomas. The crowd went wild for that slick-haired Italian kid.

The teams traded baskets the whole way, and everyone knew the game would go down to the wire. But I hate to tell you that the nail-biting finish and who won is not my point here; believe, if you want, as most do, that Dante hit the winning bucket as the buzzer blared. My point here is Dante's *look*.

Late in the fourth quarter, tight game like I said, all probably seven hundred in the gym going nuts. And their big guy gets a board and hands it to the guard, who calls time. Teams circle their coaches in front of their respective benches. And standing on the edge of the circle, the coach facing him and talking right at him, Dante looks away, past the cheer-leaders doing a quick routine, nearly at me but behind a few rows. He sees Beatrice Ricci and his face changes. Read it in his memoir—he'd been smitten by the Beaut since he was nine, but then who hadn't, young and old, men and women, too. But that's just it: we were all struck by her.

Anyway, he gives her this adoring look, like I said, past the cheer-leaders and nearly at me so I caught it, I assure. I can see it now. I can smell that sweaty gym, can hear the shouts. As cold as it was outside, it was that hot inside. And in the middle of their routine, this one cheerleader looks Dante's way. Suzanne Pitino, a beautiful girl in her own right, intercepts Dante's look. The most amazing, simple little moment— she thinks he's coming on to her. Suzanne then, now this was funny at the time, gets knocked off-balance by the look, misses a high-kick-clap combination, and nearly falls flat. She catches herself but keeps stealing glances back at Dante, as the buzzer sounds for time-in, and the guys hustle out and spread back over the court. And I thought I might have been the only one who got it—there's always a witness, remember. I turned back a few rows behind me to see Beatrice, hard to say what registered behind those amazing green eyes. Bea had all virtue, was more beautiful because of some kindness and glow, it sounds corny to try and describe (read a Dante best-seller some time). But she knew, certainly, the look was for her. Yet it didn't take ten minutes after the game before Suzanne and other on-lookers passed it on that Dante was after Suzanne.

Now I've told you that my wife's the romantic, the one who'd find this incident so deep and tragic (once I tell you the rest), it's, well, like one of the guy's novels if you ask me. She sits on the couch still, now, with that book-jacket photo of the deep-tragic-smiling Dante. And I'm sweating up the living room, trying to keep the dogs from tail wagging her mug off the coffee table in their exuberance. And I'm thinking, *what about Suzanne*?

So to finish the incident, Dante somehow gets the idea that he can use Suzanne like a "screen." He uses that word to a friend of his that I used to lend my history notes to, and I used to ask about the young romeo. Like in our basketball practices, I'm thinking, when a teammate slides in between a defender and the shooter, the screener never appreciated even if the shot falls. So Dante says Beaut's always the one, always the ideal, but since people think he's after Suzanne he'll go that way. He tells his buddy he's getting stuff for Bea and all the time giving it to Suze. He even writes her poems—this slick jock even then drawn to the way of words—one of which appeared in the school newspaper. I remember there were no names mentioned but the girl described is gorgeous, which fits both Bea and Suze, yet she's got green eyes. And then Dante and Suzanne start showing up at parties together, kissing and holding hands—seems he'd fallen for his screen—and no one would ever know there ever was a Beatrice. Except Bea herself, who won't look at Dante in the halls and doesn't return his calls, if in fact he ever did try calling like he told his buddy who told me. Such a mess, the kind of sappy shit only high schoolers get into, maybe. I don't know.

But the tragic part is next, so keep listening. It happened that Beatrice, the beaut (like the place in Montana), started dating this other fellow, a nice guy from the neighborhood who went to Catholic school. And he's driving Bea home from the movies one Friday night when a drunk slams his car into them up on Wolfe, right near the hospital. Right there, but nothing can be done for Bea. The Catholic boy and the drunk walk away, and Beatrice has a sheet over her.

And as you can imagine, when Dante hears the news he pretty much freaks. In his memoir he says he began writing seriously then, I believe he says he started *directing his grief* to the page. This after spending a few months out of school, coming down with mononucleosis, this long after Suzanne had moved away and Dante had picked up another screen for the one he professed to adore. You know he must have been pissed, after dancing with all but the one he wants, to find the band packing up their instruments and he's run out of time. So sad, my wife says, so tragic that poor man. She's read the memoir, too, of course.

And I can buy it, to a point at least. But he used Beatrice, set her up behind the screen where he could use her. She's in every story he ever wrote, in one form or another. I look at my wife on the couch with her sleepy eyes and her robe open just enough to reveal collarbone and cleft. We met in college, she grew up in Massachusetts where there probably weren't as many Poles or Italians. We watched "The Sopranos" on TV, and I think now Dante looks like a cousin of one of them. On the dust-jacket, taking himself so seriously.

My wife and I went to the movies the other night, watched a story about a guy who switches plane tickets with another and the plane crashes, you've probably seen it. The survivor feels horribly guilty and sorry for himself, looks up the widow of the guy who took his seat. Falls for the widow, but can't bring himself to tell her how he knows her. Dante wrote that screenplay, as you might have guessed. And in that one, Bea's the widow. Except in the end she finds out who he is, is real pissed, but at the very last she takes him back. In some of his stories it's like this, she forgives at the end; in others, he's left the tragic figure who blew his best shot at real love. In his latest, the best-seller, she dies before he can get to her and explain and apologize. Great stuff. Stories built on lies, really.

I tell this to my wife, since in a way cynicism and romanticism are two sides of the same reversible raincoat. Or windbreaker, isn't it, the one that's plaid on one side and beige on the other; that's reversible, isn't it?

She says yes, and no, I don't think you can wear that one inside-out. She says without the lies it's a much more interesting story. It *always is*, she says.

Could Dante have written the great stories if he didn't have this ideal heroine to inspire him, I ask. I tell her the whole thing I just told you, the tragic high school tale she knows the most of from the memoir, just from a different angle. Say he's honest about his love for her, she says, and he tells her. Maybe he marries her and he writes *better* stuff, more real. Because he's got dogs tracking mud into the living room and kids with chicken pox or worse, diseases; he's got parents who fight and struggle and die, and he's got a whole world of issues, of sorrows to address.

Then why do you have the book out, looking at the photo and keep saying that poor man.

Poor fool, I say, she says. And what about the damage, she says, what about what was her name, Suzanne, and the other one he used. What about Bea, who'd never be in the car with the Catholic boy for the drunk to hit, if not for Dante and his lies, his look toward Bea that the poor girl, Susan?, just gets flattered by. Like the movie, what if he's honest with her—they probably don't end up together, but that's for the best. He's a cad, and he lies.

The interesting story, she says again, is always the one where characters have the balls to tell the truth.

Isn't that because so few do, that the novelty is the honesty, I'm asking. Sure, she says, your figures are right, but it's not a *because* thing, it just is. And your dogs are tracking mud on the carpet and I'll be in the bedroom, she says, flashing more collarbone and cleft, a little sexy half-smile, motioning for me to follow.

Sounds good, yes? Romantic, *warm*. And untrue. Sounds Hollywood, perhaps, that last line, but not Baltimore.

So let's get it straight, separate the truth from the fiction, the what really happened from what I wish had happened. Starting with this morning, running the dogs up to Patterson Park, well, we didn't make it that far. If you check out a city map, and drew a line from here, Little Italy to the park, The Crabber's bar would be a point on that line near-exactly halfway. This is fact. And every Sunday morning, or nearly every, I set my sights on the park. I head for the park and end up parking at Crabber's.

Like this morning, and I tie the dogs to the parking meter where they get attention and nuzzle and slurp at kids and other passersby. While I step inside for a quick pop. A bloody and a draft to chase it. And another. Nods and greetings and even jokes from the rest of the crusty crew manning the barstools, tugboat workers and third-shifters and all the gradations between, some family-men and women, too, like myself. A couple pops then, and feeling the smoothness in my joints and mind, too. Thinking I could lounge here all day, catch the Ravens game on TV from my prime seat. The dogs slip in between this vision and me, a little yelp reminds me of home.

So we trot off down Thames Street, past the chemical infused soil and concrete vacant lot that was the Union Carbide plant and now can't be built on for several hundred years. I read that the Russians finally closed the Chernobyl site just last week, and I doubt there's much demand for that farmland. Anyway, the dogs and I make it home and I step inside. They prance and leap around the living room to my waiting wife, who sits cross-legged on the sofa with the newspaper. And that's back to pretty much where I began here, isn't it? Except to add that the Dante Verdadi novel on the coffee table is one *I* picked up—I've read every word the guy ever put in print. And to correct, too, that my wife's not staring at the dust-jacket photo. In fact the book sits under half of the morning *Sun*.

Years ago I used to drive down Calvert, past the newspaper offices and production warehouse, the back of the huge brick building where the vans loaded and headed out in the middle of the night. For a time, seemed like daily for years, there would be a handful of picketers pacing out front, protesting I don't even remember what, their sandwich board placards reading *Sun Lies* and on another, *More Lies*. I don't know if they're still out there or not, since it's been years since I took that route to work. But often when I pick up the paper, I see the masthead and think of those signs. I can hear them in my head, though it was a purely visual thing.

And sometimes I think of that movie of the Tennessee Williams play, the one with Paul Newman and Elizabeth Taylor, and Burl Ives as Big Daddy or Puff Daddy, something like that. They're out for the dying father's money, but they won't come out and say that, only talking about their love and concern for him. And Daddy comes up with the word *mendacity*, that a drunk Newman repeats later and again. I think of that sometimes.

So I stand in the doorway, a little winded from the jog, the last stretch maybe a mile, eight or ten unevenly spaced city blocks. My wife looks up from the Arts section and smiles a sad sort of smile that makes me feel all the more ashamed. I act normal, which is nothing like being myself, which is to say I'm consciously *trying* to be myself and so must appear like a kind of stilted version. I have no idea what she's thinking.

She lowers the Arts section to her knees and asks, pretty much the way I originally told you, "I was reading about that writer Dante Verda-di—didn't you tell me a story once about you and him in high school?"

And she means the Beaut story, like the place in Montana, and the story of the game and the look Dante gave, the one intercepted by Suzanne so many years ago. The story I started here with, with the birth of Beatrice Ricci just up the street at Hopkins. She *was* a beautiful kid, and no doubt the hospital staff would've noticed, though I really can't say that for certain.

"Yes, you're right," I tell her, heading into the kitchen for coffee, raising my voice as I pour. "I'll remind you—hang on a sec. You need more coffee?" So casual, sounding so casual.

I stand in the kitchen doorway then, unsure, thinking. It's not even that she'd care, my wife of seven years whom I love and have always, not that she'd care if she knew I slipped off for a few pops now and then. She'd worry, of course, about my depression and the alcohol's effects, about my job performance perhaps. I'd be pretty certain she knows anyway. It's not like I'm having an affair, or killed somebody and never fessed up. But I don't say anything.

Why didn't Dante just walk up to Beatrice after the game, grip her shoulders, say *Beautiful one, I've loved you since I was nine.* And tell her if she felt the same, why don't they give it a shot. Saying hey, Bea, it's not like your real love and I switched plane tickets and the flight went down, you know? I'm the guy you love. Instead, I've put this thing between my wife and me, not even the drinks but the evasion, the secret.

It's there and we both know it.

We all hide things, we all got secrets, you might say. I say it sometimes, too, and nearly believe it's the same thing. I stand sipping black coffee looking at my wife of seven years, thinking *maybe, but.* I see the spine of Dante's book under the newspaper, and I can picture his smiling, compassionate face on the back cover. My wife wasn't looking adoringly at it when I walked in, did I come clean on that? (She does wear the robe, though, and when she looks up past the paper and to me I can see smooth skin of collarbone and cleft.) But the one obsessing on the photo was me, the romantic, the liar, and trying to drink my way to feeling wiser than Dante; and in the end of my tale thinking I could slip off to the bedroom with my wife.

It don't work that way, I know. But how *do* it work then? Maybe Beatrice could've told me. Maybe Suzanne. And, probably, my wife. If I'd ask her, I think, standing in the doorway looking toward her, then focusing onto the novel that sits beneath the newspaper on the coffee table between us.

Gutted

Tuesday, August 3, 1989. 7:03 a.m.

Joseph Dromski gazed upward along the length of the crane, squinting through the already stifling haze. His reddened eyes followed the steel arm to where it reached out over the beams and girders, the skinless skeleton of the skyscraper under construction. He wondered just when it was, and how, he had lost it. "Christ, I'm tired," he said aloud.

It seemed to him that there had been definite events that had caused it. Lost promotions that had gone to less qualified, as favors and pay-offs. Jackie running away, what, seven years ago, eight? Joseph could not see the incidents as the skidmarks they were, merely warning signs on a long, steadily descending stretch of highway. And he did not wonder how negativity and hatred had replaced their opposites in his life, for it was such a gradual process.

And so it was that he did daily now things unconscionable ten years before, justifying his personal evolution in steps as it paralleled his perception of the world's decline. Each step could be justified from the one preceding it, yet Joseph Dromski had no conception of the huge number of such steps; they ran together in his mind which latched onto only a handful of specific events that must explain, he would tell someone across the bar, the laziness and lack of morality in today's youth or the warring in the Middle East. And so as he stared through the haze at the crane's arm, he tried only to justify the action of the previous step, last night ... Careless, he thought. Stupid kid.

Joseph Dromski watched the crew spreading slowly out over the site, and he, too, moved sluggishly toward the elevator cage. But as it lurched into motion, lifting him over the city, he felt none of the thrill he remembered once feeling. He sometimes saw it now in the eyes of the younger men, and he thought them foolish, unrealistic. Wise up, he sometimes told them (he'd told Teddie). Wake up and smell the coffee, and the burned toast, he'd chuckle, watching their eyes to see if his blows registered.

Tiny sweat droplets formed on his balding head, and inside, the dull throbbing began again. "Christ, it's hot," he told no one in particular.

Joseph looked around the elevator, peering guardedly at the grim faces of the other six riders, men he had known, it seemed, forever. He remembered when their moods were light and easy, and the men looked up to him, quick with a joke and the next round of Pabst. But now they hardly looked. So they're guiltier than I, Joseph took this to mean, and knew that soon he could believe it ... One more step.

The sun sliced through the wire cage and left lined shadows on the gray overalls of the riders. Their clothing now matched their faces, appearing like a prison chain gang.

Monday, August 2, 1989. 5:19 p.m.

Maggie sat on the concrete steps of the brownstone that was like all other brownstones, anywhere, and waved to Ted as he let her father out and drove off. She liked Ted, had dated him from time to time, and he had lately taken to coming into the bar some nights near closing time. Yet after a couple of drinks he would leer like a predator, over-tipping and bragging about "going places." He acted as if he deserved her rather than wanted her, and at times he spoke of life in the cynical terms he had learned from her father. Jackie had escaped before he could be so influenced, yet Teddie seemed sometimes to lap it up so eagerly. What were they doing in the middle of these nights, she wondered.

"You look like a hooker on the corner of Rush," she heard her father say. You should know, Maggie thought, not meeting his eyes. "Find a sailor to slap you around a little, huh?" And he was past her and into the building.

Yet the remarks no longer drew blood as they once had, as when Jackie had first left. Maggie silently prayed that this was not because she was drained like her mother, an embalmed body in which no blood

Gutted

remained. She thought again of Teddie, who was apparently unaware that he, too, was losing blood to this man.

Maggie remained on the steps, listening, as her father heavily climbed the wooden steps inside, angrily but without the energy to be. Bitter.

Joseph Dromski entered the kitchen his wife had made even hotter by using the oven. Without a word he took a beer from the refrigerator and slumped into the leather-cracked stuffed chair in the front room. He unbuttoned the straps of the gray overalls, revealing a sleeveless tee-shirt sweat-stained the color of his teeth.

"Do you think you might sometime serve something *cool* in weather like this?" he called toward the doorway, switching on the television to drown her possible answer.

But she offered none, only acknowledging another check on a mental calendar, another day unchanged. Della had felt her energy, her life in these past years, escaping in tiny wisps, sucked out through the door that each evening he reentered. More and more it seemed locked from the outside behind him.

He used to tell her it was she who had changed, but recently he had begun telling her the opposite—that change was demanded and she had not. "You've got to modify," he'd say. "You've got to get tough."

"They'll kill us, Del," he used to tell her, before he had modified. Before he began working nights and talking less.

And Maggie told her not to listen, to take the blows and think of her own dreams, of returning to teaching, or just getting out. But Della did not sleep well, and her dreams she tried not to remember.

She, too, wondered how and why so much had been lost. She did not understand the steps involved, could not trace it. I still miss Jackie, she thought. If I could get past that, I know I'd be better for Joseph. "He's takin' you, Ma," she heard her son, could it be eight years ago, "surer than if he was beatin' you with his fists ..." Thank God, at least, for that, she had thought at the time. Yet now, as she held the counter, the nauseating emptiness warm inside her, she was not so sure.

"Do you work again tonight?" Della asked, calling over the television, spooning chicken casserole onto a faded china plate, its blue flowered design worn unrecognizable. He did not answer, and as she handed him the meal his eyes did not leave the screen.

Maggie remained on the front steps, listening to the television news pouring from the second floor window and thinking of her mother. Finally she rose and checked her watch, knowing she would be early for work.

Tuesday, August 3, 1989. 2:12 a.m.

Joseph Dromski awoke with a start as the filter of the cigarette held loosely between his fingers seared his knuckles. He swore under his breath and stared across the room, completely disoriented. Worn furniture was bathed in blue-gray radiation light emitted from the silent television. Joseph stared blearily through the smoke at the small rectangle of light in which Groucho Marx was miming "You Bet Your Life." The emcee handed a schoolteacher from Iowa fifty dollars for using the word attached to the foot of a suspended duck. ". . . a common household word, something you see every day," Joseph mocked thickly. And then all was silent again save for an occasional passing vehicle on the still stifling street outside.

Joseph Dromski glanced at his watch now and rose quickly. He found his work boots lying neatly beside the door and mechanically tugged the laces through eyelets, pulling them tight as his hockey skates decades ago. He did not hear his wife breathing unevenly in the bedroom whose door stood ajar.

If we could finish this place tonight, he thought as he closed the door and slipped down the wooden stairs, maybe I could get some sleep. Yet as he stepped out into the moonless August night, he was wide awake, his mind actively calculating.

It had been a fine old building, 1920 maybe, and if the yard man believed even older, the bricks could sell for at least twenty-eight cents apiece. At least twenty-two hundred in the truck meant he could cut Teddie his seventy-five—for two hours work, more than I ever made at his age, the ingrate—and still have, what, five hundred plus in his pocket. That would buy a long nap, and maybe an afternoon at Arlington with the ponies.

The truck turned over grudgingly on the second try—the damn thing runs better in a Chicago winter, he thought—and Joseph drove slowly toward the south side, not worried that Teddie may have waited as he overslept. He'll get paid, Dromski told the rearview mirror, nodding at the deserted streets.

Behind him in the brownstone, Della Dromski lit a cigarette and sat up in bed, feeling somehow better the moment the door closed behind him. Endurance seemed the only goal on nights like this.

Yet it had not always been this way, she counseled herself again. She remembered the winter nights watching from behind the glass as he glided over the ice so swift and full of boyish determination. And then the breezeless summer nights like this one, passing back and forth warm pints of beer on a blanket by the lake. Watching the barge silhouettes far away and the stars. Kissing, laughing. High school, she thought. And then the wedding and the Army and the children and still, she thought, they had been happy. Yet somehow, she could not place exactly when, it stopped feeling the same.

It was partially now, Della thought, that dammit she still loved the man. And partially her upbringing, for her mother would never have imagined leaving her father, whose drinking bouts and violence were much more common than her own Joseph's. She had taught Della perseverance and preached forgiveness, always forgiveness, and as Della did now, had often blamed herself. And when Maggie pleaded with her to get out, she could never muster the strength to abandon that boy on the blanket by the lake so long since gone.

Della Dromski rose, stubbing out her cigarette, and entered the warm kitchen. With resolve she began laying out bread and mustard and sliced ham, the ritual and the mere motion of it a comfort.

She could not continue to hear the voices of Maggie and Jackie in one ear, and Joseph in the other. Her love went out to both sides, yet she was torn and unsettled.

Della listened to the steady, scuffing beat of the ancient coffee percolator. Outside, a car engine neared and quieted. She heard Maggie's footsteps on the stairs, and looked up to see the front room an eerie blue-gray as the television played on silently without audience. She turned back to her work.

Tuesday, August 3, 1989. 2:37 a.m.

Maggie closed the door quietly, wearily, and saw her mother's back to her at the counter, bread laid out in neat rows before her. She knew her entrance had been heard, and moved behind her mother, kissed her cheek.

"Take these over to . . ." her mother began, then stopped, thinking My God, that was just like *him*, and tried to smile. "Honey, how did it go tonight?"

Della felt suddenly defensive, not wanting her daughter to say a word. Embarrassed to be making him sandwiches in the middle of the night. She turned her head slightly so that Maggie's words might be channeled into her right ear, Joseph's ear.

Maggie loved her mother, and she knew what her mother had begun to ask. She understood her, and part of her loved the unfinished order. Was this where she was different from Jackie, she wondered, and more like this woman at the counter?

Yet the part of Maggie that did not love this "slip" by her mother, the unanswered love her action represented, the weakness . . . this part of Maggie hated her father, suddenly and deeply. She realized this feeling had existed for as long as she could remember. Jackie, she thought, help me now.

Maggie had watched her father gouge into people as his own self-hatred went unacknowledged. She felt him trying to take from her all that was inside her, because he had relinquished all that was inside himself. And she had watched him take away her mother's self-respect and her dreams, almost laughing that it was so easy.

Maggie had watched this since her youth, and had found her mother in tears, or worse, like this now, many times. And she had been there to comfort her. But did she respect her mother for taking all this—for letting him destroy her because he felt wronged? Part of Maggie despised this weakness in her mother and in herself.

Maggie hesitated. "I'll run the sandwiches over to Daddy," she said. "I'm still wired from work, could use the air. I know the area they're working—Teddie told me the other night." Her mother looked up seriously.

They stared at each other for a moment. Della's eyes sought an answer, what two construction workers could be doing in the middle of the night. Then, Maggie thought, they seemed to dart, to withdraw the question.

Gutted

"I love you, Mom," Maggie said simply, pouring hot coffee into the thermos.

Tuesday, August 3, 1989. 3:21 a.m.

Joseph Dromski waited by the truck in near-total blackness, sweating. He saw no lights on in the apartment building opposite the abandoned brick structure where he stood, and no sign of human life at all on the other sides, a small park and a dusty, littered vacant lot. Ted emerged from the condemned building, his shirt perspiration soaked, pushing the wheelbarrow laden with clay-colored bricks.

"That's got to be about it," Teddie panted. Joseph frowned, seeing room in the pickup for maybe, he quickly calculated, seventy more.

"A few more," said Joseph Dromski, looking at the truck.

"The interior walls . . ." Teddie began, frustrated, catching his breath. ". . .shouldn't try," he attempted, faltering, knowing it was dangerous to spark Joseph's short fuse.

As Joseph helped him stack the bricks into the bed of the truck, Ted knew that he would reenter the gutted structure. Joseph finally stood still and waited, as Teddie lifted the wheelbarrow the last time.

"Greedy bastard," Ted muttered under his breath, cursing more himself, for a lifetime of yielding in this game of chicken. He rolled the cart through the doorless entryway and into complete darkness.

Tuesday, August 3, 1989. 3:29 a.m.

Maggie had passed and rounded the same block twice before she recognized her father's truck. In the blackness it was barely visible beneath the structure that stood, she could tell, without glass in the windows or occupancy of anything but pigeons and rats.

Her Volkswagen stalled, the engine dying, as she saw the barrel-like form of her father and the tall, massless skeleton of Teddie pushing a wheelbarrow. The men exchanged words, but in the silence from a block away she could not make them out. What were they doing?

There was a moment, then, of total absolute silence, which Maggie thought she had been granted to understand something. Something you already knew, Jackie would tell her. But as she watched Teddie reenter the hollow structure she thought, I've missed it.

It was not, she would think later, violent or deafening, even played upon the background of complete silence. It was soundless, like a film she suddenly remembered seeing in grade school, of an earthquake somewhere out west. Buildings fell this way, she remembered thinking. Without narration or description; without emotion.

The last brick . . .

And then she remembered Teddie, as three of the exterior walls of the building in slow motion collapsed upon each other like a house of cards. The coffee in the thermos on the seat beside her remained hot.

Maggie turned the key and the car sputtered. The engine caught. She sat for a moment comforted, concentrating on this low rumbling, grateful. And she spun the car around, in the rearview mirror seeing the figure of her father leap into the cab of the truck. She accelerated, screeching around one corner and hitting the lights, stopping only when she felt out of reach and the telephone booth appeared in her path.

She was quite calm with the police, she thought later. Speaking evenly and giving no names, saying please just send an ambulance quickly I know nothing more. And just as calmly and rationally she somehow knew there was no hope. He has taken from Teddie what he took from Momma, and me, and God knows who else. What he took from the building itself . . . And we will all eventually collapse, she thought, our insides looted but the facades left apparently unblemished, betraying no damage.

Maggie packed quickly, leaving a note in her mother's handbag, nothing more than Jackie's address. Yet she knew her mother could not follow her now.

As the first streaks of hazy light appeared in the rearview mirror, Maggie saw the silhouette of the city, the skyscrapers rising proudly from the darkness beneath. And only then did the tears begin to fill her eyes and fall silently onto the work shirt she had never changed. There was something different about these tears, she thought, for they were not shed and lost in the night to be found again the next. They meant something, for they came with motion, and change. She gripped the wheel tightly, staring straight ahead.

Gutted

Tuesday, August 3, 1989. 7:18 a.m.

The elevator cage stopped at the top of the city, and the man closest to the gate hesitated a moment before sliding it aside. And it seemed to Joseph Dromski that the shadows of prison stripes remained on the overalls of the seven men long after they had stepped out into the sun. "Christ, it's hot," he said.

Welding Girl

On the morning of her brother's accident, Lara stood for hours in the registration lines at Tech. She was steamed at her mother who only could drive her there at seven a.m. when she knew the student adviser signatures couldn't be had until after eight-thirty. And for the trip Lara had rated only the back seat because her mother had "a client," an unemployed unwed mother with screaming baby, in the front seat being chauffeured to a job interview. The young woman had to be at the job site at eight and might need Lara's mother's Spanish translation services, too, and Lara wouldn't mind going a little early, her mother had said, right love? And as soon as Lara's Ford Fiesta was out of the shop she'd be "like, totally independent again," her mother added, embarrassingly, and wouldn't a little walking to the bus stops do Lara good, maybe? Breathing in the sharp, invigorating winter air and even losing a few pounds without even trying, not that she was at all concerned that her daughter was "too heavy."

While her brother, Wesley, was stepping into his overalls and lacing up his work boots, Lara made it to the front of one line only to be told she needed to be in another, upstairs, which turned out to be longer. The other students around her seemed to be quite a cross-section, she noticed, from young unemployeds looking to study car mechanics and welding to preppy dressed types pursuing real estate or computer programming, pregnant women who could be her mother's clients talking about cosmetology, others speaking foreign tongues and bound for ESL courses. Yet Lara felt no affinity, no connection with any of them. She munched a granola bar her mother had thrust at her in the back seat on the way over, and she stared at her course listings without reading.

While Wes drove to his new job at Capital Tree Services, drank a cup of coffee with the two others on his crew, then climbed into the cherry picker truck, Lara reached the front of the second line and sat down in front of an advisor, a middle aged balding tired looking man with tiny bits of English muffin and strawberry jam, Lara guessed, on his upper lip. He took up her registration papers and course list, and grumbled something. But at her Technical Business Writing course, W-2300, he misread the numbers and his face brightened. "W-2800," he said, "that's a fine course there, so what drew you to Welding?"

The technical writing course was a bone Lara had agreed to throw her parents, who saw her scribbling stories and poetry and had struggled to find a practical use for something Lara had gravitated toward on her own. She hated the idea of something so dry, so, well, "technical," that was just it, she thought. Like a lawn mower owner's manual. So while her brother was climbing into the bucket of the truck and the hydraulics hummed and the steel arm lifted him up into the massive pin oak, Lara looked at the tech college advisor and said, "I've always wanted to learn to weld, since I was a little girl. I can't explain it," she said, and looked down at her chewed fingernails, a gesture of vulnerability that she enacted almost unconsciously, which nearly always yielded results. In her mind she pictured some vague welded sculpture—some of her poetry sometimes took on a visual form in her mind—and hatched an idea that she could use welding as some new medium of expression. Plus, she thought, as a bonus, her parents would be so pissed if they knew.

At the time her brother leaned out of the bucket with the pole saw and lost his balance—something he the athlete, the one who had always moved so smoothly and ever so balanced—and flipped out and tumbled, "gracefully," said a woman onlooker, a neighbor to the homeowner whose yard featured the giant pin oak in need of trim, Lara was signing the registration papers. Wesley hadn't hooked himself in the harness, feeling it too restricting in the way some oldtimers view seatbelts. Lara's brother fell nearly eighty feet through the branches, almost catching himself at one point but unluckily the limb he grabbed broke off and ended up beside him on the ground. The pole saw stayed in the tree, angled naturally horizontal and so nearly invisible as another branch. It was two days before the saw was missed and a crew returned to retrieve it.

Lara's welding class runs fifteen weeks, meeting Saturdays starting at 8 a.m. until 4. The first class comes on the Saturday following Wes' accident, and she is awake in bed at six, sweating and anxious while her brother, still in the hospital, also awake, stares at the ceiling without the ability to move his legs at all, his arms more than a twitch of fingers. Lara lies in bed wishing she'd corrected that advisor or, better, that she'd signed up for the Nursing Assistant course to be of some use to Wes. But of course she'd not known of her brother's accident until after she'd registered, then after she'd taken the bus to within a half mile of the garage where a mechanic was installing her new radiator; in fact, she'd more likely have signed up for Auto Mechanics 1100, if she hadn't been almost tricked into the welding course that morning.

That is how she thinks of it now, sweating in bed at dawn on a Saturday morning, as if the advisor had somehow conspired to get her from Technical Writing to the welding shop. Maybe they needed one more student, she thinks, or needed at least one female, for some quota. As she climbs from bed, Lara thinks of Wes, her golden-boy brother, the school-record holding distance runner, the rock climber, the handsome rugged guy who belonged on the cover of *Outdoor Athlete* magazine. They'd never been close, much because she'd envied him and all that came so naturally to him, and she'd come to believe what others did, that they as siblings were opposites in all ways. And now, she thinks, she does something he cannot do, in fact will never do again: she climbs out of bed and feels the cool tile floor beneath her feet, and walks slowly to the bathroom.

* * *

In the classroom, across the hall from the welding shop, are seated a dozen males, mostly in their twenties although one guy, it turns out, is 68, and a couple more are in their forties. Perhaps half African-American, a few Hispanic, all seeming to know each other, they stop their joking and laughing when Lara steps into the room. A few nod at her, polite, not unfriendly. She's the only white, overweight, woman in the class.

Lara chooses a desk near, but not too near, the front, trying to space herself naturally in the dispersion of the students already seated. Most have large textbooks on their desks, several with welding helmets, *shields* she'll learn to call them, in front of them. When the instructor enters, the guys greet her, Lara thinks, warmly, familiarly, admiringly.

It's as if she's—the teacher is a woman, a tall African-American woman with broad shoulders and amused eyes—as if they're a team and she's a former star who graduated a year before. Lara thinks of her basketball team when she was thirteen, before they moved here, before she put on so much weight, and the high school girl who helped coach them. Older, admired, but not unapproachable. One of them, certainly. And the welding teacher greets most of the guys by name, genuine and upbeat, like cousins at a reunion cookout. It turns out nine of the twelve took her Welding 2700 course last semester. So Lara's feeling, that she'd crashed a party, was not misplaced.

Their instructor's name is Jasmine, at first as much of a misnomer as Lara. That's Lara whose name and spelling come from her mother's love of *Dr. Zhivago*, and *his* love, Lara-with-no-U, played by a lithe wispy Julie Christy in the movie her mother watched again and again. A "Jasmine," Lara would've guessed, would be long and thin and like the vine itself, long-armed and legged and with fingers much more suited to the piano than a welding electrode. It is over a month later that Lara really notices Jasmine's hands, how long-fingered and graceful and strong, like birch branches.

Jasmine takes the roll and gives an overview of the course. They'll be working from the text in the classroom, where they'll have regular written tests, and across the hall in the welding shop they'll be learning shielded metal arc welding, called "stick," and also TIG, MIG, as well as cutting and brazing. And then they begin reading from the book aloud—a paragraph per person—while Lara and those without books look on with one who has one. She pulls her desk across next to a guy they call Ken, an optimistic faced twenty-five-year-old with an established good relationship with Jasmine. He nods to invite Lara to share his text, and when it is her turn to read she worries about her stale breath and stumbles over a few words, but no one seems to notice and Jasmine thanks her when she finishes. She reads:

A **weld** is a *localized coalescence*—the fusion or growing together of the grain structure of materials, the joining together of metals or nonmetals produced either by heating the materials to required welding temperatures, with or without the application of pressure, or by the application of pressure alone. . .

The words strike Lara unexpectedly, somehow beautiful and she thinks for a moment she might cry. God, she thinks, that would seal the deal—they'd never let another woman into welding. And imagine Jasmine's disapproval, disappointment. Lara's voice cracks once, but she manages to compose herself to finish the paragraph.

And then an hour later they head across the corridor to the welding shop, where they don the gloves and shields and green flame retardant jackets not so neatly arranged in huge steel equipment trunks. For the first exercise, they'll work with a gas torch. They learn how to connect the gas and oxygen, and how to check for leaks using soapy water. The exercise must be a rerun for some, Lara thinks, but they don't show it.

Once Ken and Damon, another of Jasmine's old-timers, measure and mark with soapstone six-inch squares on a half-inch thick plate of metal, they line up to use the cutter. Lara hesitates, not sure whether to hang back or volunteer first. Jasmine demonstrates how to work the oxygen and gas tanks, the red acetylene gas hose opened first, the flame struck, and then the oxygen that shields and sharpens the flame. Lara stands close, only jumping back slightly when the flame is struck. Jasmine adjusts the gases, first the acetylene until the flame no longer smokes, then introducing the oxygen to focus the flame into ten tiny quarter-inch-long jets. Lara feels an attraction to the flame, feels power in the sound of the steady whoosh of the gas. Jasmine heats the edge of the steel until the sparks begin, then presses the gas-mixing trigger and begins to cut the half-inch-thick plate along the soapstone line. The sparks of molten metal fly from the opening the torch creates, splashing and bouncing on the smooth concrete floor. Lara finds the display moving in a way she will try to put down into written words one day. Jasmine cuts freehand along the soapstone lines, along the two sides of the six-inch metal, the flame hissing and the sparks showering and bouncing, and then she's cut through and the perfect little square falls clanging to the shop floor.

Lara ends up cutting third, behind Ken. She grips the torch, a brass gun really, she thinks, opens the valve for oxygen and next in line, Damon, strikes her a spark. The torch comes to life, the flame making a powerful wind sound that makes her think of the directed air nozzles above seats on airplanes. She adds oxygen until it stops smoking, then mixes in the acetylene, adjusting her flame to sharpen it as Jasmine had done.

"Good, *there*. That's it," Jasmine tells her to stop adjusting. And

Lara bends toward the steel, preheats the edge of the soapstone line until the sparks start to splash down, and she begins to cut, moving the torch somewhat haltingly along the line. Lara watches with fascination and even pride as the sparks shower and dance, and the flame melts a gap in the steel. And then, so quickly, her square of steel is loosed from the large plate and is clanging onto the concrete floor.

She rotates the brass knobs to cut the oxygen—first because it is feeding the flame—and gas, and hands the torch to Damon beside her, and passes to him the shield that is just slightly tinted, the dark green of sunglasses. She picks up the spark-striker, and when he has the gas on, she lights his torch, careful not to flinch the way Damon had when lighting hers. She thinks that the guys might notice any girlish gestures, and she wants Jasmine and her classmates to know she's not the type.

On her way home after the welding class, Lara stops at the hospital to visit Wes. Only three years in age separate the two, yet Lara has always found her brother hard to approach. He was always so confident without being cocky, lean and muscular and naturally tan somehow in the middle of winter. All traits that make Lara see herself as so different, opposite, and make him hard to speak to. Yet now he's smaller, beneath the sheet, vulnerable, unable to do anything for himself. He tries to smile when he sees her, but she thinks he looks terribly sad. As Wes nods in and out of sleep, Lara tells him about her welding class, how their parents think it's Technical Writing, how the torch felt in her hands. She's not sure he's heard a word of it.

* * *

The next Saturday, a bright, raw cold morning, while Wes remains in the hospital, Lara returns to class. While her brother has regained some small movement in his fingers, he has been apprised of the spinal damage that will probably keep him in a chair for the remainder of his life. Which is not to say, the doctors point out, that his situation is hopeless. He can continue to have his once-vibrant muscles stretched and worked, and some movement could return. There is also stem cell technology that might be his godsend, so he mustn't let the leg muscles atrophy. But like most all faced with similar challenges, Wes has spent the days since the accident in a haze of painkillers and leaden depression, the desolation a condition he's told might be with him for a year or more. In between the frequent visits of doctors and staff and rehabilitation aides, he thinks

122   Welding Girl

often of suicide. Nothing in his life is as it was, what, just two weeks before. While Lara drives to her welding class just before eight a.m., Wes is laying wide awake thinking of the Saturday before the accident. He'd gone hiking up to Hanging Rock and rappelling on a cold sharp day not unlike this one. From his hospital bed, he can see the sky. He moves his fingers but cannot raise his arm even enough to point to the window, like a child, he thinks, just learning to speak, to say *sun*, to say *clouds*, to say *blue*.

In the second welding class, they read aloud from another chapter on safety, and also on stick welding. Lara's paragraphs concern the types of light—ultraviolet, infrared, and visible—and how they can damage human eyes. She reads about flashburn, when ultraviolet light sears eyes in seconds, the skin in minutes, first and second degree burns. And then in the shop later she wears the cheap and scratched welding helmet, the shield that belongs to the school, with its plexiglass window so dark not only do none of the dangerous lights get through, but almost no light at all.

She partners with Ken, who's probably unwilling but too nice a guy to say so, and watches as he plugs up and turns on the transformer, connects the work lead to his metal. He nods to her and they flip down their shields, then he taps the long electrode, the "stick," to the steel and so strikes his arc. But all Lara sees through her shield is darkness, then the flash of bright yellow as the arc is struck.

And then she watches as Ken moves the electrode along the chalk line on the metal, in smooth little "C" motions, laying a straight heavy bead. Then he pulls the electrode away, breaking the arc, and the two of them flip back their shields. Ken bangs along the bead with a tack hammer, chipping off the slag. And what is revealed is beautiful, Lara thinks, what the guys have called "a roll of dimes on its side." Lara has never really noticed welds in the world before but now she starts seeing them everywhere, on the steel baker's rack in her kitchen to the bumper of her little Ford Fiesta to the I-beams of the new strip mall next to her mother's house.

Yet once Lara gets her chance to stick weld, because she's working in darkness, she struggles just to get her arc struck. Then when she does, when the current jumps from electrode to her steel piece, she moves the electrode too close, touches the metal so that it welds itself to the work, her "stick" annoyingly stuck. To extricate it, she must raise her shield to see, then she has to work the electrode back and forth until the weld breaks. And then flip down her helmet and try to light the stick again. Her first efforts look as much like a roll of dimes as she looks like a skinny girl, but Ken at least remains silent, not critical but she feels his disapproval.

And then later Jasmine when she comes around, she's kind and unfazed, acting as if it's normal frustration and telling her simply "Okay now, stick with it." When Jasmine dons her own shield, a yellow and black lightning-bolted number, and sits on Lara's stool to demonstrate, a couple of other classmates gather around. They watch her steady, unhurried movement of the electrode, smooth little C's in a straight line. She finishes a five-inch bead and touches the reddened metal with the hammer to absorb some heat before chipping off the slag. When she taps the dark burned residue and it breaks away to reveal shiny, uniform rows of waves, a roll of dimes or the surf, Lara wants to burst in applause.

And even if Lara's ugly welds are inconsistent, heavy, and crooked, she still gets the thrill of chipping off the slag. There's excitement, anticipation that builds as she completes the weld. But also a calmness that, like the rest of the process really, she thinks, is indescribable. She thinks it is something of a different dimension than words. She who values words and how they can be combined, built one attached to another in her poems, to describe something. But here in the welding shop is something else. Even as her welds worm crookedly, and the steel she lays down is unevenly distributed, unmistakable is the primitive power in her left hand when she's struck the arc and feels a strength, watching the steel melt, the molecules reorganizing and joining as one before her, the coalescence from their textbook, amazingly an action that she has caused to occur. She's transfixed, even transformed, for the few seconds before she lifts her shield.

But the first few weeks in the shop are anxious ones for Lara. She lays on sweated sheets Friday nights and is awake long before the alarm set to go off at 6:30. She feeds and walks her stinking and beloved manic-depressive mutt, relieved for the motion. She has time to review the last chapter the class had read in the welding textbook. She has to force herself to eat a bowl of cereal because her nervousness takes her appetite.

Welding Girl

And in the shop, she continues to have trouble getting her arc struck, seeing little through the scratched lens of the semesters-old, much abused shield. When her turn to weld comes, she flips down the helmet into near-total darkness before she scratches the tip of the electrode across the steel and the light flares up. Once the light shows, of course, the current is passing from the stick to the steel workpiece, and Lara has to maintain that tiny separation between electrode and steel to maintain the arc. Touch the electrode to the work and the arc is gone, the melted steel of the electrode sticks to the work. Allow the stick to stray too far from the workpiece, even a half an inch, and the distance is too great for the arc to jump across, so she loses it, too.

She feels her forehead and hands sweating beneath the shield. The perspiration fogs the already scratched tinted window, and again Lara wants to cry. Wants to give up, say it's not for her, to walk out right that minute, two in the afternoon of her third week of class, mid-March, when her brother Wes continues half-hearted efforts at rehab, barely moving fingers in his right hand, continuing to think of suicide. While her mother continues her good works, aiding the unwed mothers, frets over Wes because she has to have something to worry about—she'll create or invent something if her schedule is too clear of worry, although at this particular time her docket is understandably crammed full. Which takes her concerns from Lara, at least, who her mother thinks is taking the eight-to-four all-day Saturdays course in Technical Writing, or is it Accounting, Lara can't recall what she told her. Her mother hasn't even noticed that in the near month of sweats and anxiety of welding, Lara has lost almost fifteen pounds. Lara feels strangely ambivalent about both these issues: that is, her mother's worry directed elsewhere is both a relief and somewhat upsetting lack of attention; and the pounds she's shed are of course welcome but also gone as a part of her, a detail of her identity. In the tense concentration under her shield, however, Lara can think of none of this.

There is slight but noticeable progress. Week three, in the afternoon, Jasmine comes around to help out and check on Lara's work. They're working on simple butt and "T" joints, and Jasmine holds one of Lara's welds, heavy and a bit crooked, but Jasmine doesn't frown the way Lara expects. Doesn't show distaste.

"Okay now, Lara," she says. "Now I know you might not be fully pleased with this, but it is a completely acceptable weld." Not pretty, but it will hold, Lara thinks, a tiny bit of satisfaction flushing her cheeks.

* * *

But then, in the fifth Saturday, just after noon, something happens. Lara had been partnering with Darius, and she'd just clipped in a new, footlong electrode stick, had grounded her pipe to be welded, when Jasmine called lunch. Lara started to get up with the others filing for the door, but hesitated. The room had become suddenly quiet—no hissing and popping of other welding going on, no one using the electric grinders that scream against the metal so that most of them wear earplugs when someone is operating one. Lara sat back down on her stool. Not hungry anyway, she'd taken the electrode in her left hand, and in the air just above her work she traced her welding plan, the C's that would fill the joint between the two pieces of steel pipe. Then she lowered her shield, struck her arc, and began.

And for a few seconds a strange and amazing thing happened, and Lara understood Jasmine's words. "Try to watch your weld pool, your puddle and not the end of the electrode. Push the pool," she said. And in that short period Lara started not only to *see* that molten puddle of slag. She began to feel the movement of the pool in her own body; or her own body *became* the pool somehow. It could have been hours or days or a second—Lara had no sense of time, was in a timeless place.

And then an hour later, while the shop is once again full of activity and screeching machines, Lara is hitting the four tack welds around another set of pipes to be joined, when Jasmine makes her rounds, this time with her clipboard to note the progress of the students. Lara finishes the tack and raises her shield when she sees the instructor. Jasmine picks up the pipe that Lara welded while the others were at lunch. She turns it slowly in her hands that Lara suddenly notices are beautiful, long-fingered, strong but graceful at the same time, like Jasmine herself.

"Whose work is *this*?" Jasmine asks the five now gathered around the work table where Lara is still sitting. "This is *good*." She looks around for someone to take credit. Everyone wants to, Lara can feel it. Darius nods to her. "You did this, Lara?" Jasmine says admiringly, even proudly, as if it were her own work even, Lara thinks. "I'm going to grade this right now, because this is most excellent work."

And it was at that moment that Lara realized that the feeling that had come over her, out of body, at just a few seconds of the drawing the rod over the gap between the pipes, the feeling was something another person could recognize. Not that it wasn't significant to Lara, for it would have been, whether anyone ever saw the work or not. But Lara had felt connected for the first time, to this hot and ancient and primitive process she suddenly loved, loved beyond all reason. And in addition, it mattered to her that someone else recognized the quality of her work. This was part of it, too, Lara thought. And what *wasn't* a part of it, for chrissakes, Lara might have said even a week ago, in harsher words even. Because, don't forget, she was the fat girl—the fat person, one, *and* the girl, two, words that had defined her in the class and everywhere else for as long as she could remember.

But now, while her brother Wes sits in a wheelchair trying to exercise his right arm, moving only his fingers but moving them perhaps a quarter inch more than he had the week before, Lara watches Jasmine's long fingers turn the pipe she'd welded. And Lara feels something she can't describe, though in her poetry it will have to do with the heat and the light. When she visits her brother after class, she'll try to describe the process and her feeling, and she'll have to give up for lack of adequate words. Wes will listen, doubtlessly a part of him envying his sister, a feeling he's probably never experienced. And a part of him still so dark, so hopeless.

Two weeks later, after a Saturday of some frustration, what Lara views as digression in her skills, it happens again. They are working gas metal arc welding, or MIG welding—a process that uses argon as the shielding gas. She'd been partnering with Darius, and he left early, not returning after lunch. Lara works the station alone, and for a few seconds that afternoon she once again feels herself being drawn closer and closer to the molten pool, *becoming* the pool is how she later thinks of it.

As she moves the electrode—in MIG it's a kind of gun, a pistol that delivers the steel wire—moves it in smooth tiny C's back and forth and all the while forward along the crease, she somewhere stops watching the electric light at the end of the electrode. Just as Jasmine has said, she's watching instead the pool, the puddle of molten steel that the fiery bright current is melting. "Pushing the puddle," that's what Jasmine says.

And even more than that *watching* the pool, pushing it in little waves across the gap between the steel pieces, she *is* the pool. For those few seconds she is not the fat white girl in the shop. She is not fat, white, female because these identifiers require a physical form, and she for those seconds is, indescribably, without a body. Gone is her frustrating mother, who cares so much for everyone that Lara feels sometimes just one more, not even a young single girl with a baby that her mother helps to find home and work and childcare and often substance abuse counseling. Gone is her often depressed and paralyzed brother who spends six hours each day exercising his near useless arms, and having his motionless legs extended and worked over to maintain some muscle tone. She is nowhere but in the molten steel, is no one. And the feeling is fleeting, so that she can't just summon it at times of stress or frustration or anger. In fact, it's three more weeks before she feels it again.

These Saturdays—she's now in week twelve of fifteen—when Lara enters the classroom the others acknowledge her. Most will offer a "w'sup" or nod. Brief eye contact which she'll return in a way she couldn't at first. No one has mentioned Lara's weight loss, but she's seen their glances down her body, knows they couldn't help but notice, probably twenty-five pounds or more since the class began though she hasn't stepped on a scale, hasn't felt the anxious dread-need that drew her to it before. Some lose weight due to worry or grief, Lara thinks. Like her mother since Wes' accident. But others seem to shed pounds because of activity and positive change. Lara appears to have lost even more weight because her posture has changed in the past weeks. She sits straighter at her desk, and when she walks her head is often up, her eyes sometimes meeting others'.

Jasmine enters the room a few minutes past eight, apologizes, says hey to Darius and Kevin, nods to others, and gives Lara a wink. As if she's glad to have another woman in the room. Lara sits up even straighter in her desk seat, flushing slightly in her cheeks.

An hour later, they're restless over the text and Ted, who already mumbled when he came in at eight-twenty-five that he'd overslept and got no breakfast, reads a paragraph describing the Fillet Weld. Two "L"s, pronounced like what Lara's mother would say to a service station attendant back when gas was affordable: "Fill it." But Ted reads it as "filet," like the word before "mignon" on a fancy steakhouse menu. And Jasmine cracks up, and everybody else follows. Ted laughs, too, then, and corrects himself—"fill-it"—and adds, "Told y'all I was hungry."

When Ted finishes reading the paragraph, Lara and the others feel loose and comfortable in the room, like a team or a large family at a reunion. Yet if one were to try to acknowledge the connectedness aloud, Lara thinks, it would evaporate. There's a pause of warm silence before Jasmine speaks, the last of the laughter still in her voice. "Okay, now, I think we've had enough reading for today. Let's get to some 'hands-on' over in the shop. First, though, let's take a little snack break, if that'd be alright with you, Ted."

After a break, they try their hands at gas tungsten arc welding, or TIG, the most challenging type of welding because it necessitates using both hands simultaneously, as well as one foot for a kind of "gas pedal" that controls the speed and heat. The only one left-handed in the class, Lara guides the electrode in her left hand while she feeds the steel wire with her right. Her right foot presses a pedal, like speed control on a sewing machine, and she strikes her arc.

Lara's first efforts at TIG are awful. She takes some solace from how the rest of the class is struggling also. Even Ken, so much the seeming natural, even Jasmine herself has trouble coordinating the three variables. The poor functioning, much abused equipment doesn't make TIG any easier. At twelve-thirty, Jasmine calls lunch and apologizes for the faulty equipment. "When we come back, we'll go right to MIG welding," she tells them. "It's much easier, your wire gets fed automatically. And the machines *work*. I'll talk to the department head about getting the TIG stuff fixed. It's hard enough without malfunctioning machines." The class sighs collective relief, and all except Lara file out of the shop. When the huge room is empty and quiet, she sits back down on her work stool. She loosens the brass collar and inserts a sharpened tungsten electrode into the torch head.

And in the silence, Lara experiences it again. A few minutes, a series of seconds, really, during which she loses herself in the weld. For just a few seconds she leans in and pushes the pedal about a third of the way down. Her left hand holds the electrode at about fifteen degrees from vertical, and she strikes her arc. Her right hand feeds the filler metal wire, which nearly touches the electrode and the work. She moves the electrode, and the wire, in tiny C's, in tandem, like dance partners, and at the same time travels left to right down the butt joint. At the end of the line she breaks the arc and lifts her shield. Lara couldn't tell you if the elapsed time had been thirty seconds or thirty minutes that she'd been at it. Like a dream, the time seemed long but was actually quite short. But she feels different, somehow transformed. She lifts her metal with the clamps, dips the joined pieces in the water-cooling trough, then places it on the lower shelf of the work table with all the other students' work. As she walks out the shop door to head for lunch, she looks back at her piece among all the other pipe welds and T-joints and butt joints and lap joints, and she can pick out her own work from twenty feet off.

But thirty minutes later, when she steps back into the shop, the other students are all hard at work. Abandoned, gladly, is the TIG welding, and the class has taken up the easiest, the MIG. No speed pedal, no hand-feeding of the wire required, the MIG electrode automatically delivers the steel wire at a preset speed. The guys are working in pairs, and the MIG equipment seems functioning at all seven work stations. Lara sees Ted in the corner station running clean straight beads, one beside another so that his work-piece looks neat like a fresh-plowed field. On the other side of the shop, Darius controls the gun expertly and smoothly, and Lara will see later when she gets a closer look that he's written his name in steel, the script letters neater than if he'd used a ballpoint pen. Walt is working on T-joints and lap joints, has a steel sculpture of zig-zag metal squares, like a set of stairs clamped to his work table. Lara remembers her inspired TIG joint fashioned when the others headed to lunch, and she glances under the work table at the shelf where she left it.

Apparently the class has run out of clean pieces of steel to work with, since several of the old work pieces are gone from the shelf now. Lara surveys the work stations one by one and smiles when she sees her piece. Her neat lap joint is nearly out of sight on the inside of a steel box Walt is MIG welding, but she recognizes the tidy bead she'd laid down. She didn't get a chance to show it off at all—and while a handsome weld, it would be easy for someone to lay down one as good with the simpler MIG process. But she had pulled off a near-perfect weld by the TIG process, coordinating the electrode in her left hand, the foot pedal, and feeding the wire with her right hand. Lara wished Jasmine had seen it, but part of her didn't mind, either. Lara had accomplished it, and she held the satisfaction inside her. No one else needed to know. She heads over to the work station where Ken has his shield down, is laying down MIG weld beads like a pro.

After class, when she visits the hospital, Lara tells Wes of her weld, and tries to describe the feeling, the primitive power and losing herself in the molten metal. He still seems quite depressed, but when she shares her shop stories his eyes sometimes brighten. He sometimes smiles, and at these moments appears almost hopeful. Lara applauds his progress in finger and arm movement, which he downplays. The small steps forward are imperceptible to him, he tells her. But she can see some small satisfaction in his face.

* * *

Two Saturdays later, the class meets for the last time. It has been fifteen weeks since Lara began. And fifteen weeks since her brother Wes was paralyzed by the fall from a skyscraper pin oak. When she stops at the hospital today, she'll be helping him pack up and head home, to a small ranch house bought with insurance money and upfitted with features for handicapped accessibility.

In that fifteen weeks time Lara has lost over thirty pounds, almost without conscious effort. Wes, from hospital food and inactivity, has gained some weight. The pounds soften his features in a not-unattractive way. Lara think he looks as handsome, is the same man, she tells him. Only different somehow, too, she thinks. And now, as Wes ambivalently tries to prepare for some future, and says his goodbyes to doctors and staff, steeling himself for all things unknown ahead, Lara is at the tech college finishing her course.

At the end, they come together in the classroom, and they exchange handshakes and brief hugs, the kind athletes sometimes give one another teammate, right hands clasping and left arm reaching around the other's back, an embrace then with right hands between them, fingers hooked and fists together at their chests. Lara feels a part of something and a wave of emotion flows over her. She doesn't want to cry but can't help it. She thinks the young men will razz her, but instead they seem touched.

Jasmine, not a tearful type, thanks them, saying how much she enjoyed teaching them. "You've been a really great class, and I'm going to miss you. But keep in touch and let me know how you all are doing," she says, her voice dropping low and emotional, "and if I can ever do anything to help you, call me." She gives them two phone numbers and an email address. Walt gives her a thank-you card with a gift certificate to Home Depot, and the others each individually meets her eyes and offers thanks. Jasmine is moved, they can tell. Perhaps to cut short the emotion, maybe sensing an awkward silence, she remembers, "I've got my camera—we have to get a group picture."

So they head across the hall to the shop, and while Ken tries to line up Jasmine's digital camera on a work table, sets the timer, they compress in front of him, suddenly awkward. "Bunch up," Ken says, "I can't get us all in." And so they try to group closer and Darius is joking that all that "tender emotion" of a minute ago, across the hall, "is gone like smoke." They all laugh at the truth of this. Then he starts on this riff about how nobody better put this photo up at home "'cause I'm a wanted man" and he don't need the authorities knockin' on his door saying somebody recognized your picture on Jasmine's fridge. They're loosened up again now, and Ken gets the red timer light to flash, jumps over to the table and into the picture. The light flashes, freezing them for a split second.

Lara is thinking just then that she'll see many of them next semester, since she's just decided to return for fifteen more weeks, an easy choice really. But still she knows that returning then it won't be the same. Time will have passed, was in fact passing already, so that just like Darius, the social commentary spokesman said, even the photo antics and the hugs would be tough to pull off now, moments later. So they file out of the shop, some seeming embarrassed by the emotion. Lara takes one last look back, sees the shelf of all the work pieces, thirty or more steel shapes all covered in various welds. She stops for a moment.

Lara looks at their semester's work, the laps and butt joints, the T-joints, the verticals, the stick welds and MIGs and even some TIGs. Lara moves slowly closer, stopping maybe ten feet from the shelf, a distance from which she can see the individual welded joints, her own and her classmates'. She notes Ken's pieces, strong almost heavy beads she believes she'd recognize anywhere—his welding signature. And she notes Tyson's and Damon's, Ted's, Walt's. And the loose, somewhat inconsistent welds of Darius, much like the young man himself. Lara sees on one piece of Darius' metal a bead that stands out, steady and firm consistent ribs, solid and almost light somehow. Beautiful. And she knows that's where Jasmine had stopped by and demonstrated on his steel.

And while her brother is preparing to sign his own release form, Lara's eyes scan across the shelf to her own metal pieces. Beads of some variation, but they are welds that will hold. And she sees and recognizes the early semester efforts and the later, smoother and more consistent, the last beads not unlike Jasmine's in quality, but in a hand, a signature all her own that she can pick out unmistakably from the rest. She turns then and walks quietly to her rusty little Ford, and it heads, without Lara's conscious effort, for the hospital.

Wes sits in his wheelchair pulled up to the little desk in the room that has been home for fifteen weeks. He's looking down at the release form, the pages of small print. Then Lara watches as he turns his head to allow sight of his right arm, shoulder to elbow to forearm, wrist, and fingers. He looks at his arm as if it's detached, a prosthesis. But then he wills the fingers to move, and they do. He lifts the arm and reaches out for the pen the nurse holds to him. Wes grips the pen and slowly scrawls his name at the bottom of the page and adds the date. Lara recognizes his name, of course, and something of the slant of his script, the shape of his letters, familiar and she'd know them anywhere. But still there's something different to them, too. Perhaps he thinks: something new.

Ghosts of Doubt

He stands before the class, the lectern his wheelhouse, the teen or twenty-something-aged students his sea, the sky in the back windows his horizon. The worn paperback before him lays open to a page. If he were to brush it to the floor the spine would strike first and the leaves would fall three-quarters right, a quarter left. The book would lay open on page 63, just as it does on the podium. Like a hymnal from which only one song has been chosen, again and again. Today is October 11, exactly fifty years since the day he'd shipped out, in 1944. He always notes this grim anniversary, but it's never felt so heavy.

Hunter is not, and never was, a captain. More like the one the natives call *Tuan Jim*—Lord Jim, the title character in the novel open on his podium—he is something like a first mate. In 1944 he is twenty, the age many of his students will be, when he teaches in the decades to follow. Headed to England in October, he's a private assigned as Chaplain's Assistant. And two months later, he's leaving from Southampton aboard a Belgian troopship chartered by the British Admiralty, the *Leopoldville*, crossing the English Channel on Christmas Eve, 1944. Private Hunter and 2,234 others from the 66th Infantry Division, U.S. Army, are reinforcements for the rapidly escalating Battle of the Bulge.

Hunter and the other soldiers are not worried about the nine-hour crossing—just twenty miles but lengthened by the evasive zig-zag pattern of British Captain Charles Pringle. But they feel themselves in a kind of uncomfortable limbo, on the water between the English mainland with its ties to home, and France where they anticipate engaging the enemy. They are missing family back home on Christmas Eve and, looking forward a few more hours, they are imagining actually facing the vilified Germans.

At just after six p.m., unseen in the rough Channel waters, a periscope rises, rotates like the head of an adder, sighting the convoy and the troopship now just five miles from the French port of Cherbourg. Moments before, in a cramped bunk below, Hunter had felt seasick, so he had gone up on deck for some air. The German U-486 fires a single torpedo. Hunter is standing near the starboard rail, midships, when the *Leopoldville* shudders.

"Please turn your texts to page 63," Dr. Hunter tells the sea of blank faces before him. He does not hear the sighs, the stifled groans. The literature class meets three times a week, and each meeting for the past two weeks has begun with Hunter's same statement. By this time, the books of most students will fall open automatically to the page, just as Dr. Hunter's own copy. "Would you read for us, Gavin." He picks a different student each time, "In the long paragraph where Marlow is describing Jim, beginning 'He was so extremely calm...'" The calmness is not a feeling Hunter shares at this moment.

Gavin reads the narrator Marlow's words surprisingly well, slowly and smoothly with some gravity. "'Why I longed to go grubbing into the deplorable details of an occurrence which, after all, concerned me no more than as a member of an obscure body of men held together by a community of inglorious toil and by fidelity to a certain standard of conduct, I can't explain.'"

"The 'occurrence' is of course what, Melanie?" Hunter interrupts.

"The incident on the ship, the *Patna*," she answers, her inflection somewhere between statement and question. "What Jim is on trial for," she finishes, not describing what happened, leaving Hunter to wonder if she knows.

There were no trials after the incident on Christmas Eve, 1944. After what was negligence, dereliction of duty, abandonment, no charges were filed. Hunter recalls a U.S. Inspector General's report in 1959 and a British Admiralty Board of Inquiry report not declassified until the late '60s, both brief, vague, and reluctant to assess fault in the tragedy. He remembers the Belgian Embassy's 1992 response no one read, full of ridiculous lies. Alleging that the Belgian crew of the Leopoldville performed admirably, and all lifeboats were deployed, filled with soldiers. When the reality was that the few lifeboats released carried only the Belgian crew and their suitcases. They abandoned the soldiers on deck. Dr. Hunter sighs. "Please continue, Gavin."

". . . I see well enough now that I hoped for the impossible—for the laying of what is the most obstinate ghost of man's creation, of the uneasy doubt uprising like a mist, secret and gnawing like a worm, and more chilling than the certitude of death—the doubt of the sovereign power enthroned in a fixed standard of conduct."

"What would you say, Jennifer, makes up the 'standard of conduct' Marlow speaks of? In Conrad's world here in *Lord Jim*, what qualities make up one who adheres to such a standard? What *is* the standard of conduct?"

She's one of the brightest in Hunter's class. She hesitates, searching his face, he knows, for clues to exactly what he is expecting to hear. Now, after weeks on the same page, the class has stumbled onto many correct answers. "Courage," she says. "Honor. Sense of duty, obedience, self-discipline, bravery. Especially in adverse conditions. . ."

From the rail of the *Leopoldville*, some soldiers actually see the silver torpedo streaking just below the water's surface toward their ship. Private Hunter misses it, is lighting a cigarette in the last of the daylight. After dusk, smoking on deck is forbidden since the enemy might see the match-lights. But he feels the shudder. Like the rest of the able troops, then, he makes his way to his company's emergency deck location— they'd been told where to go, but not what to do when they got there—to await further orders. On deck, conjecture is rampant, but many realize the ship has been hit. Still, there is no panic, and the situation seems far from dire.

Below decks is different. When the torpedo strikes, three hundred men are killed instantly. Many of the dead and wounded are washed out the gaping hole in the starboard hull into the sea. Remarkably, some of these survive. As water floods into the cramped compartments of the lowest, G Deck, soldiers gasp along the ceiling beams for air. In the cold and dark, many can be heard screaming and praying as hatches are sealed to prevent the water flow, trapping them below.

Up on deck, soldiers congregate, uniting with their companies at the preassigned areas to await orders. Many witness the Belgian crew members carrying suitcases and belongings, releasing and lowering lifeboats. Loudspeakers announce the torpedo hit, tell the men to remain on deck, that tugs from Cherbourg will arrive shortly to tow the *Leopoldville* into harbor. Still most feel little worry, even though the departing crew never attempts to instruct the soldiers how to release the never-before-used lifeboats. Their explanations would have been in Flemish and French, so useless, anyway, to most of the American soldiers.

Below deck, many are pulled or carried to safety by the heroic efforts of compatriots. Soldiers form human ladders in the openings left by blown-out stairs, and some climb to safety amid shouts in water and darkness beneath them. Bodies float past. Shortly after seven p.m. the ship has begun listing badly to starboard. Private Hunter waits on deck with his company in the glare of the generator lights. He does not smoke though it would be allowed now, the prohibition a safe conduct issue when, on a lightless deck, the flare of a match could be visible to the enemy. The faces and posture of his comrades show their obedience, cold, and fear.

"Marlow tells us later, of course, what became of the eight hundred Muslim pilgrims on board the ship on which Jim was first mate," Dr. Hunter addresses the class, somewhat wearily. He feels vaguely nauseous in the stuffy classroom. He moves toward the window nearest, thinking to let some air in. "Can you tell us, Adam, what happened to the *Leopol*—, er, *Patna*, what the crew did, what Jim did, how they reacted?"

The chosen Adam—Hunter well knows the type—is a fraternity boy from a wealthy family whose majors include getting drunk, high, and laid. He shrugs, sits up slightly at his desk, scratches his cheek of a couple days' fuzzy beard growth. "Jim's ship sinks, but he saves himself, gets off with the crew. The pilgrims drown, I guess."

A few groans from opposite corners of the room. Hunter's class is now a sea of confusion, students calling out corrections to Adam's retelling. "It doesn't sink!" calls out one. "He doesn't save himself—he chickens out!" "He breaks the code," says another.

At this last, Hunter seems startled. Not noticing that even in the heated exchange, several students are asleep and others, weary of the familiar territory being re-explored, have the glossed blank eyes of reptiles. "Okay, okay," says Dr. Hunter. "Remain calm." Dr. Hunter has nearly reached the window. Two hands on, and now a simple lift.

An hour later, the tugs have not come. Had they arrived, they couldn't have towed the stricken ship anyway, since the *Leopoldville* has been ordered to drop anchor because the ship is drifting toward German-mined waters. The *HMS Brilliant*, a British destroyer in the convoy, pulls alongside the *Leopoldville*. The sea is violent. Army troops line the *Leopoldville*'s rail, watching. Swells of more than twenty feet hamper efforts to tie on, and when the men working do get a cable attached it snaps, like fishing line. From the Brilliant's deck, British officers exhort, "Jump, Yank!"

The *Brilliant*'s pitching deck is twenty feet below the deck of the *Leopoldville*. The ships are held close by ropes and nets, but in roiling seas the hulls crash together and swing apart. The soldiers must time their leaps, jumping when the British officer hollers "Now!" Frighteningly, the signal to jump comes when the hulls are farthest apart and so about to swing back together. Many soldiers slip, miss-time their leaps, hit the water. The ships crash back together, crushing hundreds. The hulls of both ships are stained red. Hundreds of soldiers paddle in the water, clinging to debris and each other, even drowning one another to save themselves.

By eight p.m., the Belgian crew of the *Leopoldville* is long gone. The bow of the *Leopoldville* turns up at an absurd, 45-degree angle, the stern goes down. In less than ten minutes she disappears, hundreds of soldiers on the rails clinging as she goes under, more than a dozen tugs and rescue boats now circling an open hole of ocean.

"*Survivor Guilt*," Dr. Hunter repeats the student's question. Devin's, wasn't it? "Interesting: Jim could feel such a thing even though it would be near a century before the feeling got named that way. Of course we feel things every day, every minute, that don't have specific, categorical names." Hunter again begins to feel the choking lack of air. He moves back toward the open window as smoothly as possible, not wishing to attract undue attention.

"But about the *Patna* and its *sinking*. I asked Jennifer to remind us the historical or factual background for Conrad's story. Certainly there were other ships whose crews abandoned the passengers to save themselves. Jennifer, you were going to tell us of the *Morrow Castle*, too, although that was many years after Conrad's story."

Hunter does not at this moment think how many in his stifling classroom have actually read the novel they're trying to discuss. He does not think, as he sometimes does, that some haven't even cracked Conrad's book, and some have sampled only small bits, or worse, skimmed the Cliff's Notes. After decades of teaching, Hunter still pleads with and exhorts and cajoles his students to read, to take an interest, to relate literature to their own lives. There are some "unreachables," of course, but Hunter also has had his share of surprises, the unpredictable successes as well as failures. Some, he has thought sometimes but does not now, some learners are wired such that they will obey a command to jump, while others, inexplicably, will freeze at the rail. Cling to it even as they go under.

Hunter knows of no foolproof way of reaching students who are unreceptive. He only tries—and this he does think now—to instill some if not respect then at least understanding of honor, or appreciation of Jim's code of conduct. And let them also see the doubt that Marlow speaks of, the creeping ghost that since that frigid night in 1944 will haunt Dr. Hunter always. They stood at attention, for godsakes. In his dreams they stand saluting on the bow as the ship slips below the water, a scene he never actually witnessed. Because by then Hunter was aboard the *Brilliant*, having regained consciousness. He was cold, dazed and so cold, chugging toward Cherbourg harbor. But that Christmas Eve, hundreds of soldiers had stood awaiting orders to abandon ship that never came, obedient to the end, adhering to their code of honor. And for no reason he can imagine, Hunter survived while so many others did not.

"... and so with the ship on fire, just five miles from shore, the crew then abandoned the *Morrow Castle*, leaving the passengers. 133 died, September, 1944," the young woman's voice continues. "Are you all right, Dr. Hunter?"

"Of course, of course," Hunter lies. He inhales deeply. He may have the flu, he thinks then, since he cannot otherwise explain involuntary shivers that propagate like waves through his neck, shoulders, and down his spine.

"And thank you, Jennifer, for that history." Dr. Hunter wills relaxation into his shoulders, sighs. "Now could we talk a moment about Jim's new start? I mean the job offer in faraway, primitive Patusan. Do you remember the analogy Marlow uses to Jim, the phrase Jim says of, "that was jolly well put!" How Marlow describes what is between Jim's past and the new job in front of him?"

A terribly leading question, yet so vague, Hunter thinks disgustedly. But in the sea of faces before him, the dull eyes of passengers on a long bus ride, there is one pair that seem to gleam. It's Adam, strangely, who does not blurt out an answer but dutifully raises his hand. Hunter nods to him, not overly optimistic.

"It's a *door*, isn't it?" Adam pauses. Hunter nods again. "Something about Jim slamming the door on what came before. And Marlow even says something about how, in Patusan, it'll be like Jim *never existed*. Jim likes this idea. Probably says 'Jove!' like he's always doing." This last gets a laugh from the class. Adam flushes, embarrassed like one who starts in on the wrong verse of a church hymn.

After the war, Hunter has his own new start. College on the GI Bill, grad school, marriage, children. A teaching job at a small and well-regarded private university. Friends, family, a couple of published works of literary criticism. All the while keeping the areas of his life, the compartments, separate. Sealed off from one another. There is some leakage, of course, but for the most part he has lived by moving through these separate areas, like the colored chalk boxes of hopscotch, rarely landing on more than one at once.

"Yes," Hunter manages a slow answer. "A door." A hatch, he thinks. A bulkhead. Darkness, freezing water rushing in, securing hatches even as screams for help and prayers and shouts in anger, desperate anger, are heard from the other side. Fainter as the hatches are secured. Acts practiced, army protocol, designed to keep the ocean out of undamaged compartments, to keep the ship afloat. In the case of the outdated cruiser the *Leopoldville*, these efforts may have only bought minutes. Perhaps minutes when some leap to safety, but many others are trapped and sealed away below. Again, Private Hunter sees none of this, standing above on deck when the torpedo strikes, but he's heard it from survivors and sees it in dreams. Pitch darkness and freezing waters rising from legs to waist to chest, then finally over his head, drowning the screams around him.

Dr. Hunter shivers again and tries to shake the memory, thinking *door* godammit, not *hatch*. A door that, once slammed, seals off the past. He almost believes it, himself part-romantic, and so wanting to believe it possible. That the horrible past could be closed off, and a new life begun, what an idea! Jove! he thinks.

"So can we talk about Jim as a 'Romantic,'" Dr. Hunter asks then. He is uncomfortably far from "page 63," which may encourage the class but leaves him anxious. "Can we talk about the relationship between a *romantic* and one who adheres to a strict standard of conduct?" This clarification makes him immediately feel a warmer sense of relief, while the question elicits stifled groans from several quadrants of the classroom. "Can Jim be *both* at the same time?"

Private Hunter stands at the rail in the numbing, deafening wind, his right arm braced around a stanchion, soldiers numbering in the dozens on either side of him. Listing badly to starboard, the *Leopoldville* pitches broadly in violent Channel waters. He watches as the *Brilliant* pulls alongside, sees the tow-cables the British officers try to tie onto his stricken troopship. The gusts smell metallic, roaring over the shouts from the soldiers on the ships, engulfing their words and carrying them helplessly out to sea.

The two ships' hulls crash together, the *Brilliant* dented and becoming stained the gray of the Leopoldville, then separate, crash together and separate. The tie-on cables snap, Hunter's ship a bulldog tethered with sewing thread. To his left, a boy from Indianapolis, from the 262nd, who Hunter has just met and spoken to, a boy who looks twelve—Christ, we all look twelve, Hunter thinks—stands frozen on the rail. Soldiers jump toward the deck of the *Brilliant* on either side of them. A British officer is timing the wave swells and the coming together and separations of the two ships. He shouts "Jump, Yank! Now!" when the ships are farthest apart. Some can't abide the leap of faith, won't believe the *Brilliant*'s deck will move back under them if they obey the command.

Hunter puts an arm around the Hoosier beside him, who is muttering about "No orders to abandon ship." In fact, he's right: No abandon ship order was ever given. The boy stands stiffly, frozen worse than by cold.

"We've got to jump for it, buddy," Hunter screams into the chilling wind.

Too quickly the kid steps one foot on the rail, then the other. The ships mash together, and he dives. The ships separate, and the boy from Indiana hits the water not three feet from the *Brilliant*'s deck. Hunter watches the hulls swing back and crash into each other. And when they separate again, there is a broad red stain on the *Brilliant* where the boy had been. Hunter climbs the rail himself, focuses on the face and voice of the British officer. When the two ships are farthest apart and the voice screams "Now!" Hunter leaps from the rail, across the roiling Channel waters as the *Brilliant*'s deck slides under him twenty feet below. His body strikes the deck, his head thumps, and he's knocked unconscious.

"Doctor Hunter. Doctor Hunter?" It's Allison's voice. Hunter stands at the lectern, still as a sleeping horse. "Did you want me to read a passage?"

Hunter gazes out at the sea of faces all staring back at him with looks of concern, of amusement, even derision. He thinks perhaps he blacked out, hopes only for a second or two. His wife would be worried, had she seen him then, he knows. He still feels so cold, thinks *I should shut that window*. Begins to recognize the faces of his students, the classroom, the details of this place where he's taught for over forty years. He holds the edges of the lectern, his ship's wheel, with both hands firmly. He remembers then the question that the girl's voice had posed him.

"Yes, yes, please, would you read for us," he looks down at the book laying open before him. "In the long paragraph on page 63 beginning with the words 'He was so extremely calm . . .'"

Halfway Again

Dad's Cabin

If there's a time of day when I wonder most what the point is, that time is early morning. The hour my dogs and many people feel charged and full of purpose. About six, when the first sun hits the old windows of this cabin my dad built almost entirely by himself, I'll lie here on the iron cot with its loud springs and its horsehair mattress, heavy as a bundle of asphalt shingles. I'll wonder sometimes why with his skills he didn't make himself a nice bed, will think of him on this creaky lumpy thing with a woman and almost laugh.

In my recent routine, I've been awakening early. I'll rest beneath the Army blanket, keeping especially quiet while the first rays get prismed through the wavy old glass of the cabin windows. I'll lie here for perhaps fifteen minutes, barely breathing so as not to wake the dogs asleep beside me. And I'll think of my father. My father, K.P. McCauslin, perhaps you've heard of him. A locally somewhat-famous activist and radio talk show host, a vibrant and robust figure right up until the end. A surprising and sudden end, a heart attack while swimming in the quarry not a half mile from here—*his* routine, each morning in summer. That was just over a year ago now; he was 63.

So I'll lie under the thin wool, Army-green blanket, smelling the cold fall air that breathes through the pine boards of this cabin my father built nearly twenty years ago. And watch the sun slant through the bubbled-glass windows he salvaged from a two-hundred-year-old farm-house that was being demolished to make room for a shopping center, a common practice even then. They're stunning windows, twelve panes over twelve, oak-mullioned. The glass distorts the view ever so slightly when looking inside to out, or outside to in. This morning, as always between 6:10 and 6:20, the light from the windows or the breathing of the house perhaps, wakes the dogs. This never ceases to amaze me, the precision of what might also be some canine internal timer. The clock beside the bed reads 6:17.

They're a mismatched pair, an eleven year-old lab-mix and a hound who's just two. But they both always awake like it's their first morning on Earth, so optimistic-seeming, wide-eyed and full of some mystic purpose that thus far eludes me. They're starving, they must go out, they've got to check on everything around the cabin, in and out. And all of it has got to happen immediately.

I've been observing this early morning routine for about the last nine months. This since I moved back here to Sanford, in upstate New York, when I had sort of lost my compass and my dad died, and my marriage fell apart and I stopped drinking so much, though not necessarily in that order. I awaken early, and usually I'll spend some quiet time around the cabin, composing myself while completing some light chores, washing dishes maybe or sweeping the kitchen or front porch. And then I'll head to the radio station between eight and nine. We broadcast Don Imus's show from the city, 7 a.m. until 10. There's no live local programming until later anyway, so no need to be in too early.

As is my custom, I feed and water the dogs, then grind some coffee and set it to perking. The small bit of exercise—rotating the old hand grinder—and the scuffing sound of the percolator, are both calming and invigorating somehow, like cool rain or a heavy sigh. And while the coffee drains through a giant aluminum pot my father must have lifted from the Rotary Club or some church basement, I can walk to the mailbox for the morning paper. It's a quarter-mile down the gravel drive, from the clearing around the cabin through hardwoods to the clearing by Hill Road. The air this morning is cold, crisp. As the sun gets higher, the day will be warm, 60s or even 70 probably, and the air will smell of leaves and apples and turned earth, but right now it smells of nothing but cool hints of these. For now, it may not even be 45 degrees, but by the time I reach the mailbox, much of my body's stiffness is gone. I open the paper, standing by the empty quiet road. The headline of the Rochester *Democrat & Chronicle*, September 12, 1998, reads "The Judgment Begins."

It's of course a reference to the judgment of the President. His perhaps impeachable offenses as unearthed by the crack team of Independent Counsel Kenneth Starr. The headline type is as large as "Lusitania Sinks," impossible to pass over, but I flip to Section D as quickly as I can. Mornings are the most difficult times for me, the periods when I feel the most depression and lack of purpose. I'm thankful, to God, to something, not even as much for the clear fall day as for the simple existence of Sports. For the clarity and beauty of games, their honesty and candor. And the mountains of statistics that explain and don't, describe and give structure to what is, at its best, play.

But as I walk back toward the cabin, my mind begins clouding with all that gets in the way of this play, the greed and over-management, the big-business aspects—mainly it's about money, all of it—and in the early morning depression I am cynical. But the problems have existed as long as there have been professional sports, and probably since the very first competitions of any kind. I wonder about the Olympics in ancient Greece, back when Nike was just a goddess. Tell me there weren't payoffs, wagering, and back-room deals even then. To make a statement about good clean play like the one above seems hopelessly naive.

Still, as I near the cabin and the dogs bound up, I'm thankful for Sports—what our radio station, AM 630, WSPT, devotes most of its airtime to, by the way. And thankful at least not to be President, on this morning or any other. Although anybody would probably tell you that's about the most purposeful job on earth.

The lab-mix, "Shag" (not for his hair, which is short, but because he probably loves fielding fly balls as much as I do), brings a tennis ball to me in the front yard, eager to play. His compatriot, "Heel" (the one thing he cannot, will not do; and alternately, in my mind, "Heal," perhaps for what I want him to do for me), is interested only in the attention the ball gets from Shag and me. Heel seems mystified by the power of the ball but plays at rapture, as if by sticking it out with us (or in with us), he'll somehow, someday understand. The sun is high enough now to be blinding off the tin roof, illuminating, too, the shaft of an antenna my father constructed at its peak, a giant lightning rod attracting news of the world. In the days of his most active participation, AM 630 concerned itself with much more than sports. But that was then, I think, heading inside for coffee.

That was the '60s and '70s, when it seemed there was more to believe in or fight for. Or cheer for, I think, remembering being nine in

1969, when the beloved Knicks, Jets, and Mets all won world championships. I've got a faded pennant for each of the three that I've moved from place to place for years, that now hang over the fireplace in the cabin, that I can see as I step inside.

I pull the little black spigot and fill an old Red Wings mug, the one with a chip on the rim just where my lips go if I grab it with my left hand. I light a cigarette, sit with my coffee and smoke, staring toward the pennants and not thinking much of anything. About 7:45, I race the dogs to their pen, an enclosure both huge and secure, a shady place that's theirs, the vet tells me, where they feel safe. And I grab the newspaper, a road coffee, my baseball mitt, and head across town to WSPT.

My rusted gray Datsun pickup turns over on the first try and its heater—the most reliable part of the vehicle—has the cab warm in minutes. Inside the truck, like my dogs in their pen, I feel secure somehow. Glad to have somewhere to go. Alone, apart from home and work, and human connections, yet somehow a part of them, too. There's a warm sadness about it that's almost *good.*

About halfway to the station, a few miles from my dad's cabin, I click on the radio. Imus and Charles are all over the presidential scandal, the report released now telling the lurid details of misconduct. But it's Friday, the second week of the college football season, and the baseball pennant races are in full swing. There's Mark McGwire of the Cardinals just surpassing Roger Maris for the single-season homers. There's golf and the NBA lockout and Rupert Murdock buying the Manchester United soccer team for a billion dollars. So much sports, my co-workers Carty and 'phree often say, and so little time. And you want to talk about oral sex in the Oval Office? Yawn. And nearing the station building, I'm once again glad for the existence of Sports.

The Station and Some Particulars

WSPT Sanford, AM 630, is housed in a small, one-story building on the west end of a block that marks the edge of the small downtown area. Before my father's renovation, it was for decades a barber's home and office. My dad always liked the symbolism, a place of "communication, be it hair-waves or airwaves," he'd laugh, and he left the red and blue pole outside the door. To the west of the wood-and-brick building is a perhaps two-acre vacant lot, a field low and grassy, an area that floods whenever we get heavy rains. The moist ground helps conduct the signal from our antenna, "the big stick" we call it. Just 300 feet and hardly huge by industry standards, yet late at night we've taken calls from as far away as Cincinnati and Detroit.

I pull into the gravel lot behind the old barbershop at a little past eight, shutting down Imus's voice and listening to the engine tick, softly cooling. Entering the two-room structure, I hear the New York host's voice pick up again, it seems just where he left off, still verbally rummaging through what's now the "Oral Office." But Imus is at least playing low in the station cabin, from a boom box on the entry desk. In the glass sound booth, one of the local high school techies, Roger, is monitoring the equipment, making sure Imus stays on the air. He looks up as I enter, brushes long straight black hair from his face, and waves.

I wave back, then put arms out, palms up, and mouth the words "Where is everybody?"

Roger almost smiles. Even though I've only been back here in Sanford and working at the station nine months, I see Roger most mornings and we've hit on this little routine. Maybe it makes us feel like we've got a work ethic when those around us don't, I don't know. Anyway, to my question Roger acts his part from the silence of the glassed-in booth. He points toward the two desks of the sports show hosts, Kevin McCarty ("Carty") and Anthony Duphree (the "'phree" or just "Free"). Then Roger, a Sanford High football and hockey star, huge, black-framed glasses, long hair askew (he looks like one of the Hanson brothers from "Slapshot"), does a little pantomime of a golfer swinging, the way Johnny Carson used to. As usual, as part of *their* routine, Carty and 'phree are out on the links this morning. (The guys play free most mornings, in exchange for mentioning the course on the air that afternoon.)

Next Roger nods his head toward the desk of Vivian Lee, who calls herself a "personal trainer of the heart and mind," and who takes calls six nights a week from 2 a.m. until 6 a.m. Roger nods toward Vivian's desk and then drops his head abruptly, eyes closed, motionless. I do my part, looking over to her desk, where she sits straight-backed, head 90-degrees tilted forward, dead asleep the way some people do on airplanes. Her straight black hair hangs vertical down around her head, longer than Roger's even, hanging like that of the magician's beautiful assistant as she's being levitated. In front of Vivian on the desk sits an imposingly thick book, on its spine printed *Infinite Jest*, by a writer named Wallace. Beside the book, also asleep, is Vivian's cat, Spencer. (No, not "Spinster," she's told Carty more than twice.)

Roger finishes the act with a shrug, and I point to him, mouthing 'How 'bout you?' And he usually does the patent mime thing, the 'trapped in a box' bit where he feels the invisible walls around him. Which always cracks me up because he *is* in a glass box.

And with this little formality observed, Roger and I each get back to our business. I set some coffee to auto-dripping in the kitchenette (such a silly word; sounds like it's got an Easy-Bake Oven, remember, with the little light bulb that cooks brownies). Roger's back to monitoring the show from the city. I head to my desk with a couple papers and *The Sporting News*, to work on some topics for the guys' noon call-in show. The Imus in the Morning broadcast plays low, and behind me at her desk, Vivian Lee sleeps on. It's hard not to just watch her.

But the brief time-gap, a little appreciated in-between-ness, gives me a chance to tell you a bit more about the players in this, our little upstate, small-market radio sports melodrama. I do this ("this" being both describing the players *and* this whole undoubtedly-thus-far sleeper of a performance, that is, the story before you) not to enlighten you (who no doubt are envying the slumbering "personal trainer" here, the not-the-actress Vivian Lee), but in order to enlighten me.

"This" is my thus-far unsuccessful but haven't-given-up-all-hope-yet attempt to deal with one or more of the following: What is it that's so important, or mystical even, or entrancing or engaging about sports and sports talk? How can I not *know* how I feel, or be unable to state even an opinion, which is, isn't it, the basic premise of talk-radio? How can I feel both "a part" and "apart"? And what's my father got to do with all this—a therapist somewhere nods sagely—and my ex-wife, and other human beings on this earth? This is the stuff, I think, that finds me down in the mornings.

Which is, apologies, an extremely longwinded introduction, especially by one who is not even a radio host (merely the son of one), who's never even been on the radio excepting some little-kid blurts into the mike when Daddy's out of the room. An extremely drawn-out lead-in to the promised description of "the players."

The Players

K.P. McCauslin. My late father, born Kevin Patrick to second generation Irish Protestant parents; 1935-97. Career stats are impressive, any would admit, and some say he's got Hall of Fame numbers. An incredibly likable, gregarious guy who was a gifted all-around player. Built or rebuilt two houses as mentioned (the cabin and the radio station building, the old barbershop I mean), excelled in business back in the '60s when a lot of salesmen were getting bad names, then turned to radio activism in the late '60s and '70s, protesting the war and championing Civil-Rights, environmental and 'politicians are assholes' movements that still carry some weight today.

Born pretty dirt poor, Kevin Patrick McCauslin lettered in three sports at nearby Penfield High, was Class President and most likely to just about everything. Learned to cook in the Army, serving (quite literally) in Korea, where the "K.P." really stuck. And by all accounts led the league in meals served and fewest complaints for chipped beef on toast (no "shit on a shingle," at least to his face), records that I believe still stand.

After the war, K.P. held several different sales jobs (yes, vacuum cleaners among them, though no *World Books*), and he later found himself in building supplies, later contracting for a while. The radio station was an opportunity brought to K.P. by a childhood friend, Harvey Keane, who was not really, "keen" that is. It was Harvey who'd brought K.P. any number of such grand "opportunities" over the years, all good or noble, all "can't misses." Water purification systems, back then when the upstate springs were probably cleanest in the eastern U.S., and a radio broadcasting school for the blind are a couple that come to mind. But the failing-radio-station buy-out actually worked, for a while. Harvey convinced K.P. that radio talk was how they could really reach people, help people, even save people. And like water purification up here today, talk-radio, too, is viable, profitable, though perhaps not at WSPT; and maybe Harvey was ahead of his time, was keen after all.

So my father and Harvey bought the failing, government subsidized farm-news and swing-music station, AM 630, for a song. Got themselves an FCC license "to operate in the public's interest" (just like we do today; same wording anyway), and started bashing President Johnson and the refusal to withdraw troops as early as 1965.

The next fifteen years were the most fun my father ever had, I think. Not only was his license jerked and reinstated three times during that period (twice more than "Laugh-In," my dad used to say, and Rowan and Martin were household names), but he got to sound off about everything. Harvey looked on, listened, smiling all the time. The programming then included (as it does today) news and farm reports, but much more politics and much less sports. Through the '80s and until his death, K.P. McCauslin hosted numerous shows, including a "No PhD's Therapy Rap," where he talked to callers about anything and everything. He related so well to people, genuinely loved them all, and his funeral last year was attended by eight hundred people (which is about 780 more than attended Roger Maris's a few years back in Fargo, S.D.).

But my mother, who divorced K.P. and left the upstate snows for the Carolinas in the late '70s, gave a mixed review of my father's memorial service attendance. You know, she said, everyone *did* love your dad. And he loved them all. But he'd spend as much time telling some lady how to grow hydrangeas or stop a leaky faucet as he would taking me out for a meal. Or hitting you fly balls (she actually said "foul balls," I have to smile). Always the Army cook, she said, and so big on equality, he only had a jar of peanut butter and he wanted some on every slice in the loaf. He loved everybody, she said, but he loved everybody the same. She was crying when she said this, for whom I don't know, but it strikes me now that I'm not sure this would be the kind of stat that gets him into 'the Hall,' or keeps him out.

Harvey Keane. Already mentioned so I'll keep it brief. Tall and so thin (he'd have to move around in the shower to get wet, Bill Russell used to say), an all-state cager and tight end later at Cornell. Quiet and optimistic. As kind a man as you'd ever be lucky to meet. Certainly unlucky, in business and financial senses, at the track as well. But like the giant invisible rabbit who's Jimmy Stewart's buddy in the movie, this "Harvey" is as good as they come. Still a kind of (fittingly) silent partner in the radio station (now WSPT), Harvey got enough from K.P.'s will to cover the station's debts and leave him with something to live on. Or actually, since K.P. had little to pass on in the way of assets, it was a part of the life insurance that my mother, by previous arrangement, slipped to Harvey.

I see Harvey now, mostly in the tavern, a couple of times a week, and I keep him apprised of what's going on at the station. He in turn tells me what he likes that he's listened to, and more often, silently, gets across what he doesn't like. If they're in the tavern, I might nod over in the direction of Carty and Duphree, and occasionally Harvey's nodded back, with a shrug or roll of the eyes, an unspoken word I've taken to be "youth," but I've never been sure.

Anyway, I promised to describe the rest of the players, and I'm promising now to do it up briefly, because by this time I imagine you've got the heavy eyelids of Ms. Vivian Lee if you're not sawing logs outright. And then I promise to get on to a little action. For isn't this crazy so far, a story about sports that *nothing happens* in? But before I go on, let me not mislead: if you're looking for shoot 'em ups or car chases, sex or violence, you may be disappointed. Now there is a gun, right in this very office, and there's a knife—well, a very sharp letter opener—too. But remember what I said, how this whole thing's really more *for me*, to answer those questions, remember? And remember, too, that it's all like radio, and as my father used to say, you gotta listen really close to hear what they're actually talking about.

So, on to Miss Vivian Lee. She wasn't even in the plans (my father's, years ago); she's a kind of "walk-on" to this team, someone not recruited and never expected to be on the final roster. Mid-forties, maybe older, but with that kind of lean and healthy look, undoubtedly prettier now than she was at 25. She's got a call-in gig from two to six in the morning, coming on just after Dr. Ruth Westheimer's "Love Line." Vivian sometimes gets callers like Ruth's, callers that might fit categories like "truly heartbroken" or "just-been-ditched," "bored and lonely" or "bitter and armed." We do the same kind of pigeon-holing of the sports junkies who call Carty and Free. But Ms. Vivian also offers a wide range of practical advice on a variety of other subjects, too. She's sort of a kinder, female Bruce Williams.

But sometimes she'll get no callers, or the same predictable regulars, mostly older folks who want to talk about gall bladders. So on quiet nights or when she doesn't, presumably, want to talk to 88-year-old Miss Louise Hipp of Elm Street, Sanford, she'll read aloud to her insomniac audience. Stories and poetry from journals named for rivers I've never heard of or colleges without Division I football teams. It looks like she was reading to the audience from that huge paperback last night. Last week, she read a story by Raymond Carver, "What We Talk About When

We Talk About Love," and I can't get it out of my mind. The characters, their relationships, the reader's voice all keep resonating in me.

But other than that, what can I say? Long, very black hair. Not tall, but thin. Moves beautifully with back straight, shoulders back, light on her feet like a dancer. There's a state School of the Arts campus nearby, and it could be she danced there years ago. We may not have exchanged more than five words at any one time. No one can tell me much about her. Carty and 'phree just laugh: "Have you listened to her show?" Incredulous, but as if that explains everything.

So Kevin McCarty, "Carty." Twenty-four, graduated from Hobart, a native upstater. Recruited out of high school to play both football and baseball, and by his junior year chose football exclusively. Irish Catholic, dreamed of playing at Notre Dame (and don't they all, Rudy?). Instead ended up blowing out his knee—a tailback, he could carry the ball as fast then as he talks now. But the injury. And so after surgery, he tried to return to baseball but couldn't cut it. He'd lost a step, 'phree says. Ask Carty and he'll say he'd be with the Red Wings, at Triple-A, or even the Orioles now if it wasn't for the knee. Six feet, 185, handsome, likable, cleancut kid. Takes himself a bit seriously, takes women much less-so; he's the one who coined WSPT's borrowed catch-phrase: We're what you're talking about when you're not talking about *getting some*! And I'd argue these two are hardly mutually exclusive, if you listen to his show.

Carty's career goals: sees himself in the big markets, ideally NYC, within five years. Thinks Imus's rise back to the top is nothing short of Lazarus's. Strengths: hits to all fields with power; arm strong but erratic; potential leader, sparkplug, but also a potential trouble-maker. His mouth gets ahead of his reasoning mind sometimes (as does his Johnson, frequently). Other weaknesses include falling victim to the Bleeding-heart-Homer-syndrome (see later explanation of caller identification types). That is, Carty often fails to see reason when it comes to the possibility of Notre Dame losing at *anything*, darts included. Which, if you happened to see the Irish beat up on Michigan last week, has made him particularly difficult to be around this past few days. (Yesterday: "NCAA college football rankings are out, and the Irish only get *one* first place vote?! Is there a just God?")

Carty's biggest fears involve the things beyond his control: that the station could get bought or sold, and the programming would be changed; or that automation would come in and replace him before he gets the chance to get 'called up to the Bigs.' He's clever, got his first break basically by hanging around under the basket until he got credit for a tap-in. This was well before I came back up here, but I've heard it from a reliable source (an eight-foot rabbit). Seems the old sports call-in host called in sick, and told Carty to inform the manager at the time. Instead Carty says nothing, does some homework, and when the host's show comes on, there's Carty behind the mike. He spouts a bunch of stuff from a well-researched *Sporting News* article, shovels a bunch of 'check me if I'm wrong but I calls 'em like I sees 'em' sort of horseshit, then gets some fraternity brothers to call in with "the suck-up" act (again, see later list of caller categories). The majority owner of the station (nameless here, for protection, though not Rupert Murdock) happened to be listening and promoted Carty *on the air*, a fucking call-in promotion. And ratings, for a brief time, soared. Much to the alternate glee and green-in-the-gut envy of the then-established star-host, "The Free Himself."

Anthony Duphree. Called Anthony by his mother, Tony by his high school friends, and just "'phree!" to his solid listener base in the upstate area. Major strength: opinionated, and with a clearly declared philosophy. Major weakness: of course, the same. His nickname says it all. Free market, free action, free speech, free ride if you can get it. Professional ballplayers have every right to shop for and grab the best deals. And much of the problem, as I see it (and I started here thinking I had no opinions whatsoever), is that his "freedoms" all have to do with money. Even his defense, ludicrous, of Latrell Sprewell choking his coach—"like any of the oppressed striking out against an oppressor," he said, even mentioning the Revolutionary War for chrissakes. And he might have found some support had Spree not tried then suing his coach Carlissimo and the NBA, looking for monetary damages when *he* did the damage. But our man 'phree stayed true to his principles, which in many cases I can abide. And I defend, of course, even envy, his right to state a firm opinion; and respect if not often his Republican views, at least his consistency.

Anthony is 27, and like his partner, Carty, he shares an ambition for the big markets. But Duphree comes from money and so has less to worry about, less to fear in the event of a takeover or buyout. He'd hate to see it (he *loves* his job, is passionate about sports), but after studying Economics at Hobart and U. of R., close to diplomas from each, he sees the business reality of sports or anything else, especially radio. If Murdock or anyone, 'phree says, so be it; they got every right. But he'd hate to see the programming change. Like most markets, ours could probably support more in the way of Spanish-language radio, perhaps Christian Gospel, Nostalgia, or Children's programming. Were someone to buy WSPT, because it'd probably come cheap, and change the format, what of all of us? As 'phree says, I'd be hatin' it, but I'd rather be simplifying the wishbone offense for a bunch of seven-year-olds than trying to extoll the virtues of beach volleyball to a gospel choir. But enough, for now, on Anthony Duphree. Except to say that, like Carty, he's clean cut and handsome, fast both in the athletic (he ran track at U. of R.) and Dr. Ruth senses. 'Phree "could build a corral for all his fillies," is how Harvey put it.

And let me add one more angle on 'phree, and Carty, too, and sports-jockeys in general. This one is about money. While the guys get free golf and all sorts of free tickets to events, as well as complimentary stuff like balls and gloves and shirts and caps, they better be adding these benefits as salary-dollars because otherwise they might qualify for welfare. Not quite—they pull around $13,000 for all their "celebrity"—but it's like any business, I'd guess, in that only the elite few in the biggest markets make any real jack. Luckily for Carty and Free, they're pretty saavy bettors when it comes to college and pro football and basketball. This, I figure, must be what keeps them in the kinds of clothes the ladies admire.

Now I could go on, describing the second-string, the trainers, the minor players on this team. But I promised some action, at least. Yet before we go to the phones, let me issue a small caveat. Look out for me, Jackson McCauslin.

I don't mean that in the intimidating sense at all. I'm just a fairly skinny white kid from Sanford, a guy who went south to college and stayed until recently. A regular guy who did some teaching and house-building like his father, worked in offices and stores and a few bars and restaurants. Who went to more school and taught and worked in some more taverns. Who married and divorced and lost a father about a year ago. And who's back "home" with some questions. The caution, or more like advice, is for you to remember what my dad told me about radio—I'm saying something here, maybe not even in words, so you've got to listen *real* close. Damned if I know what I'm saying. But apologies, and back to business.

At precisely ten, Roger switches us over to the news show we pick up from the city, and it's a little before eleven when Carty and Duphree pull up from the golf course. They don't come inside, but I can hear them out front on the narrow strip of grass, the little lawn you could cut with a weedeater. They're flipping a baseball back and forth. From inside, I hear laughter, and the sound of the ball's pop into the leather mitts. I close my eyes and listen, the leather against leather in different tones. The *thwack*, sometimes, that's one of the most beautiful sounds on earth I think.

I listen for maybe ten minutes—pop, whock, the sounds spreading in time as their arms loosen and they spread farther apart. I watch Vivian while I listen, thinking if she opens her eyes now I'll be caught. Maybe ten years apart, Vivian and I. And I'm maybe halfway between her and my father in age. She's closer in years to me than I am to Carty and 'phree, though I don't put much stock in chronological age anyway.

I realize that I need to get the guys inside, to talk over issues they're planning to discuss during their show. I walk to the front screen door and step out onto the small concrete slab that's almost a tiny porch. I call for them like a mom in summer when dinner's on the table.

Sometimes they'll call me out, and we'll play a little of what kids around here call "running bases." One guy's on foot while the other two have gloves and cover two bases. The object for the runner is to make it safely from base to base. It's fun, the most challenging for the runner, and looks like a major league run-down play if executed right. The runner takes off at the throw and generally makes it about halfway. Then there's the throwback, and hopefully he gets a couple steps back to draw another throw, then advances maybe halfway again. It's nearly impossible to score, but it's exercise and helps when we need to let off some steam. Today, though, there's no time for a game.

To my call, Carty and Duphree play along, acting like the good, irresponsible kids they sometimes are, dropping their mitts and ball on the grass and jogging for the door. Inside Vivian has awakened and slips quietly out through the screen door I'm holding for the guys, her thick paperback in one hand and Spencer baby-style in the other. She looks at me as she leaves, not embarrassed at all, and gives me a little smile that's almost coy. I can't quite place it. Later I'll wonder if I smiled back. I'm uncomfortable, holding the door, a mother hen, and I'd hate for Vivian Lee to think of me as some authority figure. The guys and I sit down then to talk over the sports events of the day.

To be sure, my role is mainly clerical, administrative. I'm here as a favor to Harvey, to try to keep things afloat here, I'd thought. But Harvey, according to Carty, 'phree, and Jim Beam, Harvey sees it as a favor *to me*. Sit at your dad's old desk for a while, see what he was doing while you were down south, or the like. Up here to visit a couple times a year is all, that's the kind of translation I got from Carty. But it's no real matter to me, whose favor and who's favored. I've got my own questions, remember? My issues, that I try not to "cart" around the way Carty does, showing his ass if you ask me. (And whoah, wasn't that another opinion from the one who can't figure how he feels about anything?)

But to finish on the favor (and my personal economics), I tend bar over at Job's Tavern three nights a week for cash, and I've been amazed at how little I spend. Living in the cabin Dad left me, there's not much more to pay for but a power bill, dogfood, beer, and smokes. For now, and maybe for once, money is not one of my concerns. Strange, I think. But apologies again, and as promised, let's go to the phones!

The Callers

"Hell-lo!" Carty's voice booms, loud but smooth as Carl Lewis over a hurdle, "You're on the air!"

This first show is Carty's. The second, during the popular "drive-time," four to seven in the evening, is Duphree's chance to shine. So while Carty talks, 'phree sits maybe ten feet away, working the *Telos* phone system. Free's got the toughest job now, because he's wearing the headphones and taking the incoming calls. He finds out the callers' names, where they're calling from, and what sports issues they want to talk about. He types the caller demographics into the keyboard, and the information comes up on the monitor that sits in front of Carty.

Carty's microphone is mounted to the countertop, comes up and out on a metal arm, like those modern-art desk lamps. The mike's a *Shure*, that's the brand name, as in 'It *shure* is a piece of shit,' is what the Free says about it, and he's right. Roger, the techie, says it's the cheapest thing out there, but that a nice *Electro-voice* runs you two grand, not the kind of cash we've got lying around. The microphone's got scratch marks from where Vivian's Spencer bats it around like a tether ball, and the support arm always has a stripped bolt so it's dropping down all the time, forcing the speaker to either bob quickly down with it or have his voice drop off the charts. (Better *no* sound, though, than what you can get late at night, sitting close to your radio, when Spencer takes a swing at it.)

So Carty's greeted the caller, the red bulb that signals "on air" is lit above the counter, and the wingnut slips on the microphone arm. The crappy *Shure* pendulums down, and Carty can't drop his head fast enough. Instead he blows on the mike, a couple quick breaths, with a quick glance over at 'phree who's stifling laughter, listening to what sounds like static over the air. Carty then hits the panic button, the cut-off-caller button we have to use sometimes since even with screening and a seven-second delay, sometimes callers get out of control. So Carty's cut the caller. He grabs the mike quickly, and as he's retightening the wingnut he says sorry to "Clay in Rochester—your cell phone just went out of range." Duphree is cracking up now, not mourning the loss of another who wants to talk about Mark McGwire.

My ill-defined job during the shows is to try to help out in any way possible, but since we've only got the one *Telos*, four incoming lines, there's not much I can do. I answer phones sometimes and jot down callers on a pad in front of 'phree, but basically I'm a fifth wheel during the shows. And I've sure as hell got no control over what *they* say or do, so I sit back and try to enjoy the show.

We try to have at least one back-up caller on hold for just this type of situation, but being a small market, that's not always possible. The hosts sometimes have huge gaps of time to fill, which can give me some anxious moments, but Carty and 'phree love it. Thankfully now there's a little more than a breath of dead air before Carty hits a flashing light and has a "Robert from Sanford" on the show, wanting to talk about the Merchant League softball All-Star game next week.

"Yeah, mmm. Yes," the voice goes from squeaky high to froggy deep. "Yes, Mr. Carty. First-time caller. But," quickly added, "long-time listener."

Carty looks at the monitor, where Duphree has typed, continues to type: "COLD? FLU? ...KID??"

"Yeah, welcome, Robert. What's on your mind, man?"

"Yeah, *yes*," the voice choking, ridiculously deep, "I respect your opinion, and I was wondering what you thought about Mack getting picked for shortstop on the 'East' team?" A pause then while 'phree and Carty exchange a look, a smile, a shake of head. Carty's not going to give him anything.

"Like Mack, he's not that quick, not so good going into the hole. And he's only batting like .278, worse with runners on."

Another pause, during which Free types: "IF KID, WHY NOT IN SCHOOL?" Then a noise in the background, the caller's background, something rustling, a voice then that sounds a lot like "Get back in *bed*!" Duphree, snickering, types: JUNE'S SURE PISSED AT THE BEA-VER!"

Brave kid, though, he pushes on. "Like Phillips maybe, or even Egan of the Revco team, do you think maybe one of them would be, you know, a better choice?"

Finally Carty speaks. "Robert," he asks. "What's Phillips hitting with runners on? What *about* Egan?" Carty's testing. He knows as well as 'phree does that Phillips is anemic at the plate, his average hovering right around the Mendoza Line. He's wondering if this caller *is* a kid, one smart enough to throw Phillips out as bait.

The froggy voice hesitates. Carty nods to 'phree, quizzically. They're partners grappling with the same question.

". . . not sure about Phillips, but Egan's over .300 with runners on, and he's got better range!"

Duphree types "*BOBBY* EGAN!" at the same time Carty speaks up.

"Listen, son. Your dad is a fine fielder, but let's be honest about the RBIs—" And with that Carty hits the panic button, punching 'play' on a commercial tape for True Value Hardware that fills the speakers. Kind of low-blow tactics from the full-of-himself Carty, probably sore about a bad round of golf. During the hardware ad, beneath the information about the new caller on line 3, Free types in: "CATEGORY 5—AMAZ-ING."

Which requires a bit of explanation. A digression, but the prom-ised list of caller categories, as compiled by Kevin McCarty, Anthony Duphree, and Jackson McCauslin. Posted above McCarty's desk, right next to his poster of O.J. Simpson, rookie year with the Bills—a team *I* remember, but Carty wouldn't even have been born yet—wearing #36 on his jersey, a collector since he wore #32 the rest of his career. The "Caller Categories" list as follows:

1. THE SUCK-UP. Calls in presumably to hear his or her own voice. Main quality: agreement with host (about everything, including shoe brands, hair styles). Adept at repeating host's points, often word for word, although sometimes using creative synonyms, sometimes re-arranging the host's ideas as if to make them original. In this category you sometimes find "the Homer," whose favorite team is also the host's. Also, "the Regular," like *Cheers'* Norm, often a suck-up and "insider" who knows the host off the air.

2. THE KNOW-IT-ALL. Very common. Main quality: unshakable belief in correctness of his or her own opinion, often at odds with the host's. Often has carefully chosen statistics which support the 'one true view.' Often a smug, strongly delivered monologue, like the host's own, with no tolerance for interruption. Sometimes angry or belligerent, often childishly deaf to reason. Variant, "the Ass," who knows mean when he hears it, who will (by transference) criticize host for meanness to callers.

3. THE CONSPIRACIST. To him or her, even the smallest of sports issues or events relates directly, causally, to huge unseen forces. These forces—favorite targets being big business, big media and television, owners, gamblers, Mafia—control all human affairs, whether the host is willing to admit it or not. A cynic, a zealot, this caller is potentially dangerous, unpredictable (the kind the 7-second delay was invented for), but is often a stimulating, provocative guest.

4. THE IRRELEVANT NON-SEQUITUR. Probably least intelli-gent of all types, this caller has a point to make and blurts it out. Point often has nothing to do with show topic or host's comments. Sometimes a conspiracist as well. Can be well-supported, valid point, however. Of-ten colorful, completely unpredictable; usually more annoying than dan-gerous.

5. THE GENUINE QUESTIONER. Rarest type, often with no par-ticular opinion or unswerving viewpoint. Often young people, charac-terized by a strikingly honest, often heartfelt tone of question. Earnest desire to hear the host's opinion and reply, will often hang up to listen to

the host's answer. Polite, unassuming, an often touching—these words J. McCauslin's, not the hosts'—genuineness separates this caller from all others.

So there you have it. And now that you've got this list, the very same list the professionals at WSPT-Sanford use, you can play along at home, in your car, in your boat.

At the station, Carty and Free play daily. It's like a variation on the license plate game kids play on car trips. To Carty and 'phree's memory, all five categories have been hit only once in a single show, and that over a year ago and before my time. But today feels lucky somehow, especially since #5, the toughest, rarest type, has already been bagged. Duphree slide-rolls his swivel chair across the sound booth to Carty, and they exchange a high-five slap.

"Hell-lo, you're on 630 Sportstalk! What's on your mind—uh—David, from Penfield?"

"Yeah, hey Carty, man, first-timer!" Free cuts Carty a look, skeptical, and even I'm thinking this guy's voice sounds awfully familiar. Still, I read over Carty's shoulder, that he wants to talk about McGwire (and who doesn't, this week?), and Carty decides to let out some line for this fish. 'Phree is concentrating hard, staring at the list of categories we've got printed in bold black and red magic marker.

"So you want to talk about Big Mac and number 62, David? What's your point—anything we haven't heard ten times this week?" Carty's understandably cynical, I think—we *have* heard just about every angle on what is, truly, a feel-good story. Still, he's bucking this caller a bit hard.

"Okay, hear me out," David continues, undissuaded. "How much you think Steve Trachsel got from the Vegas boys for serving up that meatball that *I* could've 'taken yard'? And—"

Duphree is fast and furious, typing: "CATEGORY-3!!" (Except it comes out "CAT#HORY" as he's so excited. Only two down, yet I'm thinking 'phree can feel it, the sweep of all five categories. Carty's excited too, is sensing the possibility, and I can tell he wants to hear this David out, to see how far outside he'll take it. Keep him on the line, Free is whispering like a federal agent tracing a kidnapper's call.

"Hold on now, David," Carty tries. "For one thing, Mac likes 'em low and this one was high and tight—" But the conspiracist hasn't heard.

"How much do you think the network paid to have it set for Tuesday night, primetime? How about the Mob? I wish *I'd* have known it was coming—I'd have put some cash on it myself. I tell you, Carty, the fix was on!"

When David starts in on the 1919 "Black Sox," Carty hits the panic button, just to keep from laughing on the air.

To digress for a moment more, there's another small but bold-black-printed sign on the wall next to the caller categories, nearer my desk than the others'. It reads simply ". . . NO COMMISSIONER," and serves as a cue-card for responding to callers with baseball gripes, anything from blown umpire calls to players' unsportsmanlike conduct, from inflated player and owner salaries to insanely high ticket and hot dog prices. The words explain all, the way "alien abduction" does for Fox Mulder. So the argument is both strong and weak.

Now Duphree, given his *laissez faire* philosophy, refuses to invoke the term. But Carty will sometimes, when a frustrating caller, often a conspiracist, tries to implicate huge dark forces at work. Carty will get in the last words, simply "No Commissioner," and hit the panic button. I applaud this. Not to get into this whole subject too far—the "state" of baseball operating since 1992 without a governor, a subject I surprisingly *do* feel strongly about—but I put the sign on the wall and I've no reason to pull it down no matter what Bud Selig says about his interest in the public good. Apologies for the break in the action, and now back to the show.

"Two down, three to go. Line 4 looks good this time," Duphree chimes next.

"Hell-lo, you're on the air!" Carty answers. "Gary from Canandaigua, what's on your mind?"

'Phree has typed in that Gary wants to talk about Mike Tyson, who is legitimately in the news, is trying to get reinstated to box again. Can't seem to apologize, though, or to promise not to resort to cannibalism in the ring again. A convicted rapist, for chrissakes. (And another opinion from the one who can't decide how he feels, huh?)

Anyway, Free's got a funny look on his face, like he's making a decision he's not sure of. Carty shrugs okay, moves his right index finger on top of the panic button just in case. "So, Gary, what did you want to say about Iron Mike?" Carty asks into the microphone, which is beginning to show signs of slipping down again.

"Well, I was thinking about Tyson, and the President," Gary starts out, and I'm thinking Carty should cut him off right there. No way this guy can be good, except maybe for ratings and angry mail. But 'phree is typing furiously—"CATEGORY 4—Hold on!" He wants the irrelevance noted.

"—and remember in the movie, *Raging Bull*, when LaMotta, De-Niro right? When he's asking his manager 'Did you fuck my wife?'"

And as Free busts out laughing, showing four fingers and then a thumb's up, Carty's already hit the panic button and we're all three thinking we know what the seven seconds' delay is for.

"Good *get*!" 'Phree's delirious now, using a term we usually reserve for guests or interviews of some importance, a Red Wings player mayber or a college coach who agrees to speak on-air. But he's rightfully excit-ed, since we're more than halfway to the category-sweep with two easy, common ones left; just the Know-It-All and the Suck-up remain.

And true to the odds, not a half an hour later, after another irrelevant and another genuine questioner, a couple of blurred-category callers, a couple of commercials and sure enough, Free's got a good bet for the fourth on the line. Knows it from the start. Types onto Carty's screen: "Frank from Honeoye Falls—wants to talk about Roger Maris' Hall of Fame chances." Then adds quickly: "Possible Category 2—get *stats*!"

Now "Frank," it turns out, is also one of the at-least-daily callers who have to hear their own voices on-air. Which means they try to leave their radios turned up during the call.

"Hello, Frank, you're *on*," Carty announces. Carty's voice travels both across the phone lines to Frank's den, and through the air to Frank's radio in the same den. The voices arrive, quite naturally, at slightly dif-ferent times. That, or Frank lives in Carlsbad.

"Yeah ('eah'). I don't ('ah-dough') think ('ink') Maris ('heiress') should *EVER* ('ver, ver') go in the Hall ('oh-ith-all')" Frank shouts, like they all do. And his voice booms into the phone, to Carty's, then back out our antenna and booms back out Frank's Bose bookshelf speakers.

It must be the 'category sweep' possibility that enables Carty to summon reserve calm, and ask with only a slight quaver, "Would you mind turning down your radio, friend?" Most of these types get the pan-ic-button cut-off in a New York second. But Carty lets him play on.

Sure enough, Frank's got major issues with the Maris reconsider-ation. He's pumped himself up as a complete know-it-all, so smart, no doubt with his Roger Maris career numbers in the *Baseball Encyclopedia* in front of him. But acts like he's reciting the numbers—batting averages, RBIs, homers in years other than '61—from memory, even pausing as if struggling to recall the exact figures. He's got all the statistics, plus the tired argument about the loaded Yankee lineup, and how pitchers *had* to give Maris strikes with Mantle on deck. This point, too, he acts like he originated—what an insight! And then, as if he wasn't already a lock for Category 2, this Frank starts riding Carty about how he treated the earlier caller.

"You were *mean*," Frank, the now-"Ass," too, tells Carty angrily. And amazingly, he's not mad about the way Carty treated the boy home sick from school, little Bobby Egan. This Frank wanted to hear the caller's ideas about *Raging Bull*. "You just cut him off in the middle of the point he was making, a good point about a great movie," Frank pouts. And gets the same result as the boxing enthusiast. Click.

And I'm smiling, too, happy for them—because I know now (and how) they'll get their sweep. But I'm not an insider with them. Plus that last caller kind of struck me, I'm not sure why. But I just keep picturing that newspaper photo I saw, years back, before anybody threatened his home run record, back when Maris died. Twenty-some-odd people standing at the grave, freezing rain coming down in late winter, Fargo, North Dakota, and some of folks without even gloves or umbrellas. Such a desolate scene. I'd like to see the guy get into Cooperstown just for that. He held the record for 37 years, longer than Ruth did, and twenty people bury him. Jesus.

But to finish the sweep—back to the happy endings—all Carty and Free need is a "suck-up," a "homer," a regular. It's rigged, of course, but 'phree sticks the lines so they're all busy except the one he can use to dial out. He rings Carty's old fraternity house at Hobart. The voice on the line, on the air then, will be familiar of course, but with a name they won't recognize because it changes every time he calls.

'Phree is giggling as a Domino's Pizza commercial plays, is typing into Carty's screen: "Caller: Ramadaheen, from Calcutta wants to talk about the fighting Irish football!"

Carty calls him "'Raymond' from Brighton," and for perhaps ten minutes the two of them rant shamelessly about the drubbing of Michigan last week, the virtues of "Mister McCarthy's show" and "that insightful Mister Duphree." They repeat each other's points regarding defense and offensive line play, special teams and cheerleading squad. And in "Raymond," Carty has the guest who's the amazing 'triple threat': a suck-up, who's also a "homer," and a regular. Talk about insiders.

But the sweep at least has put the two of them in fine spirits. 'Phree's show follows the news updates which follow Carty. And yet poor Free, with the amazing success of Carty, has no chance to top it. In fact, it's as if the listening audience, too, feels the let-down, the anti-climax. The call-ins seem uninspired, their questions and comments either contrived or unimaginative, stale. Yet the Duphree show ends with a juicy Conspiracist who links the eastern-Europe NHL players to the Bosnian crisis ("—spies on *American ice!*"), which causes Carty and Free to reminisce on-air about the earlier "David from Penfield" and his McGwire-Mob connection. So the show ends on an up note, especially since Carty and 'phree are partners, teammates, and share the credit for the rare Caller-sweep. Their spirits rise back as the show winds down.

And a little after seven in the evening, Carty and Free are headed out to celebrate, and they invite me along. I head home to feed the dogs, but agree to catch up with them later at Job's. Roger has returned (after school and football practice) to his technical duties in the booth, just monitoring the satellite shows we pick up—one on world news, one farm news, and one a stock market report—which take WSPT up to midnight, when it's time for Dr. Ruth. So in keeping with the plan, with the promised routine, allow me to take you to Job's.

The Tavern

I head home, to my father's cabin, enjoying the coolness of the coming evening and sounds only of the breeze, the truck's engine, the tires on the pavement. I keep the radio off, thinking I've had enough of words for a while.

The dogs greet me in an unconditional way I feel I don't always deserve. And they seem so grateful for everything, for their freedom, their food, just another day on the earth perhaps. Crazy. Crazy, too, maybe, to wish for their simplicity. To be relieved of the need to figure things out. I sit heavy on the porch step and watch Shag and Heel romp, thinking of what I left in the south, dogs and connections, too. And how my isolation, my obsession with it, perhaps began long before I married or divorced. Long before my father died, in fact far back into his life. If I'm seeing symptoms, then I must have to delve back farther, isn't that right? It's as if the strands—friends, meaning, family, sports even, somehow— or whatever powers there have ever been in my life, they're like the cat-gut strings on a tennis racket. I keep swinging and with each stroke they've been snapping, one by one. Now lose one string, one connection, and maybe Sampras won't play with it, but you or I could still keep a volley going. But eventually maybe too many strings are gone and the racket ceases to function.

I lie back on the porch and doze, awakening moments or hours later in the dark, very cold. The dogs have headed inside, perhaps chilly themselves, and I think of the Army blanket. I remember, too, that Carty and 'phree asked me to the tavern, that they're there now, talking sports, maybe stumbling onto some of my answers. I decide to take the opportunity, the night's invitation to "insider status." I leave the dogs at home where they seem content, grateful even, not to be going along. As I hear the crush of gravel under the tires heading out the driveway, the stick-on dashboard clock reads 10:43 p.m.

But first off, let me try to tell you about what it's like to walk into a bar *with* Carty and Free. I never knew how good looking they were until I did this. It's funny really, an amazing thing. To watch the heads of beautiful women turn, and watch their eyes grow large. To see them nudge each other to take a gander. A truck driver I used to deliver liquor with, he'd slow down around the college, pick out this one or that and drawl, "Take a reading, Youngblood." And it works the other way around, too, I found. I've looked at Carty and 'phree differently ever since that first time, walking into Job's. There's a power to appearances.

Anyway, Job's is a tavern and a sports bar, pretty much Sanford's only of its kind. Dark wood, pool tables, darts, a free throw hoop. And some truly fantastic memorabilia on the walls, plaques and home-run balls, Jets and Giants footballs. And some signed baseball cards in little plastic envelopes tacked behind the bar, the names that'd fill a room in Cooperstown. And for me, while I think I've pretty near outgrown this type of place, the crowd more like, it's a great place to work. Not far from U. of R. and Hobart, it gets a college crowd on weekends and local regulars through the week. Tips are good—at least what you lose in percentage you pick up in volume—and as one in search of purpose could say, "it finances my trip."

The owner, Lionel Job (pronounced like the rolling papers company), is a farmer by trade who added the long-vowel accent over the "o" on the sign outside to remind himself to be patient, "like the book in the Bible," he'll tell you. Maybe the bustling, interactive restaurant business requires a different kind of patience than the physical, often solitary business of farming. This is where Job's passion is, but he couldn't make a living at it, not today anyway. The tavern's a way for him to pay his bills—and he's ironically getting rich at it. But he can't give up the agrarian dream, what he grew up doing. He tells me that one day soon he'll have saved enough that he can go back to losing money farming. I think he means it.

I worked last night, Thursday, and made out pretty well. But it's nothing like the business on Friday nights. I park on Elm Street a couple of blocks toward the radio station from Job's, and from that distance I can see a small crowd standing on the sidewalk below the sign with the long-vowel "o," laughing and drinking and smoking. I approach slowly, liking the sound of my footfalls on the cement, a cadence like from a metronome, a kind of built-in purpose. For a moment there I'm glad to be out, to be at least taking steps, perhaps toward answering my questions. And then a block away, I'm thinking that if you asked, I'm not sure whether I'd say I care if I get there or not.

I slip past the dozen or so outside and stand inside the front door, appreciating the newness of the perspective, since on work nights I enter through the back, through the kitchen. I scan the room and spot Carty and 'phree at a large round table, just the two guys and five girls, a couple more standing by as if the first substitutes to enter the game. I laugh when I see them and they flag me down, happy as the dogs to see me. Crazy, me an insider, but they're probably tiring of the female attention.

Pitchers of beer rotate around the table and the conversation is nearly screams over the music, which when I arrive is remarkably a song I know, the Stones' "Gimme Shelter." I sit for a time, satisfied in the pulsing beat, watching the Cardinals game on a wide-screen television in the corner. I speak when spoken to but awkwardly, feeling fifteen again and not in fact fifteen years *older* than the young women surrounding Carty and 'phree.

The whole crowd is getting pretty drunk. It always amazes me to get to a party late like this. I sit watching the young faces and the Cardinals game (McGwire at this point 0-for-3 thus far), thinking and considering the differences among people. At least between myself and the others. Almost two hours later, I'm nursing my second beer and the crowd's thinned out. It's nearing closing time, last call, and everywhere the faithful remaining are clamoring for more drinks. They say alcoholics can't stop once they get started, but for some reason tonight I'm not thirsting for it. I'm still hoping to hear something in the conversation of Carty, Free, and the Hobart girls. Something I can ask, the kind of question that just opens things up. Not like the old folks' bumper sticker that says "Ask me about my Grandchildren," but maybe not so far off either.

I excuse myself, though no one takes notice, and thread my way back to the bar to talk with Job, who shakes my hand. He and I will have a few behind the bar some nights—it's legal in New York, for some odd reason—and at times I think I know him better, or understand him better at least, than I ever did my own father. I can't understand why this is. But I'd like to say something of this to him, to this barman-farmer with all the patience of rolling papers, but I don't know the words. How do we communicate over the airwaves, I wonder, reaching people we can't even look in the eyes. Like talk-radio, we're all strangers. I look at Job and I think that maybe he knows what I'm thinking or considering trying to somehow say. In his face I might see a comment—a "don't bother," or a "no need," perhaps. No need to put inadequate words to describe an understanding we have. But I can't be sure. We look out over the half-full tavern in silence then, before Job speaks and I know the serious moment has passed.

"There are two kinds of people in this world, Jackson," he tells me in earnest, and then his eyes crackle with Irish mischief. "Those who believe there are two kinds of people, and those that don't."

"I guess I'm the latter," I tell him back, laughing a little. "But I wouldn't mind being the other kind once in a while."

Back at the table, the Hobart sorority has broken up, the majority heading out and leaving the two (*their* choice, or Carty and Free's?) with the celebrity radio hosts, the gorgeous men of Sanford. I've got to guess part of their attractiveness comes by contrast, because folks around here aren't such perfect specimens. Farmers, millworkers, laborers of all kinds, and many with a missing finger or a facial scar, a limp or the like. Not to take anything away from Carty and Duphree. But what if there were just two kinds of people, I think crazily.

Job flashes the lights, last call, and I'm still thinking there's a chance we'll sit, maybe the five (or if Job would sit in, the six) of us, and drink some more and get to talking. Get to talking about what really happens on the radio, and what's the mystical language of sports, and what is the source of the power. I can picture the young women being most help- ful, giving a youthful and female angle on things, something I miss and might really help me to figure things out. I still think there's something I might be able to say that gets us all talking, like in the story Vivian Lee read over the radio. The story where couples are sitting around drinking and talking about what love means. But I look around the table and see the two women with worship and more in their eyes. I stand up, shaking their soft hands, formally, I think, like an elder, and say good night. I shake Job's hand again, and slap up high with Carty and then 'phree. They thank me for coming out in a way that seems immensely genuine, and I'm not sure what to make of it. Not sure what 'Caller Category' to put them in, or where they might put me.

The night has cooled considerably while I was inside, and I zipper my sweatshirt as I walk back to the truck, stopping to light a cigarette and look up into a cloudy night. The air smells like it did this morning almost, smells of a cold nothing with just a hint of leaves or apples or turned earth. I reach my truck parked along the darkened south side of Elm Street, pointing not toward home but toward the radio station three more blocks on. Hands in sweatshirt pockets, I walk past the truck. I'm not sure why I stop off at the station before heading home. Well, I do know part of it. I was looking for something, I guess.

It's after 3 a.m. when I open the screen door that doesn't lock. We've got a 24/7 license from the FCC, and we fill most of that time, though only some of it is live talk by the people here. As I said, Vivian Lee's show is a hodgepodge of therapy and music and poetry and books, 2 a.m. until six. She's there at the microphone when I walk in.

I stop inside the door—it's as cool inside as out—and I'm suddenly not sure how to explain my being there. I think about going over to my desk and shuffling papers, as if I'd forgotten something that I've come back for at three in the morning. She looks up then, noticing me outside the sound booth glass. She doesn't seem at all surprised.

Vivian Lee continues talking into the microphone, probably to some radio caller. The speakers are off in the outer office, so I hear nothing outside the glass booth. She continues looking at me, a look I can't read. After maybe a minute, she hits the buttons to play a taped commercial, and then rolls the swivel chair a few feet to the turntable, where she starts a record spinning. As the commercial ends—this I assume because I still hear nothing—her lips move at the mike for a few seconds, and she lowers the needle onto the turning record. She gets up then and steps out of the booth.

"I've never been here at this time of night before," I tell her, stupidly I'll think later. If I *had* been there, she'd have seen me. "But I listen to your show sometimes." I don't tell her how often, which is perhaps more than I've admitted here either. She near-smiles, a funny genuine look with maybe sadness burned around the edges like Confederate money I'd see in antique stores in the south. Thankfully, she doesn't ask me why I'm here.

"Your father used to drop in sometimes, about this time of night," Vivian Lee tells me. I get a strange sort of ticklish feeling in my stomach for a moment, and then it passes.

We talk then about my father for a few minutes, her saying I don't remember what, some memories of his activism during the Vietnam War and other causes. I really can't say what she said, or what I said in response. Later I'll try to recreate the conversation, will wonder about her connection with my father. And I'll wonder what they must've seen, and perhaps stopped seeing, in one another. But then, I remember feeling nothing—the kind of nothing that's something. Like when my mother called to tell me that my father, a strong swimmer and in great shape for 61, had drowned in the quarry not five miles from here. At some point then, Vivian Lee breaks our eye contact, turning toward the sound booth where we both notice the needle about halfway across the record on the turntable. She gives a little wince like she's not anxious to get back but has to. And she smiles at me, in it the almost coy quality I'd noticed this morning, and thanks me for stopping by. "Come back sometime," she says quietly, turning away toward the sound booth.

And I walk out then, back the three blocks to my pickup. I ride home with the windows down, in the chill feeling alive. I flip on the truck radio and hear the voice of Vivian Lee taking calls.

She's got a man with a gravelly voice on the line, a man I could guess at the age of and even draw a picture of in my mind, but for some reason I don't. I try to concentrate only on his words, or really not even those so much as what he means. The caller has "experienced some losses," is all he says really, but from his tone he's not talking about his hair or car keys. I picture Vivian at her desk this morning, head forward, hair long and hanging straight down. I picture her reading a story into the microphone that Spencer bats around. She pauses now as if considering all the things the caller hasn't said.

"An image I've been thinking of," she says quietly, "I'll offer it up, and maybe you can help me." Her voice is as smooth as Brooks at third, soothing. It makes me think of steady rain. "There was a philosopher, an ancient Stoic, I believe his name was Zeno," she goes on. In the truck, in the chill, I have no idea but she could be making this whole thing up.

"He was a mathematician, too, I believe," Vivian Lee tells the caller, "and he developed this simple proof, a formula that showed how motion was an illusion. Think of a journey, of mapping a journey, and find your point of origin and your destination," she says, and pauses.

"Now the philosopher said that you bisect the distance—to go a half at a time, then bisect that half again. If you continue to bisect the distance, you'll continue to have halves. Halves and more halves and more halves. Do you see what I mean?"

The gravelly voice says quietly, "I think so."

"So what I was thinking," Vivian Lee continues, "is that he's proving the opposite at the same time."

I turn off Hill Road then and onto the long stone driveway. Her voice continues.

"If the destination is your answers, that you're trying to figure out, look at it this way. Move halfway there, then halfway forward again. Then halfway again. And if you were a hundred miles away to start with, you're now, what, only 25 miles away. Keep halving the distance forward. You find both that you're really close, and that you'll never reach it. It's eternity, maybe, or just that stuff that's beyond our grasp, our words, our concepts. But what we've got has got to be enough."

Home then, and I turn off the engine, which ticks softly in the cool. I slowly relax my body, a little at a time. I close my eyes. My chin touches my chest and my back remains straight, the way some people sleep on planes.

Over the years, **_Gregg Cusick_** has supported his writing habit through work as a furniture mover, English teacher, paralegal, construction worker, retail manager, among others. His fiction has appeared in more than two dozen journals and has won numerous awards, including the Lorian Hemingway Short Story Competition and The Florida Review Editor's Prize, and has been nominated for a Pushcart Prize. He holds a Master's in English/Creative Writing from North Carolina State University and lives in Durham, North Carolina, where he bartends and tutors literacy. He can be contacted at greggcusick.com.